TRAILER PARK NOIR

RAY GARTON

Cover art and design by David Dodd

First Crossroad Press Edition

For my dear friend Paul Meredith, who had to leave a little early. You are deeply missed by many, but especially by me. I think you would've enjoyed the hell out of this book.

And for Dawn, as always.

One

The Riverside Mobile Home Park was so thick with trees, the sun scarcely shone on its residents. There were oaks and elms, willows and silk trees, maples and palm trees, and even a couple pines. They were old trees, and big, and they provided blankets of shade. As a result, the park always had a gloomy darkness about it that remained even on the sunniest days, when only spots and stripes of gold dappled the trailers and grounds. It was as if the trailers existed in their own dimension of sun-speckled darkness, of shadows on shadows on shadows, separate from the rest of the world.

Riverside had twenty units, trailers of all sizes and shapes and colors, from spacious double-wides to small trailers intended for camping. It started with unit one just inside the entrance on the right, followed by two and three and four and so on in a straight line down the right side of the park. In the rear, the straight line looped around a barn-red house in a semicircle, then became a straight line again down the left side of the park, ending with unit twenty back at the entrance. Trees and weeds grew within a curbed divider between the two narrow paved lanes.

1

In that small, run-down, barn-red house lived the trailer park's managers, Hank and Muriel Snodgrass. It had a tiny untended front yard that had become overgrown with vines and weeds and the small but colorful flowers the weeds produced. Ivy swallowed up a little long-dry fountain with plaster fairies attached to the rims of the two bowls and crawled up the sides of the house. Beside the house stood a slide, a swing set, and a merry-go-round on which the park's children often played.

Running along the right, or eastern, side of the park, beyond the row of trailers, was the Sacramento River. There was a sandy bank there among all the thick vines and blackberry bushes, where some of the residents went for picnics, or to fish. A white wood-and-metal pier stuck out from the shore from which some residents cast their lines. A sign ordered NO SWIMMING. The river's current was powerful, and just less than a year ago, it had carried away two children who had paid no attention to the sign. They had been found several miles down river, both twisted and dead. That story kept kids out of the water.

Riverside was an old trailer park, established in 1953, and it showed its age. The mailboxes to the side of the trailer park's entrance were dented and rusted. The narrow paved road that made a loop through the park was broken and potholed, and weeds and wildflowers grew up through the cracks.

The July heat was suffocating. There were some fat clouds in the sky and the heat was moist and clinging. The thermometer hanging on the wall on the Snodgrass's front porch read one hundred and fourteen degrees. Shasta County summers were brutally punishing.

Marcus Reznick left his tiny cramped office on North Street in downtown Anderson at five-eighteen. He'd just finished up the second of the only two cases he'd had lately, both divorce-related.

Divorces. The cesspit of the private investigator. Where P.I.s went to die.

He'd just told a woman named Linda Straight that her husband Alan was seeing seven different women on his UPS route. He'd shown her pictures of Alan kissing these women in their front doorways or beside his big brown UPS truck. She'd reacted with disbelief. So had Reznick at first. Seven women? The guy had been busy.

The air conditioning in his aging metallic-gold Toyota Corolla sedan did not work, so he had all the windows rolled down as he drove north on North Street.

The baking sunlight was occasionally obscured by the enormous clouds in the sky, sending large, whale-like shadows passing over the ground. Humidity made the air thick. Mirages shimmered on the road up ahead, gradually evaporated, then reappeared farther up. In the short time it took him to get from his office to Stingy Lane off of North Street, the back of his shirt was soaked through to his suit coat, which was also wet. He regretted not taking the coat off before he got into the car. He turned right on Stingy, drove east a short distance, then turned left on Park Way, which led to the Anderson River Park. Halfway there, he turned left into the Riverside Mobile Home Park. He stopped his car in the entrance, unfastened the seatbelt, and got out. He went to the mailboxes, stopped at his, and got his mail, all of it junk. He went back to his car, got in, and put the mail on the passenger seat, on top of his briefcase. He drove past the enormous oak tree that grew up in the center of the entrance to the trailer park, between the two lanes.

When Reznick had driven to work that morning, unit five had been empty. It had been empty for over two weeks, ever since the previous resident had been taken away by the police for beating up his girlfriend, and she had taken their two children and moved in with her mom. The battered old trailer in which they'd lived had been hauled away like the wreck it was. But now, a handsome, spacious, brand-new trailer occupied unit five. A metallic-onyx Porsche Cayenne Turbo SUV was parked in the carport beside it.

Nice and pricey, Reznick thought as he looked the SUV over in passing. *What's he doing* here?

Reznick drove to his trailer, unit nine, and pulled into the small carport, killed the engine. He took his briefcase and mail from the passenger seat and got out of the car, jangled his keys as he went up the steps. He unlocked the door and went inside.

The front door opened on the living room, with the small dining area and kitchen to the right, and to the left a hallway that led to the bedroom and bathroom.

His chocolate-brown Chihuahua yipped with machine-gun speed as he jumped up and pawed Reznick's shins.

"Hey, Conan," he said. He put down his briefcase and picked up the little wriggling dog. Conan licked his face. "You've got bad breath, kid. Hungry?" He put the dog down and picked up his briefcase again.

Reznick wore a grey suit with a dark red tie, which he loosened with one hand as he put his briefcase and keys and mail on the dining table and walked into the kitchen. Conan continued to yap.

"Hold it down, kid." Reznick went to the front door and opened it, then opened the screen door. Conan hurried outside. While the little dog was relieving himself, Reznick went to the kitchen, took a can of dog food from the cupboard, a can opener from a drawer, and opened it. He used a fork to scoop food into a bowl on the floor beside a bowl of water. He put a rubber lid on the open can, and put the remainder of the dog food in the refrigerator. In no time at all, Conan came back in and went straight for the bowl, his tail, his whole rear end, wagging back and forth as he ate.

Reznick closed the screen door. The swamp cooler in the hall ceiling was already on—he'd turned it on before leaving for the office to keep the trailer cool for Conan. He went to his bedroom, and changed into jeans and a T-shirt, then returned to the kitchen for something to eat. He had some cold fried chicken in the refrigerator. He put a leg and thigh on a paper plate and took them, a segment of paper towel, and a Diet Dr. Pepper to the living room, where he sighed heavily as he sat down in his recliner. He used the remote to turn on the TV. The news was on. Reznick quickly turned it to a rerun of *Friends*. He was not in the mood to hear the world's problems. He could barely stand his own.

What he really wanted at that moment more than anything—more than fried chicken or a Diet Dr. Pepper—was an ice-cold glass of vodka. It had been over a year since his last drink. He didn't keep track of the number of days or weeks or months the way some alcoholics did because he had not gone through a twelve-step program. Instead, he had done it himself, alone, cold turkey.

"If you don't stop drinking, Marcus," his doctor had told him, "you'll never live to see forty-five. It's going to kill you. It's killing you now. You've got to stop."

He'd decided he could do it without help, but the DTs had hit him hard. His body had quaked as if possessed, and he'd vomited again and again, uncontrollable projectile vomiting, until blood had come up. He'd ended up in the Emergency Room, feeling like he was dying, certain he was in his final moments of life, wondering who would care.

Now he confined his drinking to ice water, Diet Dr. Pepper, and the occasional sparkling mineral water. But a day did not pass without the cravings that puckered the inside of his mouth, when he could almost taste the cold vodka. They usually weren't this bad, though.

He'd fallen into a bottle when his whole life had come to pieces six years ago. Everything had fallen apart.

Before that had happened, Reznick Security and Investigations had been a going concern, the biggest and most successful security and investigation firm in Shasta County. He'd had plush offices and several employees back then, located in the city of Redding, just ten miles north of the small town of Anderson, where he lived and worked now. Reznick had inherited the firm from his father, who had taught him everything he knew. He'd never been happier than he'd been while working there with his dad for those years. Then, after Dad had retired, then had been killed—that had been one of the things in his life that had gone so wrong and had contributed to his existence falling down all around him like a collapsing building—Reznick had the place to himself, and he'd promptly run it into the ground.

Starting over was slow going. He had that tiny one-room office between a beauty parlor and a small accounting firm. The beauty parlor—not a salon, but a *parlor*—was the old-fashioned kind, mostly pink, with blue-haired ladies wearing too much makeup sitting under hair dryers reading magazines. A few doors down was a barber shop with an old-fashioned barber's pole spinning out front.

It was just Reznick now—he didn't even have a secretary, and there would be no room for one in his office if he did. Just Reznick and two divorce cases, with both now finished. He would've taken neither case back in the old days—he would've given them to junior investigators. Back then, he'd taken on only the biggest and most interesting cases himself, along with his father. They'd taken only the cases that got the most publicity, and he and Dad had been in the paper and on the evening news a lot back then.

Back then. His whole life seemed to be *back then*, before it all had come to pieces and he'd ended up living in his car for a while.

Conan planted himself on the floor in front of Reznick's chair and stared up at him with big, begging eyes.

"You just ate," Reznick said.

The dog made a small, pleading sound in his throat.

"Oh, all right." Reznick broke off a piece of thigh meat and held it down for the dog.

Conan snatched it from his fingers and happily chewed it up.

When he finished his chicken, Reznick wiped his hands and mouth on the paper towel, then leaned back in the recliner with the plate of bones on his lap. Conan hopped up on the arm of the recliner and settled down beside him. Reznick smoked a Winston, then, after awhile, he drifted off to sleep.

It seemed safe to sleep during the day. Somehow, the daylight held off the nightmares.

Two

In unit eight, Anna Dunfy set dinner before her sixteen-year-old daughter Kendra, who sat at the kitchen table. It was one of those tables with blue Formica on top and chrome edges and legs.

"There you go," Anna said.

"Thank you, Mommy," Kendra said.

Anna got her own meal and sat down at the table with Kendra.

Kendra's favorite food was fish sticks. They ate them so often that Anna had developed a taste for them, herself. There was a specific brand she preferred, although Kendra was not particular—she liked them all.

"How was Vacation Bible School today?" Anna asked.

"Oh, it was lots of fun. It was over too fast."

"Have you had any more trouble with that boy? What's his name? Jake—"

"Jake Tibman?"

"Yeah, he's the one."

"No, Jake's been nice to me since Miss Fisher had a talk with him. He can be nice, really."

"Well, that's good to know. He sure wasn't nice to you at first."

"He said he was sorry."

"That was nice of him."

Kendra's eyebrows rose high as she said, "Well, I had to forgive him, right? 'Cause that's what Jesus would have done."

"That's right, that's exactly what Jesus would have done."

Vacation Bible School had been Anna's mother's idea. It proved that not all of her ideas were from outer space. Anna wanted Kendra to have a Christian upbringing. She couldn't afford to send her to private school, but took her to Sunday school every weekend, and every summer, she went to Vacation Bible School. Anna did this even though she had problems with the church herself. Even in this day and age, she found there were still people whose faces puckered up with disapproval when they learned she was a single mother—not a divorcee or a widow, but a mother who never had married. To some people, it still smacked of scandal. So Anna did not go to church herself—she didn't like the stares and whispers. She dropped Kendra off for Sunday school, then picked her up ninety minutes later.

She envied Kendra her faith. Kendra believed everything told her by her teachers, and her faith that there was a loving God was solid and unshakeable. Kendra was lucky—she would never reach a point in her life when she would be faced with serious questions and doubts about the faith of her youth.

Sometimes, Anna found it difficult to believe that God was there, and if he was, it seemed he wasn't paying any attention to her anymore. Of course, she could hardly blame him—it had been a long time since she had uttered a prayer. She didn't see the point. When she prayed, nothing happened. Bills piled up, but money failed to come in to keep up with them. If it weren't for her night job, she feared she and Kendra would be living on the street. She thought that night job was probably part of the reason she'd stopped praying—thanks to that job, she was too ashamed to go before God and ask for anything.

She was signed up at a temp agency, which occasionally brought her some work, but it was always temporary. She had to be ready to drop everything at a moment's notice when the temp agency called. She had to run Kendra over to her sister's. Rose watched Kendra often and Anna was grateful that she was always so available and willing. Then she had to locate her temporary assignment. Being an outsider, she never fit in with the tight-knit group already installed at the businesses where she temped. They were all the same—they didn't welcome outsiders with open arms, and Anna was always on her own. Like in life.

At night, she did something else, something she wanted to keep from Kendra at all costs, and something her sister Rose disapproved of deeply. It was a topic they avoided, but somehow it was always there, whether they talked about it or not.

"How would you like it if Kendra did that?" Rose had said one day. "God knows she's got the looks and body for it. She should be on a calendar in a bikini."

"Rose! What kind of thing is that to say?"

"Well, it's *true*. Just *look* at her—she's drop-dead gorgeous. You're going to have to come to grips with something, Anna. Sooner or later—and probably sooner—Kendra is going to discover her own beauty, and she's going to start noticing men's reaction to it. She's going to put two and two together and behave the way she knows men *want* her to behave, and she's going to get herself into big trouble. Now, you need to have a good talk with her. You should have a few years ago. You don't want her to find out the way we did, do you?" She laughed and ran a hand back through her short dark hair. "Can you imagine Mom or Dad having a sex talk with us? I don't think either of them would get through it. We'd have to call an ambulance, they'd have to be hospitalized."

Anna tipped her head back and laughed. "I don't think anybody ever explained sex to *them*. We were accidents, no doubt about it."

They laughed together some more.

"I've talked to Ramona, and Frank talked to Bobby," Rose said. Ramona was her teenage daughter, Bobby her ten-year-old son, and Frank her husband. "We talked to them early, and made them feel free to ask questions. It's not a forbidden topic in our house, so it's not the big huge deal it is to so many kids. So far, it seems to be working."

"I know, I need to talk to her," Anna said. "I've been putting it off. I mean, who am *I* to talk to her about sex? With *my* background?"

"You can't think of it that way. She looks to you for answers, she sees you as being full of knowledge. Remember, she's a teenager, but really, she's still just a little girl."

"Yeah? Well, sometimes I feel like *I'm* still a little girl," Anna muttered.

"Get over it, you're not, and neither am I. Kendra doesn't need you to be a little girl, she needs you to be her mother. Even though Mom and Dad still *treat* you like a little girl."

"Oh, don't start with me, Rose."

"Who's starting anything? I'm just saying something that's already obvious."

It devolved into an argument, as usual, and Rose ended up leaving in anger, as usual; Anna called her a little later, as she always did, and sure enough, Rose was crying, and they went through the apologies and the declarations of love. Happened every time.

The truth was that, even with the two jobs—actually a job and a half, because more often than not, the temp job didn't deliver—Anna still had plenty of difficulty making ends meet. She had to juggle bills and do a lot of tap dancing every month. Sometimes it was exhausting, and sometimes—like when she was forced to borrow money from Rose (her parents had stopped loaning her money)—it was humiliating. There were times when she felt she couldn't go on with it, couldn't keep it up. But she had no choice. That was why she'd taken the job dancing at the Mt. Shasta Gentlemen's Club, and why sometimes, when things were especially tight, she took a little extra money from men for private favors. She tried not to think about it, even when she was doing it—it brought her too much shame, too much pain, and worst of all, too much self-hatred.

It was Anna's hope to save up enough money so that someday she and Kendra could find a little house somewhere to live instead of this dump of a trailer park. The only problem was, she didn't make enough money to save any. They lived hand-to-mouth. Except for the occasional temp job, the tips at night were the only money she made, and she had to pay a percentage of those tips to Rocky, the owner of the club. Just when she thought she might be able to put some money aside, something came up that prevented it—car problems, a trip to the walk-in clinic, and now the swamp cooler was making strange sounds and needed either to be fixed or replaced. That little house seemed so far, far away, like nothing more than a long-ago dream.

The trailer was stiflingly hot inside, even with the swamp cooler on. Something inside the cooler rattled loudly. It was mounted in the window over the kitchen table. The kitchen was just to the left of the front door as you came inside, the living room to the right. Through the kitchen was the hallway that led to the bathroom and bedrooms.

Anna felt perspiration trickle down her back and sides and she kept wiping her forehead before it dripped into her eyes. She saw beads of sweat roll down Kendra's temples, saw it glisten on her neck.

"Mommy?" Kendra said as they ate.

"What, honey?" Anna sounded tired, distracted.

"If everybody knows Jesus is coming back soon, why are they so mean to each other?"

Anna released a small, weary laugh. "Boy. If I'd known you were going to ask such deep questions, I would've gone to college. I don't know, honey. People have a long history of being mean to each other. It's part of what we do."

"But why?"

"Nobody knows. If we knew, then maybe we wouldn't do it anymore."

"Well … I wish we'd hurry up and figure it out. Is anybody working on that?"

"I don't *know*, Kendra," Anna said, an edge to her voice.

Kendra was chewing on a fish stick and her chewing slowed as she looked across the table at her mother with suddenly widened eyes. "You okay, Mommy?"

"Yes, I'm okay. Sorry for snapping at you. I'm just … distracted. Why did you ask that, honey? Is someone being mean to you?"

Kendra put a clump of macaroni and cheese in her mouth and chewed slowly. She did not respond for a long time, then shrugged one shoulder. When she finished chewing, she said, "Everybody's mean. In one way or another."

"Oh, surely that's not true, sweetheart," Anna said, leaning forward over her meal.

"They don't mean to be most of the time, but … after they talk to me a little … after they see what I'm like … the way they look at me sometimes … the way they talk to me. Or stare at me. *Especially* stare at me. Most of that's just accidental somehow. But the ones who are mean on purpose … there's something missing from their eyes."

Anna sighed as she watched her daughter eat.

The umbilical cord had wrapped around Kendra's neck. She had been deprived of oxygen just long enough to do some damage. They didn't know how much damage for a while. Later, the doctor told Anna that Kendra would never develop mentally beyond the age of eleven or twelve.

When he learned that there was something wrong with Kendra, Jack had skipped out, not only on Kendra, but on Anna, too. Anna had tried to explain to him exactly what had happened to Kendra, what had caused the problem, but all Jack knew was that she was "mentally deficient"—his words—and he refused to believe that she had come from his loins. He wanted nothing to do with either of them and he'd disappeared very quickly, leaving Anna and Kendra to fend for themselves. When she thought about Jack, Anna could not understand what had gotten into her—besides alcohol. She'd only been with him twice. Two times too many. Once would have been excusable, but *twice*? It probably had been the second time that took.

Anna closed her eyes a moment when she felt a pang of guilt for thinking such a thought—as if she regretted having Kendra. Kendra was the best thing that had ever happened to her in her miserable life. She didn't *deserve* Kendra. She thought of the life she'd led, and Kendra was an accidental godsend, a gift from heaven. She only hoped she could somehow make herself worthy of having her. She didn't feel she had so far.

Now, looking at Kendra, thinking about what she had just said, Anna thought, *She's supposed to be* retarded? Sometimes Kendra seemed a whole world smarter than Anna ever could hope to be. Sometimes she would casually say something that made Anna's jaw drop, or made goose pimples break out over her shoulders and neck. And then, in a moment, Kendra was a simple little girl again. She was a little girl with the incredibly voluptuous curves of a beautiful young woman.

She had no friends to speak of. She went to school when it was in session; the bus—the "short bus," others called it derisively, and it was—picked her up in the morning and dropped her off in the afternoon, and she came straight to the trailer. She had no friends asking her to come over to visit after school. She attended no school functions. There were some younger children in the park with whom she played at times, but that was all.

Kendra wore a red halter top and a pair of denim cutoffs that had been cut off pretty high on her firm thighs.

"Kendra, those shorts you're wearing today are too short," Anna said. "You've outgrown them. Change them."

"But they're *shorts*—how can they be *too* short?"

Anna sighed heavily. "Honey, we need to talk about sex."

Kendra put a hand over her mouth and giggled.

"What's funny?"

"It just sounds funny hearing you say it."

Anna smiled. "Does it? Well, I'm trying to be serious."

"I already know where babies come from, if that's what you mean."

"Where did you learn that?"

"I wanted to know, so I did what I do whenever I want to know something. I looked it up on the Internet."

A cold explosion of fear in Anna's chest made her gasp. Her mind flashed harshly on the kind of smut she imagined Kendra seeing on her monitor. "On the *internet*? What have you been looking at on the Internet? *Where* did you find out where babies come from?"

"From my online encyclopedia. I ask it lots of questions, and it always tells me about things."

15

Anna realized how tense she'd become and allowed herself to relax, at least a little. "An online encyclopedia," she said with a relieved smile. "I knew there was a reason I got you online."

"Can we go up on the roof and watch the sunset tonight?" Kendra said.

Anna smiled wearily. She envied the way Kendra could blithely hop from one topic to the next. Anna wished she could do that, just drop things from her mind and move on to something else, something pleasant. She could skirt past the worries that ate at her, the fears that dogged her and made sleep slow to come at night as she lay in bed staring into the dark, wondering if she'd be able to pay the next batch of bills, or worst of all, the rent.

"Sure we can, if you'd like," Anna said. "Is dinner good?"

"Fish sticks are always good."

They ate in silence, as the radio on the counter played soft rock. Kendra liked the music—it was soothing, relaxing. It made her feel good. But she also liked rap—because it was naughty.

Kendra Marie Dunfy was a girl with a desperate hunger to be naughty.

There was a little girl who lived in unit sixteen. She was seven years old and her name was Valerie, but everyone called her Val. Val was spoiled rotten and allowed to run rampant. No one in the park liked her. Kendra was the only one in the park who would talk to her. Val had said something once that had struck Kendra. She'd said, "It's *fun* to be naughty."

Kendra's life was an endless bland existence filled with unicorn stationary and puppy posters. One time when she and her mother had gone shopping in the Mt. Shasta Mall in Redding, Kendra had wandered into Hot Topic and had found some stationary she *really* wanted. It was all black, with silver and white cobwebs in the margins, and it came with a pen that wrote in silver ink. But Mommy said no. "I don't think that's a very good look for you, honey," she'd said. "But we couldn't afford it, anyway. I just can't afford to get you fancy stationary. We don't have the money."

But Kendra thought it *was* a good look for her—she was drawn to those dark things. For example, she had a stack of old R.L. Stine horror stories she was making her way through, and she'd even read some horror novels meant for adults. They'd been scary, and they'd bothered Kendra, but she'd enjoyed that, thought it was fun. Mommy did not approve of such literature, although she let some of it slide, saying, "I'm just glad you're reading."

There'd been a girl last school year who was always getting into trouble. Monica Hartwell—she always dressed in black and her long, full hair was dyed black, and she was *always* getting detention for one thing or another. Kendra had sat down with her at lunch one day—Monica had always sat alone at a corner table in the cafeteria. Kendra had introduced herself and said she liked the way Monica's hair looked, and the way she was dressed. They became friends, sort of. Monica did not seem to be the type of person to cultivate a real friendship. But they had lunch almost every day for the rest of the time that Monica was there. Monica had told Kendra about herself—just a tiny bit at a time—and Kendra realized she wasn't weird at all. She was just like everybody else, who simply dealt with things in a way that was slightly different from most. Monica had given her a lot of great books to read—horror novels, dark fantasies. Some of them had been hard for Kendra to read, but she'd diligently made her way through all of them. There were a couple she didn't quite understand, but most of them had been so scary, so disturbing—and so much fun! Monica had let her keep the books, but she had to hide them from Mommy, who wouldn't have liked them. She'd read them in bed, under the covers, by the light of a flashlight in her dark bedroom, which had made them even scarier.

Monica wasn't there the whole year. Her family moved away in March. Kendra missed her. There'd been no one else around like Monica, no one she could talk to with such ease, no one with whom she could truly relax and be herself. But something very useful had come from their friendship—Kendra now knew she was capable of *starting* a friendship. That was important to her.

She'd learned from Monica the same thing little Val had shouted: *It's fun to be naughty.* She'd done things with her friend that were *definitely* naughty, things she'd never thought about doing with a girl before, things she'd never thought of girls doing together. Fun things, things that felt awfully good.

"You ever done any of these things with a boy?" Monica had asked.

"No."

"You will. Someday."

Someday, Kendra thought.

She thought of her new next-door neighbor, Mr. Reznick—Marc. He was so handsome, so rugged-looking, like maybe he belonged on a horse. Kendra wondered what it would be like to do some of those things with him.

Yes, she wanted to do something *naughty*. The only problem was, she was never left alone. If only she could talk Mommy into leaving her alone for a change instead of taking her over to Aunt Rose's.

Kendra knew there was liquor in the cupboard over the kitchen counter. Maybe she could have a drink. She thought about that a while. What if Mommy found out? What if she smelled it on her breath later? Or what if Kendra got drunk and

Mommy came home and found her that way? Mommy would never let her stay by herself again, that was for sure.

Kendra could not allow that to happen.

She considered finding a pack of Mommy's cigarettes and having a smoke.

Kendra sighed. Her life was so bland, there weren't even any proper *opportunities* for her to be naughty.

It was like an itch—a naughty itch that she couldn't scratch. On one hand, she got frustrated with Mommy, but on the other, she did not want to disappoint her or make her angry. Kendra loved her, and she knew Mommy loved her, too.

But there it was, anyway, that smirking, leering need inside her, that needling itch to do something naughty, anything at all, something with some risk to it, something exciting. That was what she enjoyed the most—the excitement. She liked video games because they were exciting, and some of them were even naughty—you could get points for killing police officers, or even innocent bystanders! Kendra enjoyed adrenaline, and the satisfying feeling of getting away with something.

Last year, Kendra and Monica had gone on a lot of shoplifting trips. They'd left school at the end of the day in Monica's car and gone to a string of convenience stores around Redding. At each stop, one would talk to the cashier while the other lifted something. They took turns. They got a lot of magazines, paperback books, candy, and beer, or other malt beverages. There was always the chance of being caught at any moment, and Kendra had felt swollen and giddy with simultaneous fear and delight. It was an intoxicating concoction of excitement that made Kendra feel like she was really *doing* something, like she was *living*.

She missed those days, and she wanted to do something like that again—or something completely new that would excite her just as much, something she hadn't thought of yet. But she had no one with whom to do it. That made her sad for a while. She wondered where Monica was now and if she had managed to keep out of jail. She wondered if Monica ever thought of her, as Kendra sometimes thought of Monica.

Of course, all of this depended on whether or not Mommy would let her stay in the trailer by herself the next time Mommy got a temp assignment, or when she went out dancing at night. And sometimes it felt as if that would never happen.

Kendra was always defeated by the dread words, "We'll see" ...

Three

Reznick had been in the trailer park for five weeks. During that time, he'd kept to himself. Before that, he'd lived for a while in a smaller, more run-down park on River Valley Drive on the other side of the river, but the place had become *so* run-down that he couldn't stand it anymore. He wished he could afford to live in one of the better parks with mostly senior citizens who lived in expensive double-wides. Of course, what he *really* wanted was to live in a house again. But that was down the line. Way down the line. He had to build up his business again first. He still had some of the money his father had left him, but not much. The rental of his office took big chunks out of it. What he needed more than anything was not a new trailer park or a house, but more business.

After his nap, he got up and dumped the chicken bones in the garbage, then tied the bag off and pulled it out of the can. It was Tuesday night, and the garbage man came early Wednesday morning. He took the bag outside and put it in the big green can, then wheeled the can out to the edge of the narrow paved road that ran through the park.

He heard voices. He slowed down as he returned to his trailer, then stopped and listened. The voices were nearby, but he could see no one, and he could not pinpoint their source, but they were close. Then he looked up.

"Hello, neighbor," a woman said. She peered down at him from the roof of the trailer next door. She was lying face-down on the roof, leaning on her elbows.

"Hello," he said.

He'd seen her around, but he'd paid her no attention. They hadn't spoken. He thought she had a daughter, if he wasn't mistaken.

She seemed to be smiling down at him, but it was difficult to tell because her face was in shadow. "Have you ever watched the sunset from your roof?"

"No, can't say that I have," he said.

"You should try it, it's really beautiful. We've got a great view from up here. You want to come up and join us?"

He almost said, without even thinking about it, no. Then it occurred to him that if he went back inside, he would stare at the television and brood.

"We have ice tea if you'll bring a glass," the woman said.

"Are you serious?" Reznick said.

"Yes. There's a ladder on the other side of the trailer, in front. We have room for one more. I'm Anna, by the way. Anna Dunfy."

"Marcus Reznick."

"Well, come on up, Mr. Reznick. The sun's about to set."

Reznick scratched the back of his head, then thought, *What the hell.* He went inside, got a glass. Conan followed him out of the trailer.

"Can I bring my dog up?" he said. "He's small."

"Sure," Anna Dunfy said.

Reznick picked up Conan, then went around to the other side of his neighbor's trailer to the ladder, which he climbed awkwardly. Once his head and shoulders had risen above the top edge of the trailer, he set Conan on the roof.

"Oh, look at *you*!"

Reznick was faced by a second woman on the roof, not the one who had spoken to him. Not a woman, really—a girl. And suddenly, he could not move. He stopped climbing, stopped breathing for a little while.

The girl had been lying face-down on a blanket, which was spread over a large foam-rubber egg-carton pad, but when she saw Conan, she quickly got up and turned toward Reznick, sat up and crossed her legs. She sat between Reznick and Anna Dunfy.

Reznick was frozen in place by her. Had she reached out and plunged her hand into his chest and clutched his heart and ripped it out of him, she could not have stunned him more than she did simply by sitting there petting Conan. His heart had completely lost control of itself. It wasn't simply beating, it was thundering. His insides were tense. He was overwhelmed by a bone-deep hunger, a need so great that he set the glass on the roof before he shattered it with his squeezing, white-knuckled hand.

Never in his forty-two years of life—not even in his hormone-addled youth—had he ever wanted a woman so deeply, so desperately, so instantly.

"Oh, he's so cute!" the girl said.

Her mane of golden hair hung down on both sides of her face as she bent forward to pet the wiggling little dog. Even in the dim light, he could see her face—a beautiful face that glowed the way a pregnant woman's face glowed. She lifted her head and looked at him and he stopped breathing. Her smiling eyes were so big, he was afraid for a moment that he might fall

23

into them if he climbed any higher on the ladder. Her lips—had there ever been lips more custom-made for kissing? They were plump and her mouth was perhaps just a fraction too long, but it made her kind, sympathetic smile all the bigger and more pleasant. Her mouth was open as she looked at him, and she ran her tongue slowly around her lips. Creamy cleavage rose up out of the red halter top from between her round, heavy breasts. The halter top revealed an expanse of flat, pale belly. Between her legs, small golden hairs curled out around the narrow, raggedy crotch of the very-short cutoffs she wore. Her toenails were painted a delicate red on her bare feet. Her legs were long and slender and shapely.

For a moment, he felt light-headed. He clutched the sides of the ladder with both hands for fear of toppling over backwards.

"You okay, Mr. Reznick?" Anna Dunfy said as she peered around her daughter.

"Yeah, yeah, just … a little, uh … a little dizzy. I'm not, uh, you know, crazy about heights."

"Oh, well, you're almost here, just a little bit more."

Reznick was surprised by how much effort it took to pull his eyes from the girl. It almost hurt to look away from her. He climbed up onto the roof as the girl stretched out on her belly again on the blanket between Reznick and Anna.

"Just lie down on the blanket, Mr. Reznick," Anna said.

"Call me Marc," he said.

"And you call me Anna."

"And you can call me Kendra," the girl said as she smiled at him.

He tried to speak, to say hi to the girl, but nothing but breath came out the first couple times. "Hi, Kendra."

"I'm her daughter," she said. She was chewing gum. He could smell it—it smelled of grape flavoring.

Reznick smelled something else, too—just a whiff of it, a slight hint. Something … disturbing.

"Ni-nice to meet you, Kendra," he said, barely getting it out. He looked at the gentle slope of her back, the rise of her ass in the small patch of blue denim, the dimples on the backs of her knees.

"Just stretch out beside Kendra, there," Anna said. "There's room."

"Here," Kendra said, "I'll pour you some tea." She picked up the pitcher of ice tea in front of her. The ice cubes in it clattered and clinked as she poured some into his glass.

"Thank you," he said, and it came out as a whisper.

"What's your doggy's name?" Kendra said.

"Conan."

"He's *so* cute! Oh, Conan, you're so cute, you know that?"

Conan wagged his butt and lapped up the attention and affection.

"You haven't been here long, have you, Marc?" Anna said.

"About a month."

"I guess I haven't been very neighborly," she said. "I should've come over and introduced myself, or something."

"Don't feel bad," he said. "I'm not very neighborly myself. I guess I'm kind of … a hermit."

"Being neighborly is a lost art, I think," Anna said.

Reznick nodded. "Part of another time."

If he tipped his head forward, he could see Anna's face beyond Kendra's. He could see where Kendra got her good looks. Anna was lovely, and quite young. She had long auburn hair and big catlike eyes. She and Kendra shared full lips and a delicately upturned nose. She looked almost young enough to pass for Kendra's sister.

"What kind of work do you do, Marc?"

"I'm a private investigator."

Anna's face broke open in a broad smile. "No kidding? A real private investigator?"

"What's a private investigator?" Kendra said. She had not stopped looking at him since he'd stretched out beside her. She kept petting Conan, but she looked at Reznick. He felt naked under her gaze, and unable to return it. He felt if he did, if he met her eyes and looked in them for very long, he would burst into flames.

"You know," he said, looking at his ice tea, "a private detective?"

Kendra said nothing for a moment, and he stole a look at her. She frowned—two little creases appeared between her gracefully curved eyebrows—and cocked her head. It was a childlike gesture—a childlike gesture above the swell of a woman's cleavage coming up out of that halter top.

"Is it interesting?" Kendra said.

"Well, yes, I suppose it is. It's not boring, anyway."

"Do you make lots of money doing it?"

"Kendra, that's not very polite," Anna said.

"Oh, I'm sorry," she said, as if she truly had no idea it wasn't a polite thing to ask.

Reznick frowned a moment. There was something different about Kendra, something odd. He couldn't put his finger on it yet.

"I'll put it this way," he said. "I'm not getting rich."

"Ah, look at the sun," Anna said.

There was a break in the trees just ahead, and far beyond it was a line of purple mountains in the distance. Just above it stretched some flat clouds that glowed a bright pink as the sun set.

A moment later, the shadows were deeper and the park's shade became darker. The sun had set, leaving only a golden glow behind the mountains which was already dimming. The

26

pink drained from the clouds, leaving behind a rich deep purple.

"It doesn't last long, but it's sure nice while it does," Anna said. "It's free and it's something beautiful. Something to be appreciated, you know?"

Reznick gave Kendra a sidelong look. She was still looking at him. Her mouth was hanging open again, but her eyes were smiling at him. Once again, she ran her tongue around her lips. Had she even looked at the sunset, he wondered?

A breeze blew over them, and that smell returned.

It was stronger this time.

More distinct.

It hit Reznick like a kick to the stomach, then a baseball bat to the forehead. For a moment, he actually thought he was going to be sick.

He turned to Kendra. Her smile grew larger and she tilted her head again. Was she flirting with him? There was something so girlish about her—so *little* girlish.

But that smell.

It overpowered him. The memories flooded into his mind as if a dam had broken. The pain they brought with them was real and physical.

"What … what's that perfume you're wearing?" Reznick said, staring straight ahead.

"Oh, that's Ice," Anna said. "You like it?"

"Yes," he said, but once again, his voice came out in a whisper.

He clumsily got up and said, "I've got to go."

"Yes, so do I," Anna said. "I've got to take Kendra to my sister's, then go to work."

Reznick nearly fell off the trailer trying to pick up Conan. He was partway down the ladder when Kendra said, "Your glass!"

"I'll get it later," he said, and his voice quavered. He hoped they could not see the tears that were welling in his eyes. "I've gotta go. Gotta make a phone call. Forgot all about it."

The perfume's fragrance clogged his nostrils. It clung to him, pulled at him.

He carried Conan down the ladder, then went around the trailer and back to his own. He tripped on the steps going in and almost dropped Conan. He put the dog down and staggered over to his recliner. He fell into it and sobbed into his hands as the pain tore through him, the pain of memories he'd tried to bury with alcohol, memories he'd tried desperately to keep away during his year of sobriety. They flooded in now and he gasped like a man drowning. Even here in his living room, the fragrance of Anna's perfume clung to him, engulfed him, clogged his throat and choked him. It burned his eyes and made his heart ache. He gasped for air but all he sucked in was the smell of that perfume, Ice.

Conan stood and stared at him with his little head tilted to one side.

Four

I ce.

It had been Victoria's perfume. Reznick had bought her a bottle of it one Christmas. It was a cool fragrance, smooth and fresh. It had been in the air whenever he was with her. It quickly had become a part of her.

Reznick had read somewhere once that smell was the strongest trigger of vivid memories. That scent had created a painful explosion of memories in his mind, vivid, clawing memories that dug at the backs of his eyes. When he lowered his eyelids, he could see her. He wished to God that he could see her as she'd been, the Victoria he'd loved and planned to marry. He wished he could see the fair-skinned, freckled face and the wide smile, which had been too rare, the sad green eyes—the sadness never left them, and it was that sadness that killed her—and the long, luxurious red hair, which he'd taken great pleasure in brushing for her. But he never saw that when he thought of Victoria.

No, it was never that Victoria, it was the last he'd seen of her. It was the day he'd come home early to surprise her. No telling how long she'd been sitting on the bed trying to muster the nerve to do it. When she heard him come in, she'd resolved herself to do it at that moment. She'd known he would stop her, talk her out of it, take the gun away from her. Sitting there on the edge of the bed, she'd fired the gun into her temple at point blank range just as he walked into the bedroom. Just in time for Reznick to flinch at the explosive gunshot, and see half of her head disappear, see her brains splash over the wall and headboard. The dark red-black matter hit the wall with a splash and then began to dribble downward in tiny lumps and gobs as blood gushed from Victoria's nose and she was thrown to the side on the bed. The gun fell from her hand, a .44 magnum—*his* gun.

He'd screamed then, but his voice sounded far away to him. He rushed to her side, but of course, she was gone. Her suddenly-bulging, bloody eyes stared up at the ceiling. The blood from her nose glistened around her open mouth and on her chin like a black-red goatee.

A sheet of blood-speckled paper was on the bed beside her with some of her handwriting on it. Reznick couldn't read it for awhile, because he couldn't stop sobbing and screaming. He'd reached for the phone and called 911. He'd finally gotten all the information out to the operator, but when he was done, he could not get the phone back on its base because his eyes were bleary and his hands were shaking, so he let it drop to the floor.

Finally, he wiped his eyes and picked up the paper. Still sobbing, he read the note:

> Dear Marc,
> I'm so very sorry. I just can't take the
> pain anymore. I can't. I know you'll
> understand because you love me. I
> love you so much. And I'm sorry.
> With all my heart and soul,

Her signature was shaky and unclear, but it was hers. Her last words, written in a wobbly cursive on a page stained with her blood and something else—maybe tears.

He had tried to help her. He'd taken her to his doctor, who had diagnosed her as suffering from severe clinical depression. He'd tried several different medications out on her, but she'd had bad reactions to all of them and couldn't take them. She refused to see a therapist. There were days when the sadness lifted and she was able to smile a little bigger smile than usual, even laugh a little. But most of the time, that sadness started in her eyes and spread over her whole face.

Reznick had met her in a movie theater, where she'd worked the ticket booth. She'd kept her sadness to herself, even when it showed on her face. She managed to smile in spite of it, but it was a muted smile. It was still a beautiful smile, though. Everything about her had been beautiful—her ears, her nose, her hands, her breasts, her legs, even her feet.

And even her perfume, the perfume he'd given her.

Ice.

Three months after Victoria's suicide, Reznick's parents had gone into the Tower Mart off of Highway 273 in Anderson on their way to see Reznick's sister, her husband, and their children in Anderson Heights. They'd stopped at the convenience store to get some candy for their grandchildren, and a couple cold drinks for themselves. A robbery had taken place while they were standing in line at the register. The robber had panicked and started shooting. He'd shot and killed four people, Reznick's parents included.

Seeing Victoria kill herself had damaged Reznick. It had driven a spike deep into his brain. The loss of his parents only did more damage. That was when he'd fallen into the bottle and his whole life had fallen apart. His sister didn't care. She was his foster sister, actually, and they had never gotten along.

She'd always resented Reznick for being, unlike her, their parents' blood. So he'd fallen into the bottle alone.

A bottle. A bottle of vodka, that was what he needed. It was a short drive to the Handi-Spot Market on North Street. They sold liquor there.

He pulled his lips inward and ran his tongue around them. He could taste it. On ice, nice and cold.

Conan hopped into his lap and curled up. Reznick absently stroked the little dog for a while, then he put Conan on the floor and stood. He went to the bathroom and opened the medicine cabinet. He took two Xanax with a drink of water from the glass he kept by the sink. He also saw a bottle of NyQuil in the cabinet. He took it out, took the small cup off the bottle's top, filled it, and drank it down. He repeated the process, then exhaled hard between puffed cheeks. He replaced the NyQuil and closed the cabinet.

The cough syrup created a spreading warmth in his belly not unlike the warmth created by a swig of vodka. He thought it would help, but it just made him crave the vodka even more.

He looked at his face in the cabinet mirror. He wondered if he'd lost weight lately—his face seemed thinner. He had short, wavy brown hair, a rectangular forehead and a straight patrician nose. His jaw was square, his shoulders broad. There was really nothing special about him. He wasn't homely, but neither was he especially handsome, he thought. He wondered what Victoria had seen in him. What had attracted her to him at first? He'd never asked her. There were so many things he'd never asked her, never told her. His eyes crinkled on the corners as they narrowed and the corners of his mouth pulled back and his shoulders hitched as more tears spilled down his glistening-wet cheeks. He put his hands on the counter, elbows locked, and let his head fall forward between his shoulders.

"Victoria," he whispered hoarsely as he sobbed. "Victoria."

Later, the two Xanax kicked in. Reznick stretched out in his recliner, and turned on the television. With Conan curled up on his belly, he fell asleep as silent tears continued to spill from his eyes.

Five

The trailer was dark, but it was always dark, even during the day. During the daylight hours, the darkness in the trailer seemed almost malignant to Sherry Manning—harsh halos of pale sunlight glowed around the edges of the blankets and towels hanging in all the windows—except for the one living room window where the swamp cooler was—and the glow made the smoke from a cigarette someone was smoking look like something sinister as it oozed through the air, then was swept away suddenly by the current of the cooler.

She lay on the couch with a couple throw pillows under her head. She wasn't sure how long she'd been lying there, nor did she care. The television was on—*The Price is Right* had been on for a while, then she'd closed her eyes and opened them to *Jerry Springer*, closed them again and opened them to *Oprah*, and now it was a rerun of *Everybody Loves Raymond*. Sherry liked that show and watched it a lot. She squinted at the television and wondered if it was an episode she'd seen.

Sherry sat up on the couch and yawned. She smacked her lips and rubbed her eyes. Her mouth was dry and she felt … gummy. Gummy in her mouth, and gummy all over.

Andy came in from the kitchen and said, "Hi, babe." He sat down on the couch beside her, put an arm around her, and kissed her cheek. "I gotta go." He held a cigarette between the first two fingers of his right hand, and it trailed ribbons of smoke that got caught up and swept away by the swamp cooler.

"Where you goin'?" she said. Her tongue felt thick and she slurred her words. She sat back a little, reached up, and stroked his smooth face, brushed a strand of his long hair out of his eyes. She loved his hair. It was long and thick and luxurious, a rich brown, like chocolate, and she loved stroking it, running her fingers through it.

"I gotta pick up David," he said. "Him and me're gonna score some weed. Pays the bills, y'know."

"Yeah, okay. Gonna be long?"

"Shouldn't be. Don't worry, you got plenty a company." He looked down at the floor where four bodies formed sprawling lumps under a tangle of blankets.

"Who's here?" she said as she squinted down at them.

Andy frowned for a moment and shrugged. "I'm not even sure anymore. People've been in and out today."

"Do me a favor before you go?"

"Sure, what?"

She reached over and took her black vinyl kit from the end table and handed it to him.

Andy looked at the kit disapprovingly and sighed. He only smoked weed, he didn't do the hard stuff. He didn't like it when Sherry did, either. She didn't do it very often. Sometimes she got an itch for it, like she'd had the day before. At least she thought it had been the day before. She frowned.

"What day is it?" she said as he took the kit and opened the zipper.

"Tuesday." He opened the kit and went to work. "You know I don't like you doing this shit. You do it much longer, you're gonna have trouble getting off it."

"Don't worry. I won't."

Sherry liked to watch him as he held the lighter under the spoon, as he loaded the spike. As he put the tourniquet—a length of surgical tubing—on her arm. Then he tenderly felt for a vein, gently inserted the needle, and—

All the gumminess went away. In seconds, Sherry felt pristine and shiny, like the surface of a mirror, like the sharp, glinting, polished-steel blade of a knife.

Oh, yeah. She dropped her head back and relaxed, slumped on the couch as it moved through her, as it soothed every nerve to the point of ecstasy.

"You gonna be okay now?" Andy said.

"Mmm, yeah. I feel all yummy now."

He leaned over and kissed her, and she put an arm around his neck, pulled him close, and gave him a long, deep kiss.

He smiled as he pulled back. "That's nice. I want some more a that when I get back."

He stood and she said, "Hurry back."

Andy left the trailer. A moment later, she heard his pickup truck start. A moment after that, he backed out, then drove away.

Sherry licked her lips, then smacked them. Now she could function. She stood and prodded one of the lumps on the floor with her bare foot. "Okay, who's on my floor?" she said. "C'mon, guys, it's—" She looked at the clock on the VCR. "—it's almost nine-thirty. It's nighttime, guys."

The bodies began to stir on the floor. Blankets shifted and a head popped up from beneath one of them.

"Lissa?" Sherry said.

"What?"

"Hi. I'd forgotten you were here."

Lissa smiled, then wiped her mouth with the back of her hand. She smacked her lips and rubbed her eyes. Looked like Lissa was feeling pretty gummy, too. She had short dark hair and a round face and was plump. Lissa and Sherry had been friends since high school.

"Who else is here, anyway?" Sherry said.

"Rob. Remember? And Philpott."

"I remember Rob being here. When did Philpott come?" His name was Sherman, but everybody called him by his last name, Philpott.

"I dunno. Oh, and some guy."

"Some guy?"

"Yeah, some guy, I dunno who he is." She nudged the body beside her with a knee. "Come on, guys, wake up. It's late."

"You want some more, Lissa?" Sherry said.

"Oh, yeah."

Sherry opened her kit as Lissa got up on the couch beside her. Sherry went through all the motions.

"Oh, God," Philpott groaned as he slowly rolled over and peeled the blanket back. "My back."

"What?" Rob said.

"My back. It's in pain. From sleeping on the floor. How long've I been down here, anyway?"

"All day," Lissa said as Sherry injected the needle. "No wonder your back hurts. Mine doesn't feel so good, either." Her voice became quieter and quieter and her head fell back on the cushion, and a big, slow smile spread over her face. "Mmm," she said, and it sounded like a cat's purr.

Sherry pulled the needle out and put her things away in the black vinyl kit.

"What the hell is *this*?" Philpott said.

"Oh, God," Rob said.

Sherry looked down at the boys and tried to focus on what they were looking at.

There was one remaining lump beneath a blanket. A corner of the blanket was pulled back, and there was a puddle of something on the dirty old cigarette-burned beige carpet, something white and foamy and lumpy that disappeared under the blanket.

"Hey, dude," Philpott said. "Wake up." He reached over and shook the body beneath the blanket, but it did not respond.

Philpott grabbed the edge of the blanket and pulled it back in one quick movement.

A young man in his early twenties, their age, lay on the floor on his side with his mouth and eyes open. The foamy substance clung to his lips and chin. He'd vomited it onto the floor. He stared at nothing with dull, flat, milky eyes. His face was pale with a sick, yellowish hue, his messy hair dark.

"Holy *shit!*" Philpott said as he scrambled to get to his feet and get away from the body.

"Oh, God," Rob said as he got on hands and knees, then stood.

Sherry gasped and shot to her feet, still holding her kit. She swayed a little unsteadily, then found her footing. "Who *is* that?" she said. "What ... what *happened?*"

Rob said, "It looks like ... he O.D.'d."

"Oh, dear Jesus," Sherry whimpered as she pressed both fists to her chin and dropped her kit to the floor. "But who *is* he?"

"Didn't he come here with David this morning?" Philpott said.

"When was David here?" Sherry said.

They stared at the corpse for a while—all but Lissa, who sat slumped on the couch, her eyes closed.

Sherry tried to speak, but only croaked like a little frog. She did not recognize the pale, dead young man on the floor.

"Yeah, he was here," Lissa said, still slumped on the couch with her eyes closed. She opened them and slowly leaned forward to sit on the edge of the couch. "David was here early this morning. *Today* was still on TV, so it was early." Lissa slowly looked down and saw the body and gasped. "What the … who's *that*?" she said, her voice breathy.

"That's right," Rob said, frowning. "I've got a fuzzy memory of David being here."

Sherry said, "What's he doing here *now*?"

"Well, he's … dead," Philpott said.

"But who *is* he?" Lissa said as she stood.

"We don't know," Philpott said.

"Well … what are we supposed to *do*?" Sherry said.

Timidly, Lissa said, "Call the police?"

Sherry said, "We *can't* call the police, Lissa, there's a fuckin' *meth* lab in the other room."

"Oh, yeah," Lissa whispered.

"And we're stoned," Sherry said.

"Hey, I'm not stoned," Rob said. "I gotta go, anyway." He started looking around for his shoes.

"What?" Sherry said. "You can't leave."

"I brought you, Lissa," Rob said as he put his shoes on. "You comin' with me now?"

"No, you guys *can't* leave!" Sherry said. "We have to wait till Andy gets back. Andy'll know what to do. Don't go!"

"I gotta go," Rob said. "You comin', Lissa?"

"I-I don't know," Lissa said. She put a hand to the side of her head, as if it hurt.

"Come on, Lissa, you *can't* go," Sherry said. "You, either, Rob. You *have* to stay till Andy comes back."

"No, I don't need *this* shit," Rob said. "C'mon, Lissa, let's go."

"But I don't wanna leave Sherry here with this."

"Fine, then, stay. But I'm goin'." Rob went to the door and opened it as he fished his keys from his pocket. Outside, it was dark. "I'll see you guys later." He pulled the door closed after him.

They heard his car door open, then close, heard his engine start.

"I can't believe he left," Sherry said quietly. "I mean, we, we've got a-a dead *body* on the floor, and he, he just *leaves*."

"Please cover him up," Lissa said.

"Yeah, that's not a bad idea," Sherry said as she bent down and tossed the blanket over the staring body.

"I'm hungry," Philpott said.

"How can you *eat* now?" Sherry said.

"My stomach's growlin', that's how."

"Well, have some cereal, or somethin'. Help yourself."

"What are you gonna do?" he said.

Sherry sighed. "Wait for Andy to get back. I don't know what *else* to do. Maybe Andy will."

Philpott nodded and said, "Yeah, he probably will. When's he coming back?" He went to the cupboard, got a bowl and a box of Cap'n Crunch, poured the cereal into the bowl, then went to the refrigerator for milk.

"I don't know," she said, thinking, *Not soon enough.*

"What are we gonna do with him?" Lissa said, her eyes puffy. "I mean, if we take him to the hospital, they're gonna wanna know who *we* are. They'll ask about our connection to him, they'll wanna know who he is, they'll ask—"

"*Stop it*, Lissa!" Sherry snapped. She raised her hands and buried her fingers in her hair on both sides of her head. "Just *stop it*, please. My *God*, I need a cigarette. And a drink."

Sherry went to the end table, found her Marlboros, and lit one up with a red butane lighter.

Philpott stood leaning on the kitchen counter and ate his cereal.

"I wish I'd gone with Rob now," Lissa said, her voice quavering. She turned and stared down at the long lump in the blanket on the floor.

"I'm sorry, Lissa," Sherry said. "I didn't mean to snap at you. I'm … tense. I really appreciate you stayin' here with me. Both of you, thank you for stayin', really."

Philpott put his cereal down and held up a half-full bottle of tequila. "You serious about having that drink?"

"Yeah," Sherry said. She went to the kitchen, took a glass from the counter and rinsed it out. She held out the glass and Philpott poured.

He was short and pudgy with bright red hair and a face covered with freckles. He took a glass down from the cupboard and poured some tequila for himself, took a few swallows, then picked up his cereal and finished eating it, drank the remaining milk out of the bowl, then put the bowl in the sink.

"Lissa's right," Sherry said. "What're we gonna do with him without getting ourselves in trouble?"

A brief frown could not darken Philpott's open, optimistic face. "We'll ask Andy when he gets back. Maybe David will be with him and we can find out who this guy is."

Sherry thought of the corpse's open eyes and mouth and took a couple gulps of tequila. "Hurry home, Andy," she said.

Six

Steve Regent, in unit five, heard a car pull up in front of his trailer and idle for a moment. He suspected it was his ten o'clock appointment. Sure enough, the engine was killed. Regent tried to make all his appointments during the daytime — they looked more legitimate that way. But this woman insisted on meeting him at ten at night, it was the only time she was available.

Regent went to his door, opened it, and took a step down. He waved at the small compact car parked across the entrance to his driveway. She got out of the car, and he held the door open for her as she entered the trailer.

"I hope it's okay, where I parked," she said.

"It's fine, don't worry about it," he said.

He kept his trailer well-lit inside so he could see them as soon as they entered, get a good look at them. They did the same thing over at Josh Garner's house. Garner was his partner, and they usually did most of their business at the house he kept in Redding just for this purpose, but this woman had spoken to Regent and he'd been the one to talk her into it, so he'd had her come to his trailer.

She was nineteen, maybe twenty. She wore a tiny yellow shirt that exposed her flat belly, and a short, tight turquoise skirt. Her bare legs were gorgeous, maybe her best feature. Her face was okay—youthful and clean—but her legs were her selling point, her legs and her ass. Not much in the way of breasts, but she would do.

She stepped into the entryway, which opened onto the den where he kept his computer on a large desk, behind which was a long couch, a couple armchairs, a sideboard where he kept some bottles of liquor and some glasses. He led her to the right, into the living room where the couch and recliner and two other chairs faced the big-screen TV. The living room was attached to a small dining area, which was separated from the kitchen by a bar. A hallway led down to the bedrooms and bathroom.

"Have a seat," he said.

She sat down at one end of the couch.

"Can I get you something to drink?" he said. "I'm having wine. Would you like some?"

"Sure, that would be nice," she said.

He went to the kitchen and got another wineglass from the cupboard, poured some chilled white wine into it.

"Now remind me," he said as he came back into the living room with a glass of wine in each hand, "your name is—"

"Heather," she said. "Heather Winters."

Regent handed her the drink, then sat down in an armchair, which he turned to face the couch. His drink was on the lamp table beside the chair. He picked it up and took a sip, then another. "So, Heather Winters, what can I do for you?"

"Well, your ad said you were interested in helping out young women who needed money and were willing to be photographed. That you'd pay up to seven hundred dollars."

"That's right."

"Well—" She swallowed dryly. She was very nervous, and her right leg bounced up and down frantically. "—I'm curious to, uh, know what, uh, kind of photographs?"

"It's nude photography. You need some quick money? I hope nothing's wrong, Heather."

She released a quick, nervous laugh. "Well, yeah, something's wrong, you could say that."

"What's the problem?"

"I, uh … I'm, uh … my boyfriend doesn't know yet because I haven't told him. I know what he'll say, what he'll do. So I'm not going to tell him. I need money for an abortion. I'll pay for it myself and he'll never know the difference. I'll tell him I'm going down to Corning to stay with my sister for a few days. And I will. Afterward. He'll never know the difference."

"I'm sorry you have to do that, Heather," he said.

"Do what?"

"I'm sorry you have the kind of relationship that makes it necessary for you to do something like sneak around that way."

"Oh. Yeah. Well. It wouldn't go over, believe me. He'd accuse me of trying to trap him. He'd be … oh, he'd be *furious.* But he'd never allow me to have an abortion. He's very conservative and he doesn't believe in it."

"That's too bad. It's something you two should be able to share joyfully."

"Yeah, you'd think."

Heather burst into sobs, put her wineglass on the end table, and quickly grabbed for her purse. She took a tissue from it and wiped her eyes. The sobs passed quickly. "I'm sorry, I'm just … I'm not … myself lately, you know?" She snatched up her wineglass and took a couple big gulps. When she saw how little was left, she finished it.

Regent stood and took the glass. "Let me get you a refill. Unless you'd like something stronger. I have some good scotch."

"No, the wine's fine."

He went to the kitchen, poured more, then returned and handed her the glass, sat down in the chair again.

"Let me tell you the pay scale," he said. "But first, I've gotta ask—are you easily offended?"

"What do you mean?"

"I mean, are you going to start slapping me when I give you the pay scale? Because all you have to do is say you're not interested, you really don't have to hit me."

She laughed, a small, soggy sound. "No, I won't."

"Have you done any modeling?" he said.

"A little back in high school. My aunt owns a dress shop and I used to do some modeling for her, and I was in some of her newspaper ads."

"Well, here's how it works. A hundred dollars for simple nude pictures. If we get more graphic—if you masturbate, for example—then it goes up to two-fifty. Then you have the option of doing video. You can strip on video for three hundred fifty, or you can strip and masturbate for five hundred. And you get seven-fifty if you agree to give me head on camera. That, uh, that would give you the money you need for an abortion."

"Yes, it would," she said, but she barely got the words out before sobbing again. She sobbed quietly, her head down, and her shoulders jerked as she got another tissue from her purse. "I'm sorry," she whispered.

"Don't be. I only wish I could do something more for you."

"I'd need more to travel down to my sister's," she said as she wiped her eyes. She blew her nose, then stuffed all the tissues into her purse. "I don't even have enough money for gas to Corning, I have nothing once I pay all my bills, and there's

45

no one I can go to for help, and I … I …" She sniffled and shed a few more tears. Suddenly, she shook her head sharply. She stood and said, "Maybe I should go."

"No, wait. Maybe we can work something out. Maybe a *package* deal."

"What do you mean?"

"How about doing *all* of it for twelve hundred dollars?"

"All of it?"

"The nudie photos, the explicit photos, the video, the whole thing. You do that, and I'll pay you twelve hundred dollars."

She stood there and thought about it for a long time. Slowly, Heather lowered herself back onto the couch.

"Your boyfriend will never know the difference," Regent said.

"What are they for?"

"I'm sorry?"

"The pictures and videos—what are they for, what do you do with them?"

"They go on my websites."

Her eyes widened a little. "For how long?"

"What do you mean?"

"How long do you leave the pictures and videos on your website?"

He shrugged. "As long as the sites are up. You have a problem with that?"

"Well … what if he *sees* me?"

Another shrug. "Some men, they really get off on it. It turns them on, seeing their girlfriends or wives on a website, knowing other people are looking at them. Some men love it."

"I don't think Nate would."

"Does he join paysites?"

"What do you mean?"

"He would have to pay to see you. Does he pay to join websites?"

She released a small sigh of relief. "No, he doesn't."

"Then you've got nothing to worry about."

She stood and thought some more. "You get a lot of people coming to your site?"

"In the millions. I have a few different sites. They're all very successful."

"I see. Well." For a moment, she looked like she was about to turn and leave. Then she put the purse on the couch. Her voice trembled as she said, "Okay, the whole thing for twelve hundred."

"Wonderful," he said, "just wonderful." He stood and went to the end table by the couch and picked up the cordless phone on its base. "I'm going to have to call a friend over to help. I'm going to need a hand." He punched in the number, waited a moment. "Hey, it's Steve. You got some time? I've got a session set up, and I need a hand." He listened a moment, then said, "Great, see you in a few." He turned the phone off and put it back on its base. "He'll be here in awhile. He lives just north of Redding. In the meantime, why don't we get some pictures. C'mon in the studio."

Heather followed him down the hall to a bedroom with a king-size bed on one side, and lights for the photo shoots on the other. He turned a couple of the lights on, then went to a small desk behind the lights. "I need you to sign a couple forms before we do anything. How old are you, Heather?"

"Twenty."

He took a couple sheets of paper from a desk drawer, put them on the desk, and handed her a pen. "Just sign here," he said, pointing to a line at the bottom of the page. She signed it, and he pulled the first page aside. "And here."

As she signed the second sheet, she said, "What are these for?"

"One swears you're of age, and the other is so you won't sue me when your pictures and videos show up on the Internet, and gives me permission to use the photos and videos on my websites."

"Oh, I see."

Regent took a digital camera from the desktop. "Now, we'll start with your clothes on. Just lie back on the bed and pose for me. Give me your sexiest looks."

Heather slipped her flats off and got on the bed, stretched out on her back, propped up by her elbows. She went through a series of poses for him—bend the knee, raise this arm, lift that hip. Her movements were stiff, her poses rigid.

"You need some more wine," Regent said. "You're very stiff, Heather. We need to loosen you up."

"How about some of that scotch?" she said.

Regent smiled and said, "Attagirl."

Regent had discovered the greatest job in the world, and he was a huge success at it. He and his buddy Josh Garner—they'd known each other since college—had joked for years about starting an adult website. Then one day they decided to put their money where their mouth was. They got a loan from the bank for "online entertainment sites," and assembled a website made up of pictures they'd found on the Internet. But they knew they couldn't charge for membership unless the pictures were originals. They purchased the equipment they would need, then decided to try the local community college. They put notices up on bulletin boards:

WANTED: ATTRACTIVE FEMALES

Are you an attractive young woman
in need of some quick money? Earn
up to $750 posing for photographs
and video. Tasteful.

They included Regent's cell phone number as a contact.

Regent and Garner were stunned by the response. They were astonished that so many attractive young women were willing—even *eager*—to take their clothes off for total strangers.

Regent and Garner had been living together at the time in an apartment in Redding. They'd held auditions there—every girl passed. They'd set up lights and a camera in the spare bedroom. At first, most of the girls just went for the topless photos for a hundred. A few opted to pose for more explicit photos. Only one girl that first week agreed to give Regent head on camera. But she was insatiable. She didn't want to stop with that—she wanted to fuck. She invited Garner to service her while Regent recharged. She took on both of them, and they recorded every minute of it. It remained the hottest video in their collection.

Usually, Regent had to listen to them whine a lot longer than he'd had to with Heather. That was the hook—he and Garner wanted to help them out, so what was the problem? And they spilled their guts. They were just looking for someone to listen to them for a while. They didn't get it from their boyfriends, or their husbands. Really listen to a woman, acknowledge what she had to say about things, and she'd be eating out of your hand—that's what Regent had learned. So he listened to their problems, and eventually it got around to some kind of financial needs. And then he presented them with the opportunity to make some quick cash. But by then, they *trusted* him, and that was the key. He'd listened to them, he had validated their problems, their opinions, and he had expressed sympathy and understanding. To be listened to, taken seriously—Regent was surprised by how little of that women got in their everyday lives. He and Garner gave them that. And after an hour, maybe two hours, maybe a drink or two or three or more, they felt so grateful that they were much more inclined to take off their clothes for them.

Regent and Garner had four websites—Young and Lovely, which featured college-age girls; MILF Parade, featuring mostly women in their thirties and early forties; Lusty Lesbians was self-explanatory, and was made up of pictures and videos of those women they encountered who were bisexual, women to whom more money was offered for lesbian action photos and videos; and Carnal Couples, where they posted pictures and videos of Regent and Garner having sex with women in couples only, no three-ways. But now, Regent was working on something new.

Trailer Park Girls would be a website featuring only women who lived in trailer parks from all over the country. He'd purchased a mobile home and an SUV that could pull it, and his plan was to drive around the country and move into trailer parks. He'd stay at each park for a few months—long enough to get to know some of the women there, to get them to pose for him—then he'd move on to another and do it all over again. He'd keep an online log for members and write about the trailer parks he stayed in, the people he met. He'd do video updates from the road in which he appeared with nude women. The whole thing was planned out in his head.

But he'd just started. Actually, he hadn't started yet. Riverside Mobile Home Park was his first shot at this. His plan was to move east in his tour of trailer parks, but he'd decided to start right there at home. That way, if there were any problems, or if it somehow just didn't fly, he'd know without having traveled across the country—he'd know right away. He always knew right away if something was going to work or not, he felt it in his gut. Riverside would be his testing ground to see if it worked. For all he knew, there *were* no attractive women in trailer parks and they all really *did* look like Jerry Springer's guests.

Heather was not a trailer park girl. At the age of twenty, she would be featured on the Young and Lovely site. He had not yet had a chance to meet any of his fellow residents at Riverside. But he would.

———————

With some scotch in her, Heather loosened up, relaxed. She posed with ease on the bed, and she looked great.

"Now, take off your shirt," Regent said.

"My shirt?" she said. "Couldn't I take off my skirt?"

"We'll get to your skirt, but I'd like to start with your top."

"But I … I don't … my breasts …"

"Honey, your breasts are just fine. And believe me, the guys who visit my site will want to see them. Trust me. They'll want to see them, and they'll *love* them. Really. Whatever *you* may think of your breasts, these guys are going to *adore* them."

She laughed a little and said, "Really?"

"Yes, really. And where'd you get the idea there's something wrong with your breasts, anyway?"

"Nate says they're too small. He wants me to get implants."

"Well, if your boyfriend hadn't already given me enough reason to think he's an asshole, that would clinch it. You hear me? Your boyfriend's an asshole."

She laughed again. "Thanks for saying that, but … well, I love him."

"He doesn't deserve you."

"That's sweet of you to say, but … like I said …"

"You love him, yeah. Well, that sucks, it truly does. Whattaya say you take that top off and we get some great pictures of your gorgeous breasts."

She took the shirt off and tossed it aside.

"Yeah, *screw* your boyfriend!" he said as he took pictures.

Regent took a few topless pictures, then had her take her skirt off and got some panty shots.

"Now, what-say you take off those panties?" he said.

She hesitated for a long time, then removed her panties. She knelt on the bed facing him.

"What do you want me to do now?"

Regent said, "Get on your hands and knees with your back to me and let's get some shots of that incredible ass."

Heather turned and got on hands and knees. Then the sobs started again, quietly though. She tried to fight them back, but could not. When her shoulders quaked, Regent said, "What's wrong? Are you crying?"

She said nothing, just kept crying.

"Oh, well, that's okay. I'll just get some more pictures of your ass while you get it out of your system."

She tried to pull herself together. She reached up and wiped her eyes. She rolled over and said, "Is this gonna show?"

"Yeah, it looks like you've been crying. You want to go wash your face?"

"Yeah, I'll be right back."

"Second door on your left."

While she was in the bathroom, Regent heard the front door open. Garner had arrived.

"Now we can get down to the fun stuff," he said to himself with a smile.

Seven

The night had been a battle so far, a battle not yet won. The Xanax had made Reznick groggy, and he stayed in his recliner and passed in and out of sleep. Each time he woke up, he could smell the perfume. It wasn't there, of course. It was just the memory of smelling Anna Dunfy's perfume. It lingered in his mind like a ghost in a castle tower. Each time he woke, there it was, that fresh, cool scent that plunged daggers into his eyes, all the way into his brain, deep into his brain, where the blades triggered just the right synapses and he could hear Victoria's voice, see her, feel her touch.

It was some kind of barbaric torture, but it was not physical. Tormenting memories sent jolts of electricity down to his stomach and made him feel nauseated. As Letterman started his monologue, Reznick hurried into the bathroom, knelt before the toilet, and vomited his guts up. The NyQuil stung his throat and mouth as it came back up. Afterward, he brushed his teeth, rinsed his mouth out, then drank some more NyQuil, straight out of the bottle. He finished it off and dropped the empty bottle into the waste can.

When he left the bathroom, he swayed dizzily. His chest ached from all the retching. He staggered back to the living room, where Conan was running in circles at the front door.

"You need to go out, kiddo?" Reznick said hoarsely. He opened the screen door and let Conan out.

Reznick went down the steps barefoot, walked out from under the awning and carport, and looked up at the trees overhead. Even at that hour, the night was still warm—the pavement was toasty beneath his bare feet.

He had a little over two hours before his battle would end. At two o'clock, the bars would close and the stores would stop selling liquor, and he'd have nowhere to go to get it. If he could hang on that long. When he wasn't smelling Victoria's perfume, he was hearing ice jingle in a glass. All in his head, of course.

As he stood on the edge of the park's road outside his trailer, a car pulled into the entrance and came his way. All he could see at first were the headlights. Then, as it passed, he got a look at it. A black car, maybe a Crown Victoria, he wasn't sure. He couldn't tell how many people were in it. It went around the loop behind the Snodgrass house and stopped at unit seventeen across the road. The engine was killed and the lights went out. Whoever was inside the car just sat there and did nothing.

Conan came over and licked Reznick's foot, startling him. He picked the little dog up and went back inside.

By midnight, Andy had not returned to unit seventeen.

Sherry paced the living room, but did not get too close to the body under the blanket on the floor. "I don't understand why he's not back," she said. "And I don't understand why his phone isn't on. Andy *always* has his phone on, it's how he works, it's his *life*."

"Maybe he doesn't have it with him," Philpott said. He was slumped at one end of the couch.

"Are you kidding? He practically *sleeps* with that phone. Seriously, he sleeps with it on his night stand, right by his head."

"You seem pretty uptight. You wanna feel better?" He took her kit from the end table.

"I don't know. I was thinking maybe I should stay straight, y'know? Until Andy gets back?"

"Nah, you don't wanna stay straight."

She laughed. "Okay." Laughed again. "Boy, I guess I caved on that pretty easily, huh?"

Philpott went to work.

Lissa was gone. She'd called a friend and asked him to come pick her up. To make it easier for him to find her, she'd gone down to the entrance and stood waiting for him there. She'd been gone for about half an hour.

Philpott hurt her with the needle and she winced.

"Sorry 'bout that," he said.

When he was done, he set the kit aside. Sherry started to slump back on the couch, but he stopped her and slid behind her, then let her lean back on him. Philpott put his hands on her shoulders and began to massage them.

"You look like you could use a back rub," he said.

"Mmm, that feels good. Do that a little harder." Her speech slurred a little, her eyes closed.

He did, and she seemed to melt against him.

"You like that?" he said.

"Oh, yeah."

He continued to rub her shoulders.

After awhile, she said, "What time is it?"

"Uh, lessee, it's about twenty after twelve."

She clicked her tongue and whispered, "I can't believe he hasn't at least called by now. He knows I'll worry. What if something's wrong? He said he probably wouldn't be gone long, and he usually does what he says he'll do, you know? If he says he's gonna be somewhere at a certain time, he's there at that time, y'know? He's very, uh … what's the word?"

"Punctual?"

"Yeah, that's it, he's that, and he expects everyone else to be, too. That's why I keep worrying that something's gone wrong because he'd either come back soon, like he said, or he'd call and let me know he'd be late. He always does that because he knows how I worry."

Philpott stroked her upper arms, massaged them.

"I don't even know who to call," she said. "I don't have David's number. He was supposed to meet with David and score some pot tonight. But he said he'd be back soon. He *said* so."

Sherry realized that Philpott's mouth was on her neck and his hands were on her breasts, squeezing them, and she pulled away and stood, facing him as she said, "*Phil*pott! What're you *doing*?"

He sat there with his hands held out in space where her breasts had been for a moment, then his arms collapsed at his sides. "Oh, I, um … I … I'm sorry," he said. His face turned bright red.

"You're blushing, Philpott," she said with a smirk.

He tried to smile, but his lips trembled. He bowed his head instead.

She sat down on the couch beside him, turned so she could see his face. "Look, I'm tempted to take you up on it, you wanna know the truth," Sherry said. "Andy *deserves* to come home and find me fucking someone. For making me sit up and worry like this, he's got it coming."

Philpott lifted his head slowly and said, "Really?"

"But think of what it would do to your friendship with Andy. You guys've known each other all your life. You wanna bust up a friendship like that over *me*? Trust me, Philpott, I'm not that great in bed. For one thing, I don't give head. I just refuse. I mean, most men won't go down on women, and I find giving head to be a … well, an unfair thing for that reason. So I won't do it. You'd be very disappointed in me, Philpott. But thanks for the interest. It makes me feel good."

In one surprisingly quick and smooth movement, Philpott put his arm across her shoulders, pulled her to him, and kissed her hard.

Sherry started to push him away, but stopped. It was such a sincere and passionate kiss that she didn't want to interrupt it. It was a very *nice* kiss, in fact, and after several seconds had passed, she lifted her hand and put it to the side of his face, stroked his cheek with her thumb.

The kiss softened and he put a hand on her neck, stroked her earlobe with his thumb.

When they finally pulled apart, it was Sherry's turn to bow her head. She stayed that way a moment, then looked at him and smiled. "You're a great kisser, you know that?"

"Really?"

"Really. I mean … a *great* kisser."

He was on her then, his mouth on hers, his hands moving over her body, and for just a moment, she fought him. But the kiss … it was so passionate, so full of life. Finally she pushed him back and said, "Not here. Not with that *thing* in here." She glanced at the lump under the blanket on the floor. They stood and she took his hand. "Come on," she said. She led him through the brightly-lighted kitchen and into the dark bedroom down the hall. She dropped her shorts and slipped off her T-shirt, and she was naked.

"Can we turn the light on?" Philpott whispered.

"Why?"

"Well, I, um … I just thought …"

"What? Why do you want the light on?"

"So … I can see you. I want to look at you, Sherry. I want to see you."

She laughed a small laugh. "Why do you want to see me?" She was being coy now.

"Because … a girl like you, Sherry … girls like you aren't with guys like me. I want to see you. So I can remember this."

"Aw, that's sweet." She reached over and turned on the bedside lamp.

His eyes widened as they moved slowly down her body, then back up again. "My God, you're beautiful," he whispered reverently.

"And you're still dressed. Get those clothes off."

She got into bed as he quickly removed his clothes and dropped them on the floor where he stood. Then he got into bed with her.

Sherry wrapped her arms around him and held him to her. "How long have you wanted to be with me?" she whispered.

"Ever since I met you," he replied.

"No shit?"

"No shit."

They kissed as their hands explored.

Sherry started kicking her legs. "It's too hot for blankets," she said as she tried to kick them off.

Philpott pulled away from her and sat up. He swept the covers back to the foot of the bed, until they were completely uncovered. He turned back to Sherry, but before stretching out over her, he knelt on the bed beside her and just looked at her.

"What are you doing?" she said.

"I'm sorry, I'm … staring at you." He chuckled.

"Staring at me?" she said.

"Yeah. I'm ... drinking you in."

"Now you're drinking me?" She laughed even harder and the movement of her breasts made Philpott instantly hard. She reached out and stroked his cock. "Boy, you really get off on this staring stuff, huh?"

Philpott reached down and spread her legs and knelt between them. He was lowering his face to her crotch when someone pounded on the front door.

"Oh, shit!" Sherry hissed. "It's locked. Doesn't Andy have a key? Why is he knocking?"

"You think it's Andy?"

"Who *else* would it be at this hour?"

"Shit," he said as he scrambled off the bed and assembled his clothes. They dressed quickly, bumping into each other a few times.

Finally, they were dressed and in the living room. Philpott flopped onto the couch and looked at the television. Sherry went to the door.

Before she could open it, there was more pounding.

"Andy?" she said.

There was no response outside the door.

"Uh, hello?" she said. "Who is it?"

Another long silence followed and she turned to Philpott with a questioning look.

"Don't open it," he whispered.

"Who *is* it?" she said.

Still no response.

"If you don't answer, I'm calling the police," she said.

A strong male voice said, "We're looking for Arnold Garvis."

Sherry turned to Philpott with wide eyes. Together, they turned to the lump under the blanket on the floor.

"That's all we want," the first voice said. "We'll just take him and go."

"Who *are* you?"

Silence, then: "Secret Service."

Sherry rolled her eyes. "*You're* the secret service?"

"Do you know who Arnold is?" the second voice said.

Sherry looked over at the shape under the blanket on the stained floor again. "Well ... no."

"We do. And we've come for him. Just let us get him, and we'll leave you alone."

Philpott stood and went to Sherry's side. "Who *are* you?" he said.

"Someone who can make a hell of a lot of trouble for you in a very short period of time if you don't cooperate."

Sherry went to the bar and opened the small drawer behind it. She removed from the drawer a .38 revolver. She turned to Philpott and said, "I'm gonna let 'em in." She turned to the door. "I have a gun. The second you do something I don't like, I start shooting, understand?"

"Yes."

She unlocked the door and pulled it open. She saw two black figures on the other side of the screen door. She turned on the porch light, but they remained two black figures. They wore black shirts and black pants and shoes and looked like twins. One had blond hair, the other dark. They had very serious, stern, but nondescript faces.

When she pushed the screen door open, they came inside.

They were tall and bland. They turned to Sherry and the blond said, "Where is he?"

The brunette glanced at Sherry's gun.

"Under that blanket over there," she said.

They went to the lump on the floor and Blondie pulled back the blanket. They stared down at the corpse.

The dark-haired man turned to Sherry. "What happened?"

She shrugged. "We woke up and found him that way. It looks like an overdose. We don't even know who he is or what he's doing here. He came with a friend of a friend early this morning."

They spent a few more seconds looking down at the corpse, whispered briefly to each other, then turned to her again.

"Mind if we take some of these blankets?" one of them said.

"No, go ahead, take 'em."

She and Philpott stood back while the two men wrapped the body up in blankets. One stood at each end and carried the wrapped-up body to the door. One opened the door and they carried the body out of the trailer. The blond man leaned back into the door and said, "We were never here. You never met him. This never happened."

The screen door slammed shut. Awhile later, an engine started and a vehicle pulled away from the trailer.

Sherry rushed to the door and closed it, saying, "What the hell was *that*?"

"Who *was* that guy?" Philpott said.

"I don't know." She put the gun back in the drawer, then started pacing the living room again. "Where's Andy, dammit?"

"Um … care to, uh, pick up where we left off?"

"Oh, I'm sorry, hon, but that kinda blew the mood for me, you know? Mysterious men who come and cart off a dead body? There's something creepy about that."

"Yeah. Well … you want me to wait here for Andy with you?"

"Yeah, please don't leave me here all by myself, Philpott. I don't want to wait for him alone."

"Okay, then, we'll wait together."

In unit five, Regent smiled.

They were all the same, these women. No matter what they said at first, no matter how opposed they *claimed* to be to the idea, once that camera was on them, they always ended up playing to it—they loved the attention, the focus on them, just them.

Regent and Garner had spent the last two hours taking turns shooting Heather and fucking her, and she had put on a memorable performance. All that crying and wailing, all that wincing and sobbing—it had been endless, and it had been wonderful, some of the best footage he'd gotten in awhile.

Garner was in the shower. Regent wiped the sticky perspiration from his body with a towel as Heather sat on the edge of the bed, naked. She seemed deflated, empty somehow. She stared at nothing, her mouth open, her eyes a little wider than they should be.

There was a spot of blood on the bed. Regent figured that had probably come from the anal sex. She'd screamed when he'd entered her anus, and her screaming had made him harder.

"You were incredible," Regent said. "Really. I mean it. My members are going to love you."

She did not look at him or respond. She stood very slowly, then limped around the room collecting her clothes. She put them on the bed and slowly, clumsily began to dress.

"You want something to drink?" he said.

Still, she said nothing as she put on her panties, then stepped into her skirt and pulled it up her legs, buttoned it, then pulled her shirt over her head. She wobbled as she stepped into her shoes, then bent down to pick up her purse. When she stood up, her back was to him. She stood there, facing the wall, for several long seconds as he watched her.

"You okay?" he said with a smile.

"Where's my money?" she said, voice cracking.

"Sure, I'll get your money. No need to rush off, though. Let's have a drink. I'd like to talk to you about possibly doing this again. I really think you're going to take off on the site."

Heather turned around slowly until she stood facing him. Her face looked longer, somehow—as if it had been stretched. She seemed paler than before. Her hair was all over the place and her eyes were puffy. She looked exactly like what she was—a woman who'd just had a whole lot of great sex.

"I want my money now," she said.

"Oh. All right. Hang on, I'll be right back." He went into his bedroom, to a cashbox on his dresser. He got the money and went back into the studio. He held out the money and Heather snatched it from his hand.

She reached around and stuffed the money into her purse. Then she turned and headed for the door.

Regent grabbed her arm and said, "Wait, I thought we could—"

Something broke in her then, and she jerked her arm out of his grasp and turned to him with wide eyes and lips pulled back tight over her teeth, and she screamed at him, "Don't you *touch* me!" She started crying then, and it was a powerful cry that moved through her whole body and made her bend over as if she had cramps. Her sobs turned into coughs, and then she began to gag, then heave.

"No," Regent said, "not on the carpet, not on the—"

She vomited on the carpet.

"Oh, shit," he said. "You stupid bitch, you just puked on my carpet! I can't believe you. You—you actually *vomited* on my *carpet*!" He looked at her as he pointed at the mess on the floor.

63

"What, is this, is this something you *do*, you just barf on people's carpets when you're in their houses? Huh?"

She stood up straight and wiped her mouth with the back of her hand. Then she left the studio.

Regent shouted, "You stupid cunt! Get the hell out of here before I make you lick it up!"

She went to the door and opened it, went down the steps.

Regent stood in the doorway and watched her as she got into her car and started the engine. Then he closed the screen door, then the door, locked it.

"Where'd she go?" Garner said as he came up the hall with a towel around his waist. He used another to scrub his hair.

"The stupid bitch vomited on my carpet."

"Oh, is that what that puddle is back there?"

"Clean it up for me, will ya?" Regent said.

"What? Whoa, that's not in my job description. I'm strictly a camera man and a spare dick when needed. I'm not cleaning it up."

Regent sighed. "I'll have to, then. How disgusting. What a disgusting woman she was."

"Yeah, but she's gonna look amazing online," Garner said.

"I'm gonna clean that shit up in the studio, then let's go out and grab a beer, huh? We can check out the girls at the Mt. Shasta Gentlemen's Club, okay? Jeez, how long's it been since we've been out there?"

"A long time. Sounds good to me. Happy vomit-cleaning."

Kendra could not sleep. She lay on Aunt Rose's couch with the television on, the volume low. She always slept on the couch when Mommy went out to dance. Well, she *usually* slept. Mommy had a key to Aunt Rose's front door, and when she got off work, she came to Aunt Rose's house and unlocked the door, came inside and woke Kendra and took her home, all without waking up anyone else in the house. But tonight, Kendra simply could not sleep.

All she could think about was Mr. Reznick, their new neighbor. Mr. Reznick was the handsomest man Kendra had ever seen. Up close, anyway. There were some movie and TV stars she thought were handsome, but they weren't ... *real*. Not like Mr. Reznick, who lived right next door.

Lying on the couch with a funny old monster movie playing on TV, Kendra closed her eyes and saw him again. Thick and wavy brown hair, the kind of hair she would love to run her fingers through, and deep brown eyes she could dive into and swim around in like deep pools. Oh, he was like a dream. And his voice—deep and resonant and manly.

Kendra smiled as she lay there in the dark with the grey light of the television flickering over her.

She couldn't wait to see him again.

As the men applauded and whooped and hollered, Anna Dunfy collected the clothes she'd shed over three dance numbers, then picked up all the money left for her by admiring customers, and walked backstage.

Dina Noos was getting ready to go on. There were a few other girls back there, too, either getting ready to dance or to waitress, or to go home.

"What's it like out there?" Dina said. Her stage name was Desiree.

"Not bad," Anna said. "I've seen better, but I've seen worse." She put the money in her purse, locked her purse in her locker, then began to put her costume back on.

Her stage name was Kitten, and she was very popular at the Mt. Shasta Gentlemen's Club. She had a lot of regulars who came just to see her. The money was better than any job she could get in town. The job market in Redding was in pretty bad shape—she could get plenty of work if she wanted to flip burgers or wait tables part-time, with no benefits, nothing. The only office work she could get was through the temp agency, which was *less* than part-time. Stripping barely took care of their needs and left nothing for her to save up for her dream—a down payment on a little house for her and Kendra. She could not see that ever happening.

With her costume on, Anna left the big communal dressing room and went out into the nightclub. Between sets, the girls waited tables. Some chose to wait tables topless while others kept their costumes on. Anna wasn't comfortable walking around topless. Dancing naked on the stage was one thing, but just walking around from table to table with her tits exposed—she couldn't do it. She knew it meant less in tips, but she couldn't help it, it was out of her hands.

The bar was in the front of the club, the stage in the rear, and in between were tables, and against the wall some booths. There was a bar along each edge of the runway, too. The club was spacious, with a high ceiling. From outside, the building looked like a ski lodge, with an A-frame and tall windows. But the blackened windows were dark, and written in purple neon in one of them were the words LIVE NUDE GIRLS. It was located halfway between Redding and Mt. Shasta, out in the woods, of all places. But it did a booming business. It helped that it was the only strip club in the area. The next closest was all the way over in Chico.

Anna went behind the bar and got an order pad and pen. She found the manager in the kitchen behind the bar, where they made all the bar food. Paul Wagner was a little balding man with a belly and jowls who always wore a suit.

"Where do you want me, Paul?" she said.

"Take section four," he said. "Delilah was supposed to take it, but she went home sick. So I've got Candy working two sections, and you can take section four."

"Will do, boss," she said, then she turned and left the kitchen, went out from behind the bar, and headed for section four. That included all the customers seated at bars along the sides of the runway and tables to the left of the runway.

There was just another hour before closing time. Anna sighed and went to a table and took her first order.

Her third order came from a handsome man with dark hair seated at the runway. He ordered a scotch and soda, then said, "Could I have a word with you?"

"About what?" Anna said, smiling.

"What's your name?"

"Kitten."

"Well, Kitten, my friend and I, here, are photographers. We have some websites and I was wondering if you'd be willing to pose for some pictures for us."

"Pictures, huh?"

"We'll pay, of course. Think about it. Here's my card." He took his wallet from his back pocket, opened it, and removed a business card, which he scribbled on with a pen before handing it to her.

It read, BURNING LIZARD AMUSEMENTS, and below that was a phone number and a post office box number in Redding. Written on the back was his name and another phone number.

"My name is Steven Regent," he said. "You are an exceptionally beautiful woman, Kitten. You stand out here, I'm serious. You're also the finest dancer in the place."

"Well, thank you, aren't you sweet. I'll get your drink for you."

"You'll think about it? I think we could work together very well. We pay well."

"I'll think about it," she said, then she turned and headed for the bar.

Photographers. A website. It sounded dubious to Anna. But he said they would pay. And well. She slipped the card into the top of her right stocking. She'd keep it. Just in case.

Eight

Reznick rose slowly to the surface of his sleep like a bloated corpse bobbing to the surface of a still, deep lake. He opened his sticky eyes and squinted painfully at light, then closed them again. It was morning, he knew that much. But he wasn't sure where he was.

Did I tie one on last night? he wondered.

He reached up and rubbed his eyes with the heels of his hands, then opened them. He was lying on the couch in the living room wearing only his undershorts. The television was on. Cartoons. Rocky and Bullwinkle. He smacked his lips, but he tasted no liquor. Instead, he tasted bitter morning breath and the harsh remnant of NyQuil.

He'd made it through the night without having a drink, without driving down to Handi-Spot and buying a bottle. It had not been easy.

At first, he'd fallen asleep only to find himself in a dream of Victoria—a vivid dream from which he'd awakened suddenly with a ragged gasp, still smelling her perfume, his heart drumming against his ribs. He'd been in bed then. He'd tried to

69

go back to sleep two more times, maybe three or four, but the same thing had happened again and again.

Around four in the morning, he'd come out to the living room and stretched out on the couch. He'd turned on the TV, tuned it to the Cartoon Network. Something that would shut his mind down and not require any thought. Pretty soon the cartoons had blurred, the colors had bled together, and he'd finally drifted off into a deep sleep.

He swung around and sat up on the edge of the couch, put his elbows on his knees, and scrubbed his face with both hands. He looked down and saw Conan curled up on the floor beside the couch. The dog lifted his head and looked at him, then stood and stretched. Reznick sat up straight and looked at the clock on the wall, focused. It was eight thirty-three. He could easily go back to sleep, but it was time to get up.

"Hey, buddy," Reznick said, and Conan hopped up onto the couch beside him. He petted the dog, roughed him up a little. "Need to go outside, I bet." Reznick stood and went to the door, opened it, opened the screen, and said, "Go ahead, boy."

Conan dashed outside.

Reznick went to the kitchen and got the coffee maker started. By the time he was done with that, Conan was back inside. Reznick closed the screen door and locked it, then turned on the swamp cooler. He fed Conan, went into the bathroom and took a shower, and by the time he got out, the coffee was ready. He put on a pair of jeans, poured a cup of coffee, then took it outside, shirtless and barefoot. Conan followed him. It wasn't even nine o'clock yet, and the thermometer on the wall beside his door read a hundred and four. There was no breeze—the morning was still. Country music played loudly from one of the trailers.

Reznick opened his mouth for a long, luxurious yawn, then turned to go back inside, but stopped. He heard a rhythmic slapping sound. He turned around and faced the road, turned toward Anna Dunfy's trailer.

A multi-colored ball bounced on the pavement from the front of the Dunfy trailer. A moment later, Kendra appeared.

"Hello," Reznick said.

Startled, she missed the ball and gasped, turning to him. The ball bounced away from her and she chased after it, snatched it from the air, then turned to him again.

"Huh-hello, Mr. Reznick," she said. She looked at him with her mouth open.

"You can call me Marc," he said.

"Mommy likes me to call grownups by Mr. and Mrs."

"I see. Well, *I'm* more comfortable with Marc."

"Okay."

Conan hurried over to Kendra and pawed at her bare shins. She hunkered down, put the ball on the ground, and petted him with both hands, saying, "Oh, you're just such a sweet little doggy, you know that, Conan? You're a sweet little doggy."

While she played with and talked to Conan, Reznick took her in.

She wore a short sleeve red plaid shirt open over a bikini bra, and a pair of black shorts, flip-flops on her feet. Her legs were long, her sizeable breasts round and firm. Her long, honey-colored hair fell down on both sides of her face as she bent and played with the dog.

Reznick realized his breathing had increased in speed. His heart was beating faster. His palms were sweaty, and it had nothing to do with the heat. He could not remember the last time he'd wanted a woman so badly, so deeply, the last time he'd felt a physical hunger for the touch of a woman's flesh, for the sensation of her lips on his.

He remembered the night before on the roof of Anna's trailer—he'd noticed something odd about Kendra. What had it been? He'd been unable to put his finger on it then, and he couldn't identify it now, either.

He sipped his coffee, but it tasted bitter, awful. He tossed the coffee out on the small patch of grass in front of his trailer.

"How old are you, Kendra?" he said.

"I'm sixteen," she said. "I'll be seventeen in November. Mommy said she's going to buy me a big cake for my seventeenth birthday. German chocolate's my favorite. What's your favorite kind of cake, Mr. Rez—uh … Marc?"

Mommy, he thought. *How many sixteen-year-olds call their mother "Mommy"?*

"I guess my favorite would be chocolate," he said, frowning now, trying to put his finger on it. "You like Conan, huh?"

"Oh, *yes*! He's such a cute little doggy."

"Don't you have any pets?"

She stood up then, and a frown created lines between her eyebrows and on her unblemished forehead. She tilted her head to one side, mouth open slightly. "No, I don't. I've *never* had a pet. I'm gonna ask Mommy if I can have a doggy."

"You go to school, Kendra?"

"Not during the summer. But yes, I go to school." She frowned again. "Some kids, they make fun of me, because I ride on the short bus."

Mommy. Doggy. The short bus.

Oh, my God, Reznick thought. *She's retarded.*

"I'm gonna tell Mommy I want a doggy." She took a few steps until she was standing right in front of him. She spoke in a whisper. "When you see Mommy, will you tell her you think it would be a good idea if I got a doggy?"

She was so close to him he could almost feel her heat. Her eyes were the blue of denim. She wore no lipstick, but her lush lips were rosy.

"Well," he said, "I … I suppose I could put a word in."

"Oh, *thank* you!" she said. She threw her arms around him and squeezed him.

Reznick's heart stopped as he felt her breasts crush against him, felt her warmth against his body. He did not return her embrace because he was afraid that if he did, he would not let go, he would be *unable* to let go until his mouth was on hers and their tongues were together and his hand was on her breast, and he thought, *Whoa, buddy*, as his heart seemed to beat against his ribs like some kind of animal locked in a small cage desperate to get out. He smelled the shampoo she'd used to wash her hair, smelled the toothpaste she'd used to brush her teeth, and felt her breasts, still pressing against him. It seemed to go on and on, and he felt perspiration dribble down his sides, down his back, and he hardened against her, he couldn't *help* himself, he couldn't *stop* it, his erection pressed against her and she pressed against it, and her embrace seemed to last and last and —

"I'm gonna go tell Mommy I want a doggy right now," she said as she pulled away. "And if she don't agree with *me*, maybe she'll agree with *you*." She turned and picked up the ball, tucked it under an arm. She bent down to pet Conan one more time. "Bye-bye, Conan." She tossed him a smile over her shoulder and said, "Bye-bye. Marc."

"Bye," he said, but it came out a broken whisper.

Kendra disappeared around the front of her trailer.

Reznick turned and went inside before someone saw him standing there with a hard-on.

———————————

Anna leaned out the door of the trailer and said, "Kendra? Breakfast is ready."

"Okay," Kendra said, coming from the front end of the trailer holding a ball.

Anna noticed what she was wearing and said, "Hey, if you want to wear that shirt, you'll wear it buttoned up, understand me?"

"But it's cooler this way."

"Then put on a cooler shirt you can button up. You're not going around like that, Kendra."

Anna stepped back as Kendra came up the steps and entered the trailer.

"You don't think it looks good?" Kendra said.

"That's not the point. I don't want you walking around dressed like that, and I think you know why. Don't you?"

"But what about when we go to Brandy Creek and I swim in the lake? I'm wearing a lot less then."

"Well, that's different. We're not at Brandy Creek right now. Sit down, now, I've got pancakes."

"Oh, goody!"

Kendra went to the small table in the kitchen and sat down.

Anna put a plate of pancakes and some banana slices in front of Kendra. There was already margarine and syrup on the table.

Anna's parents had been crazy people. They had been abusive and unloving. But they had given her something she had always appreciated—they had seen to it that the family had always eaten their meals together at the dining room table. Well, they had eaten breakfast and dinner there, anyway. In the morning, they'd gathered at the table and, when the yelling subsided, they talked about the day ahead, and their plans for it. At dinner, they'd talked about the day that had passed and what had become of their morning plans. It was a good memory she had of growing up—one of the few—and she wanted to pass it onto Kendra. It would be nice if Kendra could pass it onto her children. But that wasn't going to happen.

"Mommy, when are you going to let me stay here by myself when you go out?" Kendra asked.

"I don't know, honey."

"I'm old enough. I'm sixteen."

"I know, sweetheart, but we've talked about this. You're sixteen, but … you're not like other sixteen-year-olds."

The heavy aroma of buttermilk pancakes and coffee filled the trailer. There was a radio on the kitchen counter and Anna had it tuned to a soft rock station. She didn't believe in having the television on during mealtime, but music was nice. Anna wore a pink T-shirt and blue shorts, feet bare.

"But I'm old enough to take care of myself while you're gone," Kendra said. "I promise I won't even leave the trailer. I can even feed myself. You've seen me. I can make cereal and sandwiches—I can even cook eggs and bacon, you've seen me, and I can make a grilled cheese sandwich, too. And soup, I can make soup. I'd be fine if you weren't here."

Anna sighed. It was a discussion that came up frequently. Kendra wanted some independence, some control over her own life. She wanted to prove that she could take care of herself, if only for a little while.

"Okay, look," Anna said. "We'll see. Okay? Maybe it would be okay to leave you here for a little while sometime. But that's not a definitive yes. We'll see."

"But that's what you *always* say," Kendra said. She sounded frustrated.

"Your breakfast is getting cold," Anna said as she sat down with her own breakfast.

Kendra chewed a mouthful of pancake, gulped it down, then said, "You *always* say *'we'll see, we'll see,'*—so *when*, Mommy? When do we get to *see*?"

Anna sighed as she poured syrup over her pancakes. How could she argue with that? Kendra was right. She said "we'll see" a *lot*—Kendra had every right to be sick of hearing it. Anna had never heard that when she was a girl. Her parents were more the "shut up," "go to your room," and "You want me to hit you again?" type and had none of the gentility or basic good nature of a "we'll see." At least Kendra would never hear any of those things. If "we'll see" was the worst thing Anna ever said to Kendra, she was doing okay.

"I'll tell you what," Anna said. "Next time the temp agency calls on me, I'll seriously consider it. Okay?"

Kendra beamed. Her eyes grew wide, as did her smile.

"Thank you, Mommy!" Kendra said, her voice breathy. It was an important victory for her, and it took her a moment to absorb it. During that moment, her face held a childlike glow that almost concealed her true age. Almost. There was no concealing those breasts, those legs.

Anna noticed men staring when they went to the Safeway for groceries—not boys Kendra's age, but middle-aged men with wives and kids. Oh, sure, other teenagers noticed her, too, but that was natural. But mostly, Anna noticed the grown men. Something came up in their eyes as they looked at her. Like some creature rising up out of the deep shadows of a moonlit forest, this thing rose up in their eyes and first widened, then narrowed them. Sometimes the men licked their lips without seeming to realize it. Maybe the jaw jutted a bit, or the chest puffed up and the gut sucked in as a deep breath was inhaled. While their heads usually remained facing front, their eyes— their *darkened* eyes with that new *thing* in them—followed Kendra. Sometimes the men were bold in watching her pass, as if they didn't give a damn if their wives saw them do it. They all reacted a little differently—but they all had the same look on their faces, in their eyes. They were hungry animals, hungry for her daughter's flesh. That darkness that rose up in their eyes was the malignant onyx-flash of lust. Their eyes dwelled on her breasts, her ass, her legs. Some hungered for her individual parts, others for her whole body.

Anna remembered a time when men looked at her that way, and she'd liked it. If Kendra were a normal sixteen-year-old girl, she wouldn't be so concerned. But she was a little girl with a big handicap—that face, that body. Those parts.

Anna could almost hear the camera-click of their minds snapping pictures of Kendra, of those parts, taking mental pictures that could be pored over in their minds later.

That was why she was so wary of leaving Kendra home alone. She was so vulnerable. There were some shady people living in the Riverside Mobile Home Park. Of course, shady as they were, none of those people had ever been any trouble, and there was no reason to think they would be. She was just making excuses, she knew that.

Kendra deserved a little independence.

"Mommy, can I have a little doggy?" Kendra said.

Anna chuckled. "You're full of demands this morning, aren't you?"

"Demands?" Kendra said, her eyebrows rising high.

"Nothing. A little doggy?"

"Yeah, like Marc's."

They ate as they talked. Sometimes Anna sipped her coffee.

"You should call him Mr. Reznick."

Kendra shrugged. "He told me to call him Marc."

"Oh? When?"

"This morning. I was talking to him outside."

"Oh. Well, if *he* wants you to call him Marc, then I guess it's okay. You like his dog, huh?"

"Oh, Conan is such an adorable little doggy! Can't I have one, please? He'd be able to keep me company when you leave me alone here."

Kendra laughed. "You're very ambitious this morning."

"Ambitious?"

"That means you're covering a lot of ground. First you want me to leave you here alone, then you want a little dog, and somehow, you manage to successfully tie the two together. Kendra, I think you should go into advertising."

"You think so?"

"Yes, you'd be a big hit."

Kendra laughed, even though she wasn't entirely sure what her mother meant.

Anna finished her breakfast. Her purse hung from the back of her chair. She reached into it and removed her cheap GNC cigarettes and a lighter, and she lit one up.

"Well, Kendra," she said, "if you had a dog, no matter *how* little he was, he'd have to be fed and watered every day. He would have to get plenty of love. And you would be responsible for all that. You'd have to house train him, if he isn't already, and you'd have to clean up after all his little accidents."

Again, Kendra's eyebrows rose high, this time with excitement. "Oh, I would, I would. I'd take *good* care of him, and I'd do *everything*."

"Hm. Well, I wouldn't mind having a little dog in the house myself. It's been a long time since I had a pet around. I miss it."

Kendra's fork dropped onto her plate with a sharp clatter and she clapped her hands together rapidly a few times. "Oh, *yaaay!*" she said. "Thank you so much, Mommy! Can we get one today?"

"Today?" Anna said, smoke fluttering out of her mouth and nose. "Well, as far as a dog goes, we'll—" She stopped herself. She'd been about to say, *We'll see.* "We have to run some errands today. We'll stop by the Haven Humane Society and see if we can find a little doggy to take home."

Nine

Dressed in a dark blue suit with a red-and-black tie, Reznick left the trailer, locked the door, and carried his briefcase to his car. His father had always told him to wear a suit when he worked, no matter what he did. He should always look his best, the old man always said.

Reznick got in the car and started the engine. He started to back out but stepped on the brake because a white pickup truck was coming along the narrow road. It drove past him and around the loop to the other side. Reznick backed out and went around the loop. The pickup truck stopped at unit seventeen. Reznick left the trailer park.

He was in the Yellow Pages and the White Pages. He wondered if he should blow some money on advertising. Maybe in the newspaper. Things couldn't go on like this much longer. Something had to change. He was actually putting reading material in his briefcase so he'd have something to do at the office. He had two novels in his briefcase—a Larry McMurtry and a Stephen King. He'd probably get through the McMurtry by lunch, if it was like most days. The King book was four times the size of McMurtry's and would take more time.

On the northern end of North Street, Reznick pulled off the road into a small parking lot, and pulled up beside a tollbooth-like house with a sign on the front that read Java-Hut. It was painted pastel violet with pastel yellow trimming, like an Easter egg. He stopped with his car window just below the window in the side of the little house. The young woman who worked in there was a fresh-faced blonde with dreamy eyes and a bedroom smile that was an especially pleasant way to start the day.

"Hello, Marc," she said.

"Good morning, Janine," he said with a big smile. "I'll have the usual, please."

"Comin' up."

It was the only time he ever wished he drove a big pickup or an SUV—so he could be level with the window and look in there while Janine moved around making his frozen coffee drink. He imagined she wore faded denim shorts above long tan legs that looked as smooth as the coffee drinks she served. Probably a very tight, round ass. Nice, smallish breasts—those he'd glimpsed from his car as she bent forward. She looked like she had the whole world in front of her—and she was trapped in that little shack selling coffee drinks. He wondered what her dreams were, and how that job figured into them. She was twenty-two, twenty-three—where did she hope to be at thirty-three, at forty-three? Or did she think that far ahead? That was what worried Reznick about the young people he met—they seemed to go along with the flow of things, no ambitions, no particular hopes or dreams, seeking not knowledge but the next entertainment, the next diversion. He wondered if Janine was that way. And he wondered with whom she discussed those things—what lucky guy got to hear about Janine's dreams? Or was she with a guy who didn't care?

"Here ya go, Marc," she said with a big smile.

She took his money with one hand and gave him the drink with the other. Their fingers briefly touched. As she made change, she said, "Any interesting cases?"

"I'm afraid not, Janine. Business has been very slow. I may just dump the whole thing and go raise alpacas, or something."

Her laughter was a pleasant, youthful sound. She handed Reznick his change.

"Have a good one, Janine."

"You, too."

He drove away and headed for his office.

His frozen drink was already beginning to melt.

———————————

Sherry awakened suddenly and bit the inside of her cheek.

"Ow," she said as she slowly raised a hand to the side of her face.

"What's wrong?" Philpott said.

"I bit mythelf," she said.

"Andy's here."

"*What?*" she said, her eyes suddenly open wide. She looked down at herself. She was lying on the bed, all the covers in a heap at the foot, in shorts and a yellow tube top—*When did I put that on?* she thought—and she sat up straight. She closed her eyes tightly when the bed whirled around. She flopped back down on the pillows.

Philpott said, "You wanna try that again a little slower?"

Sherry laughed humorlessly. She slowly sat up and moved her legs off the bed. She sat there for awhile, her elbows locked at her sides.

"What time is it?" she said.

"About quarter to ten."

"When did he get here?"

81

"They been here a few minutes."

"They?"

"David's with him."

She set her jaw and stood. "That son of a bitch had better—" She stalked down the hall and shouted, "You son of a bitch, you'd better have a good story ready!" She stepped into the kitchen and saw him seated at the bar, smoking a cigarette and drinking a beer.

"I brought a buncha beer," he said. "The fridge's full of it. Now we gotta get some *food* in there."

"Where the hell have you been?" she said. "You fuckin' jerk, you know how worried I was?"

"Yeah, I noticed how worried you was when I got here. You was so worried, Philpott had to wake you up."

Sherry turned around and reached out blindly. Her hand landed on a coffee mug on the counter. As she lifted it and pulled it back over her shoulder, Andy disappeared behind the bar. She threw it anyway, and it broke into two pieces when it hit the living room floor.

"Hey," David said. He was seated in Andy's recliner watching television. The mug fell at his feet.

"You fuckin' asshole," Sherry said. "I was worried all night. I called your cell phone, but it was turned off. Turned *off*! Since when do you turn off your phone?"

Andy cautiously raised his eyes above the edge of the bar. When he saw she was unarmed, he rose up and sat on the stool again. There were two stools at the bar, one on the living room side and one on the kitchen side, and they did not match.

"My battery's dead," he said. He reached into his pocket, took the small silver phone out and put it on the bar. "Look at it yourself."

She crossed the kitchen and opened the phone. She tried to turn it on.

"No signal," Andy said. "Nothing. Needs batteries."

"Where the hell were you all night?" she said, putting the phone back down, not very carefully.

"David and I went over to Eddie's to score some pot," he said.

Sherry pulled back and put a fist on her hip, her elbow jutting out at her side. Her face seethed. "Was Karen there?" she said.

"Well, a *course* Karen was there, she's *married* to him, isn't she?"

Karen was a sore spot. Andy had slept with her once while Eddie was out of town. The only reason Eddie had anything to do with Andy was that Eddie didn't know anything about it.

"You were there all *night*?" Sherry said.

"Well, Eddie had some weed that was … oh, man, it was some special shit, I tell ya, some stuff he'd grown himself." Andy shook his head. "Ain't nothin' ever made me that stoned since the first time I *got* stoned." He turned to David. "Wasn't that some good shit?"

"Incredible shit," David said. "It was amazing. At one point, I imagined I had a bunch of little holes in my forehead and a cold breeze was blowing in over my brain."

Andy and David laughed.

"You were *stoned* all night?" Sherry said.

Andy said, "Too stoned to drive home."

"And Eddie and Karen don't have a fuckin' phone?"

"Like I toldja, I was stoned, I didn't think to call you. I wasn't *thinking*, period."

Sherry sighed. What made her just as angry as the fact that he hadn't called all night was the fact that she was so glad to see him, she wanted to go to him and touch his face and put her fingers in his beautiful long hair. She stood there and looked at him for a while, and then she did. She went to the bar, bent over it, and kissed him with her hand on the side of his head.

"God, how I wish you'd been here last night," she said. "It was so scary." She pulled back and turned to David in the living room. "Who the hell was that guy you brought here?"

"Arnie?" David said. "Where *is* Arnie, anyway?"

"He's *dead*," Sherry said angrily. "He OD'd here last night."

"Whuh ... *what*?" David said, slowly sitting forward in the recliner. He gradually rose to his feet. "Did you say ... Arnie is ... *dead*?"

"Yes."

"Then ... where is he? What happened to him?"

She looked at Andy. "You're not gonna believe it. These men—they claimed to be Secret Service. They came and took your friend away, David. They wrapped him up in blankets and just took him away. Two men dressed in black. As they left, one said this had never happened, and we'd never seen them, or somethin' like that."

David walked toward her, until he was standing at the end of the short bar. "Secret ... Service?"

"Yeah," Sherry said. "Who *was* he, anyway? How did they know he was *here*?"

"His dad's a senator—haven't you heard of him?" David said.

"We're not like you, David," Andy said. "We don't watch the news unless they're gonna show a train wreck, or somethin', and we wouldn't know a senator from a monkey on a rock. You're a college boy, man," Andy said good-naturedly, and not without a little envy. "You pay attention to that stuff." He took a long drag on his cigarette. "We depend on you to tell us about it." Andy chuckled smokily.

"Oh. Well, if you say so," David said, but there was a flatness to his voice, and his eyes fixed on the end of the bar in a sad stare. "His dad's Senator Wilson Garvis. From … uh … damn, I forget which state now, isn't that funny? I've known Arnie all these years … and I can't … remember … what state he's from."

David clutched the end of the bar hard, as if he would fall if he didn't.

"You okay, David?" Andy said, moving toward him. "Maybe you should sit down."

"Sit here," Sherry said, bringing the stool around to him.

David perched himself on the stool and leaned his elbows on the bar.

"You know the type," David said. "He's big on morals and family values and prayer in schools. He and Arnie never got along. He wanted Arnie to follow in his footsteps and go into politics. Arnie wanted to be a biologist. It infuriated his father. The man was constantly interfering in his life, even having him followed, and attaching homing devices to him, or using his cell phone signal to keep track of where he was at all times. That's probably how they found him. They probably weren't far away. They might've even had something on him that picked up blood pressure—you know, vital signs. They … they probably knew he was dead."

"Are you *serious*?" Sherry said.

"Dead serious. The man was almost obsessive about keeping tabs on Arnie. He wanted to know what he was doing at all times. Now they're probably going to arrange a more … wholesome death."

"Whatta ya mean?" Andy said.

"They won't want anyone to know that he duh-duh …" David stopped and put his face in his hands. "That he died of a drug overdose. Couldn't have that. They'll come up with another kind of death for him. Something cleaner. More acceptable." He lowered his hands and sat up straight, took in a deep breath and let it out in a long, sigh heavy with sadness. "Arnie had too many secrets," he said. His eyes glistened and his cheeks were wet. "Drug use. The fact that he was gay." He turned sad eyes to Sherry. "We were lovers. For a long time."

Sherry took in a breath. "Oh, David, I'm so sorry."

His head jerked up and down. "I know, you didn't mean anything, and you couldn't have known. But now ... yeah, they'll have a fake death. A car wreck, or a boating accident, or something. Anything but an overdose. And I won't be able to go to his funeral. For me, he's just ... he's ... gone."

"Those bastards," Sherry said quietly. She went to David and took his right hand in both of hers. "What *else* are those people hiding?"

"Oh, lots of things. His mom is hooked on pills and his dad drinks and sees hookers. But they go to church every Sunday, so I guess it all ... evens out."

Nobody said anything for a long time. Sherry turned to the refrigerator and got a beer. She popped the can open and tipped it back, took a few big gulps. Then she wiped her mouth with the back of her hand. She found herself facing Philpott, who had been standing the whole time in the entrance to the hallway. "You've been awful quiet, Philpott. Wanna beer?"

He shrugged. "Sure. I feel bad for David. And those guys ... they're a little scary."

She got another beer from the fridge and handed it to him. "What do you mean?"

Philpott shrugged again as he opened the beer. "Who's to say they won't want to shut up the only people who know that Arnie Garvis *really* died of a drug overdose?"

A splash of cold filled Sherry's chest, then slowly passed through her entire body, until she shivered in the heat. She turned to Andy and David.

"Did you hear that?" she said. "He's right—who's to say they won't?" To David, she said, "What do you think? Will they come back? Or will they send someone else?"

Andy said, "Oh, c'mon, you're bein' paranoid now."

"Oh, really?" Sherry said. She felt genuine fear in the pit of her stomach, and she turned to David again. "You're not sayin' anything, David."

"Well …" His mouth opened and closed a couple times, but nothing came out. "You … you probably don't have anything to worry about," he said without looking at her.

"Probably?" she said, her voice low and tremulous. "Whatta you mean, *probably*?"

"I-I-I don't *know*," David said as he dropped off the stool and began to pace the living room.

"So … there's a *chance*," Sherry said. "You're sayin' there's a *chance*."

"I-I just don't, I don't know, Sherry," he said as he threw up his arms and let them slap at his sides. "I don't know what to tell you."

She went to Andy and clutched his forearm. "You hear that?"

"Don't get yourself worked up," Andy said. "Nobody's comin' to shut nobody up. And if they do, I gotta couple guns a my own that I'm not afraid a usin', and I can use 'em pretty damned good, too." He wrapped his arms around her and smiled as he kissed her. "Don't worry, hon, nobody's comin' to get ya."

"Yeah, that's what you think," she said against his shoulder. "You didn't see these guys. They gave me the creeps."

"Don't worry," Andy said. "I'll protect you from the bad guys." Then he laughed.

Ten

By lunchtime, Reznick was finished with the McMurtry novel.

His office was just one square room, with a door in back that led to a long corridor, which led to a restroom used by all the businesses on this side of the block. There was his desk, always a bit of a mess, with his computer and keyboard. Behind it, a low cupboard with a counter on top, and another cupboard above it. In the upper cupboard, he kept a few mugs, a few plates, glasses, bowls; in the lower cupboard, cleaning supplies, paper towels, and a small garbage can, with one drawer just below the counter in which he kept some utensils and cutlery. On the counter beneath the upper cupboards were a coffee maker—it was on now and the whole room smelled of coffee— a microwave, a small refrigerator, and a sink, with a roll of paper towels hanging over it. There were a couple metal filing cabinets, a small closet. He had two framed posters hanging on the walls—one of *The Scream*, the other of *Starry Night*.

It wasn't much, but it was all he could afford at the moment. Anderson wasn't the ideal location—Redding would have been better. But it was cheaper here, and right now, that was more important.

He'd eaten no breakfast—he hadn't been hungry—but now his stomach purred and gurgled and let him know it was time to eat.

A new barbecue place had opened two doors down, just the other side of Bea's Beauty Parlor. Barbecue sounded good, and he decided to give it a try. Normally, he brought his own lunch, but he didn't feel like taking the time to make one that morning.

He didn't bother locking the office. He turned right outside his door and moved through an area of vile odors emanating from the beauty parlor, into an invisible cloud made up of the tangy aroma of barbecue. Reznick tilted his head back a bit, breathed in deep through his nose, then out through his mouth. He looked at the words painted on the glass in front of the small take-out joint: UNCLE LEROY'S HOMEMADE BARBECUE.

Specials were posted on a board that rested on a tripod just outside the glass door. The door had a flat metal bar across the front of it, just like the door of Reznick's office. He pushed through the door, stepped inside, and released a pleasant sigh.

The aroma was *thick* inside. Behind the front counter were tri-tips on a spit over a grill that held chicken and ribs, and a large pot. Behind the counter stood a tall black man in a long white apron over a white T-shirt. His short black hair was sprinkled with white.

"Hello, there," Reznick said.

"Hello to you," the man said, smiling.

"Are you Uncle Leroy?"

"That's me, all right."

Reznick shook his head and smiled. "I'll tell ya—I don't think I've ever *smelled* better barbecue in my life."

"Well, if I do say so myself, it tastes as good as it smells. What do you have a hankerin' for today?"

"I think ribs sound really good."

"Ribs it is. Ribs for one?"

"Yes."

Leroy turned around and unrolled some aluminum foil.

"You've only been open a couple days, right?" Reznick said.

"Three days."

"How's business so far?"

Leroy put some ribs on the foil and wrapped them up. "Truth be told, I'll be outta here in two weeks, it don't get any better soon." He put the ribs in a white paper bag. "You get two sides with that. I got mashed 'taters and gravy, I got coleslaw, which I made this mornin', I got a green salad that's just so-so, I'm afraid, and mister, I got baked beans my momma made that'll take you outta your *body*."

Reznick laughed. "Let's see, give me ... some coleslaw and some of those metaphysical baked beans."

Leroy laughed then.

While Leroy went to the refrigerator for the coleslaw, Reznick said, "What's wrong with us, Leroy? What happened? We're two guys who are good at what we do, and all we want to do is sell our services and make an honest living. Right? Isn't that what America is all about? So how did we end up *here*, short of customers? Huh? What do we have to *do*? I read online this morning about that serial killer—have you heard about this?"

"No, I don't think so," Leroy said as he put the Styrofoam container of slaw in the white bag.

"He's the one who built a shack out in the woods and had all those women he'd killed sitting up in a row in that shack. He'd cut their throats and watched them die. Then he'd had sex with them. I mean, Leroy, can you *imagine* anything more horrible, anything more barbaric? But now they're making a movie about him."

Leroy scooped baked beans from the pot into a Styrofoam container.

Reznick said, "Now, you and me, Leroy, they'll never make a movie about us. Nobody'll ever write a book about you or me. But go to the bookstores and the shelves are filled with books about men who kill their wives and women who kill their husbands, or their *children*—and people eat them up with a spoon. And you and me, Leroy … we can't make a buck. So what's wrong? Huh? Hey. I've got an idea. Do you have any business cards, Leroy?"

"Yes, I do, I just had 'em made up."

"Tell you what," Reznick said. "We'll trade business cards, you and me, and we'll hand them out to people. What do you say? It's always easier to talk up somebody else, right? And we'll actively try to get rid of them, okay?"

Leroy frowned for a moment. "Are you serious?"

"Sure, I'm serious. Of course, if you're not interested, you just say so, and no harm done. But I think we might be able to stir up some business for each other."

The frown relaxed and Leroy smiled. "I'm sorry, but I don't even know your name, or-or what kind of business you're in."

"Oh, yeah, you don't, do you?" Reznick reached under his coat and produced a single business card. "Marcus Reznick of Reznick Investigations. I'm a private investigator. Call me Marc. I'm just two doors down."

"A real private investigator, how about that. What's your specialty?"

"At the moment, it's divorce cases. But I also find people, find *things*, follow people, do thorough background checks. I'll even serve papers, I'm not proud. I'm reasonably priced, totally confidential, and I've been in the business since I was a kid. It's second nature to me."

"You got yourself a deal, Mr. Detective. Hang on." Leroy hurried down the counter in the long, narrow room, and disappeared through a door in the back. He came back a moment later with a thick stack of business cards. He handed them to Reznick and said, "There you go."

"Thank you. And I'll go get some of mine and bring them to you."

"That's a good idea, Marc."

"Hey, what the hell, it can't hurt."

Reznick paid the bill for his lunch and left Uncle Leroy's Homemade Barbecue. He walked back down to his office. A hot, smothering breeze had blown up while he'd been getting his lunch—it was like some darting, invisible mythological creature that sucked the breath from its victims' lungs, leaving two scorched husks. He stepped up to the door of the office and found someone seated in the chair facing his desk. The person's back was to him until he pushed the glass door open, then he stood and turned.

"I hope you don't mind me comin' in here and waitin' for ya," the man said.

"No, not at all," Reznick said. "In fact, I'm glad you did."

He was built like some kind of comic book superhero—his muscles seemed to have muscles. But he didn't quite look like a body builder. Reznick guessed he was in construction, or the timber industry, something like that. His short hair had a sandy color, and he had one of those mustaches that drop down from the corners of the mouth to the edge of the jaw on each side of the chin. He wore work boots, jeans, a long sleeve plaid shirt with the sleeves rolled up and the front unbuttoned, with one of those shoulder-strap undershirts on under it.

"Are you Mr. Reznick?"

"Yes. What's your name?"

"My name's Morris Carey, but everybody calls me Mo."

"Have a seat."

Reznick went behind his desk and sat down. He put the white bag containing his lunch on the desk. His stomach gurgled.

"Well, Mr. Carey, how can I help you?"

"I'm not sure you can, see, that's the thing. I never been to no private investigator before, so I don't even know if this is the kinda thing you handle."

"Why don't you let me decide." Reznick smiled at him.

"Yeah, okay, I can do that. See, it's my wife."

"If it's your wife, Mr. Carey, then I can *assure* you that it's the kind of thing a private investigator would handle."

"Really? Okay, then, I guess I was right in callin' on you."

Reznick leaned forward a little, genuinely interested. "Tell me, Mr. Carey—what made you choose me?"

"'Cause you was in Anderson," Carey said. "Anderson's closer to me than Redding. I'm in Happy Valley."

For a moment, the smile dropped off Reznick's face. He had a bad memory of Happy Valley—a wooded, rural area west of Anderson—and had not returned there since he'd *made* that memory. He'd been hired by a couple middle-aged parents who drank too much and probably paid little attention to their children, who wanted him to rescue their son from the bad crowd into which he'd fallen. He'd run away from home, they said, and they wanted him found and brought back. They suspected they knew where he was—they gave him the address. They asked him if he carried a gun, and he said yes. They said he might need it.

Reznick had gone to the address that night, which had been in Happy Valley. It was right off Happy Valley Road—a long gravel driveway led to the house, with glowing windows some distance from the road. There were several cars parked around the house in a big clot. Reznick did not turn down the driveway.

He went on and pulled over on a narrow shoulder. He got out of his car, locked it, and crossed the road. He started down the long driveway.

Halfway there, he was accosted by an ugly, familiar smell—a smell like someone painting a car. It was the smell of a meth lab in operation.

"Holy shit," Reznick muttered.

Reznick was not a coward, and he was willing to take a risk now and then when it was necessary. But he was no idiot. He did not mess with people who had meth labs. He did not mess with the meth freaks.

He turned around and found himself looking down the barrel of a sawed-off shotgun.

"Who the fuck're you?" the dark figure holding the gun said. That's all he was, a dark figure with what looked like long straight hair, broad shoulders—and that gun somehow sticking out of the dark, vivid in front of Reznick's face.

"Marcus Reznick, private investigator. I'm looking for a young man named Rodney Pope. I was told he might be here. His parents want him to come home. I'm not here to make trouble."

"You a fuckin' cop?"

"No, not at all, I'm a private investigator, I'm not affiliated with law enforcement in any way. In fact, I usually have an adversarial relationship with them."

"Stand right where you are."

"All right."

The tall shadow moved around him, then poked him in the back with the shotgun. Reznick started walking.

"You get the fuck outta here, you hear me?" the man said.

"Yep."

"You come back here, I'm gonna be the first one to find ya, and I'm gonna blow you in half, you unnerstand me?"

"I understand perfectly."

The man moved his face close to Reznick's ear and said quietly, "I mean it—right the fuck in half." His breath smelled of garlic.

"You'll never see me around here again," Reznick had said. "You just keep walkin'."

He'd never walked faster.

Meth-heads were utterly unreasonable and dangerously violent, usually psychotic. Reznick had no intention of getting near any again, and if he suspected he might, he would turn the case down, no matter how much he needed the money.

Rather be poor than dead, he thought.

"Where in Happy Valley?" Reznick said.

"Right off Happy Valley Road."

Reznick nodded. "A lot of people live right off Happy Valley Road."

The warm, tangy aroma of the barbecue filled the office. But there was something else—Reznick could smell the baked beans, too. Not as strong as the barbecue, but it was there. It was making his stomach growl its head off.

"Have you had lunch, Mr. Carey?"

"Matter of fact," Carey said, "I haven't. This is my lunch hour, but I'm skippin' it to see you. Is that barbecue you've got in that bag?"

"It sure is."

"'Cause it's makin' me crazy."

Reznick laughed and said, "Yeah, me, too." He quickly cleared away most of the top of his desk, then reached into the bag and brought out two dinner rolls wrapped in plastic, the Styrofoam cartons and the foil-wrapped ribs. Also in the bag were napkins, a plastic fork, toothpicks in plastic and a chocolate mint. "I'll be damned," he said. "This is a pretty generous order for one."

Reznick got up and went to the cupboards, got a couple plates, a couple forks, a couple paper towels, and returned to his desk. A few minutes later, the only sound in the office was that of two men eating—teeth tearing meat, lips smacking, forks clacking against plates.

Finally, Reznick said, "Is this the best barbecue you've ever had?"

"It's fuckin' delicious, if you'll pardon my French," Carey said. "Where'd you get it?"

"Two doors down, Uncle Leroy's Homemade Barbecue. There's a stack of business cards. When your hands are clean, take a few and pass them out to friends. Stop and get some, take it home for the wife so she doesn't have to cook."

"Don't worry, she probably won't be around long enough to cook."

"What's the problem, Mr. Carey?"

"Oh, you can call me Mo."

"I'm Marc."

As they discussed Carey's problem, they continued to eat.

"The last year or so, see," Carey said, "my wife Alicia's been goin' out with her girlfriends."

"What do you mean by that?" Reznick said. "Where do they go?"

"Well, she always told me they'd go out to a bar, or maybe to the Win-River Casino. A concert once in a while. Always drinkin', they always go to a bar or club and drink."

"Do you have children?"

"We have a little four-year-old girl."

"Really? And your wife still goes out—how often?"

"Well, that's the thing, see. At first, it was once every month. Then pretty soon, it started to be once every couple weeks. Then once a week. Now it's a couple, three times a week, sometimes more."

"Have you told her you don't like this?" Reznick said. "Does she know how you feel?"

"Oh, yeah. I've tried. *That* never goes over well. It always turns into a fight."

"What's her argument?"

"Her argument? She says we married real young, and we did. Just outta high school, Melanie got pregnant, and we got married. The baby was stillborn. We waited a long time before tryin' again. I thought the marriage—that we—I thought everything was great, y'know? But *somethin's* wrong if she's doin' this two-three times a week. I'm afraid she might be gettin' herself a drinkin' problem. Mention that to her and she flies into a rage. I think she might be takin' drugs."

"Was this sudden," Reznick said, "or were there warning signs? Can you look back now and see things happening that might have led up to this?"

Carey's eyebrows were pretty bushy, and they huddled together thickly in the middle of his frown. "Y'know, there have been things, and I've noticed all of 'em, and I've even brought a couple up to her, but it was always a mistake."

"What kind of things?"

"Well …"

Carey was hesitating because that was private stuff, and he was reluctant to discuss it with a stranger.

Reznick's head bobbed up and down and he said, "I'm sorry, I should've pointed out to you by now that everything you say in this office is absolutely confidential. Everything you say stays within these walls. So you shouldn't be afraid to say anything."

Carey nodded. "Okay, I'll buy that. It's just that—see, these days, most people're real eager to go on TV and talk about how crazy their families are, y'know? But that's not the way I was raised. I was raised to keep my dirty laundry off the outdoor line, where it didn't be*long* in the *first* place."

"That's very respectable, Mo."

"Thanks. Course, it ain't gettin' me nowhere with my wife."

"What *about* your wife, Mo?" Reznick said. "What do you want me to do?"

Carey dipped his roll in the baked beans and took a big bite. He chewed for a while, then said, "Last week, I'm sittin' at home with our daughter, watchin' a rerun a some dumb show I didn't like the first time I saw it, when I realized, why should I do nothin' while she's out kickin' up her heels?"

As Reznick listened, he ate his last rib, and forced himself not to groan happily at the flavor of the barbecue.

"I know all the husbands and boyfriends of her girlfriends, see," Carey went on. "I figured I'd call 'em over and we could play poker, or play video games on the X-Box, or somethin' — *anything* besides wastin' another second on television, for cryin' out loud. So I call the first one — name's Ted Haker. Him and me went to high school together. We even dabbled in college together over at Shasta College. It wasn't for me, but Ted went off and got himself a business degree. Now he owns a small chain of electronics stores here in northern California. Ted's always fulla good stories. He's dealt with a lot of strange people over the years, and he's fulla real funny stories. So he's always fun to have around. So I call Ted. I ask him if he wants to come over and do somethin'. Ted acts kinda funny, and he says, 'Tonight?' And I say, 'Yeah, tonight.' And after awhile, he says, 'Okay, yeah, I guess so. What's Melanie gonna be doin'?' I thought that was a funny thing for him to ask, and I said, 'Huh?' And he said, 'What's Melanie gonna be doin' while we're playin' video games?' And I said, 'What the hell you talkin' about, she's out with your wife and the others.' And Ted chuckled and said, 'My wife's right here with me.' That's when

I got this cold feelin' inside. I called the other husbands and chatted, found out their wives were home, too. That feelin' got worse. That helpless feelin' you get when you realize something important to you is out of your hands, beyond your control, y'know? Somethin' that's not really lost, but that maybe you never had. It's like bein' in a earthquake. Ever been in a earthquake, Marc?"

"Yes, I have," Reznick said.

"It's a helpless feeling, ain't it?"

Reznick nodded.

"So is this feelin' ya get when you know somethin's real wrong, somethin' outta your hands. Somethin' bad."

He liked to tell a story, this Mo Carey. Reznick wished he would pick things up a bit. "What was your somethin' bad?" Reznick said.

"Melanie wasn't out with her friends—she was out with … well … someone *else*."

"Any idea who?"

"None."

"You want me to find out?"

"Yeah, that's right. On top of her goin' out so much, she's been buyin' stuff. Just things now and then. But they ain't all that cheap, you know? A dress here, some perfume there. Pricey stuff. And I don't know where she's gettin' the money. Then I got to thinkin' … maybe she ain't buyin' 'em. Maybe somebody's buyin' 'em for her."

They stopped talking to eat more coleslaw and beans and ribs. Then Carey said, "I don't know where she goes, but I think her girlfriends do now. I think they're all in on it, tryin' to hide it from me."

"You think she's seeing another man?" Reznick said.

"What *else* would she be doin' at night?"

"You might be surprised how many bad things people can get up to at night without having affairs. You want me to follow her?"

"Yeah. I don't know when she'll go out again. Maybe tonight, maybe tomorrow night. She comes home from work, throws somethin' together for my dinner, feeds the kid, and she's gone. Usually by six-thirty, seven o'clock. Not every night, but often enough for it to be … well, you know, outrageous. Here she is my wife, and I hardly see her anymore. I pick the baby up on my way home from work—she stays at my mom's during the day—then go home. I get there 'bout the same time she does. Before I know it, she's gone again."

"Give me your address in Happy Valley, tell me what kinda car she drives," Reznick said. "I'll wait for her to leave, then I'll follow her. I'd also like a picture of her, if you have one."

Carey stopped eating and wiped his hands and face on the paper towel. He took his wallet from his back pocket and started looking for a picture.

"What kind of work you do, Mo?"

"Construction. I'm workin' on the new jailhouse in Redding."

"Ah. And your wife?"

"She works in a dentist's office." He handed Reznick a picture of Mrs. Carey.

"What's her name?" Reznick said.

"Alicia."

Reznick nodded.

The woman in the picture was smiling, but she had the kind of face that would look angry and mean if she weren't. She was a plain woman with straight, stringy, dirty-blonde hair. She had a broad face with small blue eyes perched above chubby round cheeks that became more pronounced when she smiled.

"Look," Carey said. "Before we go any further, I gotta know—how much is this gonna cost me?"

Reznick told him his rates and how much he'd need up front.

"Okay, well, that's a little steep for me. But I'll handle it."

"I assume you want me to start right away," Reznick said.

"Tonight, if you can. Like I said, I don't know if she'll go out or not. If she ain't gone by seven, she's probably not goin'."

"How has this affected your marriage?"

Carey shook his head. "We ain't had sex in a long time. She's never interested. That's another thing makes me think she's seein' someone else. Hell, she don't even seem that interested in our little girl. And she's been actin', I dunno, kinda … kinda unstable lately. Mood swings, know what I mean? One minute, she's fine. The next, she's yellin' and screamin' at me, or even our daughter. Then, the next minute, she's cryin'. Real weird. I been tellin' her to see a doctor, but she won't do it, says there's nothin' wrong with her."

Carey had stopped eating and wiped his hands on the paper towel. He was getting himself worked up. His big hands closed and opened and closed into fists as he spoke.

Reznick decided to change the subject. "What's your little girl's name?"

"Brandy Michelle." Carey smiled then and his hands relaxed. "Brandy Michelle Carey, and she's the most beautiful thing you ever did see."

"I'm sure she is. Does she notice her mother is gone so much?"

"Oh, hell, yeah. She's always askin', 'Where's Momma? Where's Momma?' And I don't even know what to tell her."

"And you've confronted your wife about this?"

"Oh, yeah. And it always turns into a fight. Next time I talk to her about it, I want to be able to show her pictures, tell her I know *exactly* what she's up to, and she better stop it or I'm gonna get a divorce."

"Don't get ahead of yourself," Reznick said. "You don't want to start talking divorce until you know what she's up to. Now, let's get those things I need, and I can get started tonight."

Eleven

The phone inside the trailer was chirping when Anna and Kendra got back from running errands. Anna hurriedly unlocked the door and went inside, a bag of groceries in one arm. She answered the phone while still holding the bag.

While Anna talked on the phone, Kendra stayed outside and played with her new pet—a tiny pale-tan Chihuahua she had named Dexter. The little dog had fallen in love with Kendra at once when she first held him in the animal shelter. Dexter had licked her face frantically and quivered and wiggled in her arms. The dog was not unlike Conan, the main difference being his lighter color.

Anna came to the door. "That was the temp agency," she said. "I've got a job this afternoon, but I have to go right away. I'm going to get dressed, okay? You gather up whatever you want to take to Aunt Rose's."

Kendra stomped a foot. "But *Maah-meee*! You said the next time you had to go out, you'd leave me to take care of myself."

"Not this time, honey, I'm in too big a hurry, okay?" She disappeared from the doorway.

Kendra bent down and scooped Dexter up in her arms. She went inside, where Mommy was unloading the groceries into the refrigerator.

"Mommy, you said you'd seriously consider it," Kendra said. "And this is perfect! It's daylight. You can go straight to work instead of taking me to Aunt Rose's. And it'll still be light when you get home, light for a long time. If you get off at five. Will you get off at five?"

"Actually, I get off at four-thirty," Anna said. "You'll miss Vacation Bible School."

"It's okay, I can miss a day." Kendra put Dexter down on the floor and spread her arms dramatically. "And see? Four-thirty! It's only a little after noon now. You wouldn't be gone long at all! Just a few hours! I can take care of myself, Mommy. *Really* I can. I'll prove it to you."

Anna chewed on her lower lip as she thought. She put a fist on her hip and shifted her weight from foot to foot. She could tell someone to keep an eye on Kendra for her that afternoon. But who? There was Debra Connor in the trailer across the way, but—no, that wouldn't work, Debra visited her parents in a rest home most afternoons, she was probably already gone. She could ask Mrs. Snodgrass—if she hadn't started drinking already. That was what she would do.

"You won't go wandering off?" Kendra said.

"No!"

"No cooking. I don't want you using the stove while I'm gone."

Kendra shrugged. "Too hot to cook, anyway. I'll have cereal, or a sandwich for lunch."

"I put the cans of dog food under the sink. You might want to go ahead and feed Dexter, because we don't know when he ate last."

"Okay."

Anna sighed as she stared at Kendra.

"Whatsa matter?" Kendra said.

"I don't know. I guess … well, I'll worry about you."

"Don't worry about me, Mommy," Kendra said with a big smile. "Dexter will take care of me. And Jesus and my guardian angel will watch over me."

For a moment, Anna thought she was going to cry. She swallowed hard a few times until the feeling passed. "Well," she said, "I should get cleaned up." She turned and left the kitchen, and went down the hall to her bedroom.

Kendra picked up Dexter again. "Y'hear that, Dexter? Me'n you'll have the whole house to ourselves this afternoon."

The little dog seemed thrilled.

———————

Muriel Snodgrass came to the screen door about thirty or forty seconds after Anna rang the bell. She was a fat pasty-white woman with a big belly, but spindly legs that came like sticks out of the baggy blue shorts she wore. Her black-dyed hair—and a bad job, too—was a mess. She wore glasses with big square frames, a baggy sleeveless top speckled green and yellow and white. "Yeah?" she said. She held a glass of something on ice in her right hand. It was the kind of glass handed out at fast food chains to promote movies. This one had some kind of superhero on the side.

Anna hoped the glass did not contain liquor, not at this early hour. It looked like iced tea.

Somewhere in the house, a television played loudly.

"Hi, Mrs. Snodgrass," she said, smiling.

"Hi. Keepin' cool in this heat?"

"Barely. It's miserably hot, isn't it?"

"You got that right. What can I do for you?"

"Well," Anna said, "you've met my daughter Kendra, haven't you?"

"Sure. Real purty girl, too, she is."

"Well, you know she's a little slow."

"Yeah. Shame, too."

"I have to go to work, and I'm going to leave Kendra at home by herself for the first time this afternoon. Would you mind keeping an eye on her for me? I mean, just from a distance, you know? See if anybody shows up while I'm gone, or something."

"You expectin' someone?"

"No, no, I'm just …" She chuckled a brief, breathy chuckle. "I guess I'm just a nervous, worried mother."

"Yeah, I unnerstand. I was that way with my kids, too. I devoted my whole life to 'em. I *dropped* my life for 'em, y'know? Now, do I hear from 'em? Do they come see me? Do they call? Or even write me a e-mail? Nope. Not them. Too busy. Or they live too far away."

"I'm sorry to hear that," Anna said, trying to conceal her need to get away from Mrs. Snodgrass as soon as possible and get to work. The workers in the office at Redding Tractor and Lawn Mower needed a hand right away, and she did not want to make them wait any longer. "I *really* have to run, Mrs. Snodgrass, or I'd stay and chat."

"Don't worry, honey, I'll keep an eye out for your little girl."

"Thank you so much." Anna turned and hurried back to the trailer.

She'd called Rose to ask her to drop in on Kendra while she was gone. But she'd gotten Rose's answering machine. She'd called her cell phone, but it was turned off. Anna did not understand why Rose had a cell phone if she never turned it on.

Anna was dressed in a business-like blue-and-white suit and ready to go. She went inside and stood before Kendra, who

106

was on the floor playing with Dexter with an old sock that had a knot tied in it.

"Sweetheart, I have to go," Anna said. "Can you stand up for a second?"

Kendra got to her feet. "Don't worry, Mommy. I'll be fine."

"I guess that's my problem," Anna whispered as she hugged Kendra. "I don't like the idea that you don't need me anymore."

"Oh, *Mommy*," Kendra said as she squeezed Anna. "I'll *always* need you."

They stood that way for a long moment, then Anna pulled away, pecked Kendra's cheek, and said, "I've got to go."

Out in the car, as she backed out of the carport, Anna noticed a man walking from the new trailer in unit five. He headed toward the Snodgrass house.

She stopped backing up for a moment, and watched him in the rearview mirror. There was something startlingly familiar about him. He had short dark hair, broad shoulders—he wasn't that tall, but he was well built. And there was something about him ... *some*thing. She frowned as she watched him in the mirror and tried to place him, tried to figure out where she'd seen him before. But she could not.

Anna drove out of the trailer park and headed for work at Redding Tractor and Lawn Mower.

———

Muriel Snodgrass heard another knock at her front door. It was really more of a rattle, because someone had knocked on the metal edge of the loose screen door. That made three so far today. What did all these people want all of a sudden?

The first had been Audrey Marsh from unit nineteen, wanting some sugar, because she was baking cookies and had run out of sugar and couldn't run to the store because there were cookies in the oven. Muriel had invited her in and given her the sugar. Why she wanted to do any baking in such miserable heat was beyond Muriel.

Then it had been that woman with the beautiful retarded daughter.

So, who was it this time?

"Hank, get the door!" Muriel shouted. She was washing dishes. There stood on one side of the sink several piles of filthy dishes which had accumulated there over the last couple weeks. Muriel let all the dishes pile up awhile before she washed them. She didn't wash them until they ran out of clean ones. That way she didn't have to do it as often.

"Dammit to hell," she said as she threw the sponge into the sink and dropped a plate with a clattering splash. She rinsed the suds off her hands, dried them on a hand towel, tossed the towel onto the counter, picked up her drink, and left the kitchen.

In the hall, cats scattered before Muriel.

As she passed the living room to the right, she looked in and saw her husband Hank slumped in his recliner, big belly sticking up out of the chair, a big, round, snowy mountain in a white sleeveless undershirt. A nature program played on TV.

"Useless," she shuffled in her slippers to the front door. "Hi."

"Hello, there, Mrs. Snodgrass."

"Who're you?"

"You don't remember me? I'm Steven Regent, your newest tenant." He turned and pointed. "Over there, in unit five."

"Oh, yeah. Step back a bit." When he did, she pushed the screen door open and invited him inside.

When he came in, Muriel gave him a good once over. He was good-looking, this one. Not too tall, but handsome and strong-looking.

"What can I do you for, Steve?" she said.

"I'd like to pay my rent for three months in advance."

"Oh, really?"

"Yes. I hope that's not a problem."

"Oh, no. But I'm curious, Steve, whatcha payin' rent in advance for? Or is that none of my business?"

"Not at all. It's just that I like to get it out of the way so I don't have to worry about it every month for a while."

"Oh. Sure. Okay. You wanna pay your rent in advance, that's just fine by me."

He reached fingers into the breast pocket of the unbuttoned short-sleeve blue chambray shirt he was wearing. He wore nothing underneath it. From the pocket, he removed a check.

"That should be the right amount," he said as he handed the check to Muriel.

She took it, tilted her head back, and looked through her bifocals. "Yep, right on the money."

"Could I get a receipt for that?" Regent said.

"A receipt?"

"Yes, please." He was still smiling.

He was a looker, all right, in his mid-thirties. A genial fellow. But there was something else. There was something about that constant smile. Muriel did not trust people who smiled all the time. It wasn't natural—and usually, it was downright fake. If Mr. Regent didn't lose that smile pretty quick, Muriel was going to get rid of him pretty quick.

"C'mon in here," she said, leading him down the hall to the kitchen. Once again, cats scattered before her. The house smelled of them.

"How many cats do you have?" Regent said.

"Eleven." She put her drink on the counter, then went to a desk against the kitchen wall on the right. The desk was cluttered with papers and big envelopes and books and magazines and even a shoe box. Muriel shuffled things around until she found her receipt pad. It didn't take her long to find it—the desk was a mess, but she knew where everything was.

Muriel put the pad on a stack of books, then felt around for a pen. She filled the receipt out, referring to the check for the right total. She tore his copy of the receipt from the book and handed it to Regent.

"Howzat?" she said.

He looked at it. "Perfect. Thank you."

"You all settled in now?" Muriel said.

"Yes, I am. Everything's unpacked and in its place. I didn't procrastinate at all this time, I got all the unpacking done the first day."

"Well-well, good for you. What kinda work you do, Steve?"

"I've got a few very successful—what am I saying, *wildly* successful websites."

"Websites, huh? Pornography?"

"I prefer adult entertainment."

"Yeah, that's what they're callin' it these days, huh?" Muriel went over to the kitchen counter where a half-full whiskey bottle stood next to two glasses, Muriel's almost full. By her glass was a pack of cigarettes, a red Bic lighter, and an ashtray full of butts. "Can I get you a drink?" she said as she shook out a cigarette, then lit up.

His smile fell away then. "Nothing for me, thank you."

"I been spikin' my iced tea this afternoon," she said in a conspiratorial whisper. "So you got websites with lotsa neckid women on 'em?"

"Yes, something like that."

"You'n my husband Frank'll get along just fine. He looks at them titty sites all the time. He don't know how lucky he is to have a wife don't mind him lookin' at them titty sites. You ain't gonna have a big parade of neckid women comin' in and out of your trailer, are ya?"

"Oh, no, nothing like that at all. We do most of our work at my partner's house, anyway. We're very discreet, I promise."

"Okay. That's good. This is a family park. I can't have no pornography goin' on all over the place for the kids to see."

"Don't worry, you won't even know I'm there."

"Sounds good to me," Muriel said. "A quiet park is a happy park."

She walked him back to the front door, said goodbye, then stepped outside and watched him walk to his trailer from the porch, smoking her cigarette. She looked at his trailer a long time, and the back end of his SUV—a very expensive SUV, she knew, because it was a Porsche.

Muriel went back into the house and turned into the living room, went to Frank's recliner. "Wake up, Frank."

He did not move. He was snoring quietly. For a change. When he snored in bed he sounded like an ill zoo animal. He snored in his recliner and he sounded like a purring cat.

"*Frank!*" she shouted.

Frank jerked in his chair. "Huh?"

"Wake up."

"Dammit," he said as he shuffled around in the recliner. He reached down and clutched a wooden lever on the side of the chair, pulled it, and straightened it up into a sitting position. "What the hell's a matter now?" he said. Frank Snodgrass had a long, hound dog face, bald on top with a U of greying brown hair from ear to ear. He slowly stood as he said, "What's so damned important that I couldn't sleep a little while longer, huh?"

"There's something wrong about him," Muriel said.

"Wrong about who?"

"That man who was just here."

"Who the hell you talking about? I was asleep, 'member?"

"The man who just—Steven Regent, who just moved into unit five."

"What about him?" Frank shuffled out of the living room and into the kitchen.

Muriel followed him, talking the whole way.

"What's he doin' *here*, in *this* trailer park?"

"What kinda question is that?" Frank said. He went to the refrigerator and opened the door below the top freezer. He bent down and looked in at what was on the metal shelves.

"Well, *think* about it," Muriel said. She went to the counter and snubbed her cigarette out in the ashtray. "He's got that beautiful trailer—that thing looks new, and it didn't come cheap. And how about that Porsche SUV, huh? How much you think he paid for *that*? And he just now paid three months in rent. Three months."

"So what?"

"Well, if he's—what the hell are you *looking* for?"

"Nothin'." He stood and closed the refrigerator door. He did that all the time, and it drove Muriel crazy.

"The *so-what* is that he's here in this *dump*," Muriel said.

"Maybe he just likes trailer park living, ever thought a *that*?"

"Then why *this* trailer park? This place is an old dump. Why would he come here? He's got a lotta money, and he smiles a lot. Too much. Says he runs a few titty sites on the Internet." She went back to washing dishes.

Frank was pouring some whiskey into the empty glass, and he stopped and turned to her. "Really? Titty sites?"

She turned to him. "Yeah, I *thought* you'd like that. You an' your titty sites. I got a bad feelin' about him."

"Maybe the guy just wants to live in some outta the way dumpy trailer park, who the hell knows anything about anybody? You're always tryin' to figure out what's goin' on in other people's heads." He took a couple big gulps of whiskey, put the glass down, then came up behind Muriel and wrapped his arms around her from behind. He rubbed his hands over her belly, then slid them up and cupped her sagging breasts. "You gotta stop tryin' to get into other people's heads, my melon princess." He kissed her neck.

Muriel laughed and put her hands over his. "I can't help it. I see things other people don't. And I'm seein' somethin' in that young man. There's somethin' wrong about him."

"Don't worry about him. He's prob'ly innocent as pie. Hell, he runs titty sites, he can't be all bad."

"You know how lucky you are you gotta wife lets you look at them titty sites on the Internet?"

"Oh, yeah, I know how lucky I am. And you know the only titties I *really* want are yours."

Twelve

Kendra held Dexter in her arms and danced around in circles with him as a music video played on TV. When she finally stopped, she was a little dizzy, and she laughed.

"You like that, Dexter?" she said. She hoped she hadn't made the little dog dizzy—she hadn't meant to do that. She put him down and he immediately rose up on his hind legs and began pawing at her shins. "Hey, I got an idea," Kendra said.

She left the living room and went to her bedroom and to the closet. She had a box of balls on the floor of her closet. In it was the multicolored ball she'd been bouncing earlier that day. There were also smaller balls, and *much* smaller balls. She found one small enough for Dexter to be able to pick it up with his little mouth, then left her bedroom.

"Oh, *no*, Dexter!" Kendra shouted when she found the little dog urinating on the kitchen floor.

He stopped and scurried away, whining.

She went to him and shouted, "No! No, bad boy, Dexter, *bad* boy!" as she wagged a finger at him.

Dexter quivered and whined and lowered his head and tucked his skinny little tail between his legs.

Kendra went back and cleaned up the little puddle with paper towels. She hoped she was doing this right—she had no idea how to house train a dog. She was simply doing what made sense to her.

She went back to the living room, where Dexter was still huddling at the foot of the recliner.

"I'm sorry, Dexter," Kendra said as she sat down beside him, "but you gotta learn that's a no-no. You wanna play fetch?" She showed him the ball and he took some interest. She threw the ball into the kitchen and Dexter darted away after it, little toenails clicking on the kitchen floor. He went to the ball and playfully knocked it around on the kitchen floor. But he didn't bring it back, no matter how much Kendra called him.

She got up, went to the kitchen, snatched up the ball, then returned to the recliner. Dexter never took his eyes from the ball and followed her all the way. She threw the ball and Dexter shot off after it. Again, he did not bring it back, even though she called him.

Kendra occupied herself with this activity for about half an hour before suddenly, out of nowhere, Dexter picked up the ball and brought it back to her, dropped it in her lap, as if he'd known how to do it all along, but hadn't wanted to.

"You little poop!" she said. "You been playin' with me all along, huh?"

For another fifteen minutes, Kendra tossed the ball and Dexter brought it back. She was endlessly entertained by the way he ran, by the way he trotted back with the ball in his mouth, head held high. By the way his whole back-end waggled as he eagerly waited for her to throw the ball.

She threw it too hard and a little too far to the left. The ball bounced around in the kitchen sink. Dexter ran into the kitchen and stopped, body rigid, and looked around for the ball. It was nowhere to be seen, so he lowered his head and began to sniff around for it.

Kendra got up and took the ball from the sink, and dropped it. Dexter snapped at it as it bounced in the air a few times before coming lower, and lower, and lower, until Dexter finally caught it in his little mouth. Head high again, he trotted away.

Kendra leaned her hips back on the edge of the kitchen counter and thought about how lucky she was. Because she was real happy. She was starting to get some independence in her life. She'd been alone in the trailer for about ninety minutes— for the first time in her life. And she had a little doggy all her own, for the first time in her life. It was a day of first times.

But so far, Kendra had done nothing naughty, nothing to make her feel good, to somehow scratch her naughty itch. There had to be something she could do without getting caught—but with just enough risk of getting caught to make it exciting.

For one thing, Mommy had made her take off the bikini top and put on a T-shirt with her shorts. So Kendra went to her room and took off the T-shirt and put the bikini top back on, then put the plaid shirt over it, left it open, the way she'd worn it that morning.

Kendra was pouring herself a glass of ice-cold lemonade when she heard the piercing squeak of the mailman's brakes. She could hear them all the way there from the trailer park's entrance, where the mail truck stopped at the bank of mailboxes.

"Hey, Dexie," she said with enthusiasm, "you wanna go get the mail?"

Because of her tone, the dog got excited and began hopping up and down.

"You're not gonna run away from me soon as we get out there, are you, Dex?" she said.

The dog continued to hop, throwing in a piercing little bark now and then.

Just to be sure, she picked Dexter up in her arms and then went outside, then she held him up in front of her. "Now, you can't run away, you hear me, Dexter? You have to stay with me. Okay?"

Dexter licked her face and she giggled. She put him down on the ground and he ran circles around her feet.

The shade helped keep the trailer park cooler than it would have been without it, but it was not immune from the baking summer heat, not even in the shade. A hot breeze whispered secrets in the trees overhead as Kendra headed for the trailer park's entrance.

Dexter ran ahead of her, and Kendra called, "Dexter! Come back here!" She slapped her bare thigh and made kissing sounds with her lips. The little dog turned around and hurried back, then fell into step beside her, trotting to keep up.

Country music came from one of the trailers. It always seemed to play in the trailer park, all day long. From another trailer came the angry sound of talk radio. Kendra heard a sound ahead and to her left and saw the door open on unit five, the new trailer. A man came out holding a tall glass and a magazine in one hand. He closed the screen door behind him, then sat down on the top porch step, took a sip of his drink and put the glass next to him on the porch.

Kendra kept glancing at him, wondering who he was, what he was like, where he'd come from, and what had brought him to Riverside Mobile Home Park.

Suddenly, he looked up. Then he did a double-take. Then he stared openly at her.

She glanced at him again and again, and each time, his stare was fixed on her, lips slightly parted. Kendra began to feel the jittery sensation of self-consciousness creep up on her. She wondered if there was something wrong with her—did she look funny, was *that* why he was staring at her?

She told herself to stop looking at him, then maybe he would ignore her. She felt her back stiffen as she walked by him. One more glance—he was still watching her from the porch and she stiffened even more as she walked out of his line of sight.

Kendra never knew what it meant when someone stared at her, and it always made her uncomfortable. It seemed people stared at her a lot. Was it because she was slow—could they tell by looking at her? Was she ugly? Funny-looking? She couldn't understand it. Like she told Mommy, everyone was a little mean at one time or another.

She walked on, nearing the park's entrance and exit, the two lanes separated by the giant oak. The row of twenty mailboxes was on the left just outside the entrance.

Kendra glanced back over her shoulder and almost tripped over her own feet when she saw that man standing out in the road now, watching her from behind, arms folded across his chest. She spun back around and faced front, frowning now. She picked up her pace a little, then darted to the left, again out of his line of sight, behind the grey cinder block wall that ran behind the mailboxes. There was another wall just like it on the other side of the exit, but that one had big words on it: RIVERSIDE MOBILE HOME PARK. She went down the row of mailboxes to theirs. She opened it, reached in and removed the mail—mostly junk mail, and a couple bills—then closed the U-shaped door of the mailbox. Kendra hated the look she saw in Mommy's eyes whenever she got a new bill.

She stood in front of the mailboxes for a while, thinking about that man from unit five, the man who'd stared at her the whole time she'd walked down there. She turned around and looked for Dexter. He was a few feet away, sniffing at a rock embedded in the ground. She called him to her and he darted to her side. She picked him up. She didn't trust him so close to Park Way, which got a lot more traffic than the little road inside the trailer park.

Kendra did not know if she could bear the weight of his stare all the way back to the trailer. Maybe he would say something to her this time. That wouldn't be so bad, if he'd say hi, how are you, instead of just *staring* at her like that.

She peeked around the old cinder block wall and down the road into the park. The man was gone. With a little sigh of relief, she started back toward her trailer. Once she was back in the park, she put Dexter down again, and he trotted along beside her.

From the corner of her eye as she came upon unit five, she saw him standing there, leaning back on the rear of his SUV.

"Hi, there," he said with a big, friendly smile.

Startled, Kendra stumbled to a halt, then turned to him, unaware that her mouth hung open. She unconsciously ran her tongue around her lips.

"I'm new here," he said, still smiling. "My name's Steven. Steven Regent. Who're you?"

She looked down at Dexter for a moment, feeling embarrassed, although unsure of why. She lifted her eyes and looked at him again, and his arms were folded across his chest again.

"My name's ... Kendra," she said.

"Well, Kendra, it's nice to meet you. I guess I've been kind of rude, staring at you like I have, but you know what? And this isn't some kind of line. You, Kendra, are maybe the most beautiful girl I've ever seen. And I've seen a lot of beautiful girls, because I'm a photographer. I photograph women. And you, Kendra, you are absolutely stunning."

Along with the heat of the summer came the heat of a stinging, embarrassed blush as it worked its way up her neck and throat and up her face. She did not know what to say. No one had ever said such a thing to her before and she had no clue how to react.

"Kendra?" he said. "That's a beautiful name, by the way. It suits you."

Dexter pawed at her calves.

Kendra finally lifted her head and looked at him again. She was still blushing. She smiled and said, "Thank you. Nobody ever said that to me before."

"You're kidding. No boys have ever told you that?"

"No."

"Well, then you are surrounded by blind men, Kendra, because you are a young woman of exceptional beauty. You should be modeling, or acting, or something. I'd like to photograph you."

"You ... you would?"

"Yes, very much."

"What kind of photography do you do?" she said.

"All kinds, really."

"And you wanna photograph *me*?"

"Yes."

"How come?"

"Like I said, you're beautiful. How could I not want to photograph someone so beautiful?"

She was unable to suppress a little giggle.

"Where do you want me to ... where do you want—" She giggled again, stumbling over her words nervously. "Where would you photograph me?"

"I've got everything set up in my trailer right now. We could do it in there. And I've got central air, so it's nice and cool in there. What do you say?"

"What, right ... right *now*?"

"Yes."

"Dressed like this?"

"You look incredible dressed like that."

"Really?"

"Yes, you do. The all-American girl."

"Wow. Nobody ever called me *that* before. What's it mean?"

"What's it mean?" he said. "Well, uh, it means you are a … an *ideal*. When you think of a beautiful American girl, it's a girl who looks like you. But that really doesn't do you justice. You're something more than that."

"I … I don't think Mommy would like it."

He frowned a moment and said, "Mommy?"

"Yeah, my mommy, I'm not sure she'd want me to."

"Where's your mommy now?"

"She's at work."

"When does she get off?"

"Four-thirty."

"Then we've got plenty of time to do it and be done long before she gets here, and she'll never know a thing about it."

"That would be naughty, wouldn't it?" she said with a sly smirk, her head tilted forward slightly.

Steven Regent chuckled and nodded and said, "Yes, that would be naughty. Is that what you're looking for? Something naughty to do while you're mommy's at work?"

Kendra giggled, then said, "I'll have to go put Dexter in the trailer. I'll be right back."

———————

Regent went into the studio and looked around to make sure there were no offensive pictures out in the open. He did not want to scare her off.

He could not believe it—a retarded teenager who was *that* beautiful. It didn't seem right. Of course, if he could get her to keep her mouth closed—though even that looked somehow sexy on Kendra—she wouldn't look retarded in the pictures.

He straightened up the bed. He'd already started thinking how he'd work her clothes off.

"Naughty, she says," he muttered. "If she wants naughty, I'll give her naughty." He turned on all the cameras and aimed them at the bed.

This would be more than just another shoot. He had to do everything just right, he couldn't blow this. He had to have her. He wanted her more than he'd ever wanted any of the other bimbos that marched by in an endless parade. She stood out like a gorilla at the opera. She put all the others to shame.

When he'd first seen her, he couldn't take his eyes off of her. Skin like milk around bedroom eyes and lips that promised so much. The swing of her hips, the slight sway of her breasts. He'd never seen anyone quite as beautiful as Kendra. He wanted a lot more than just pictures of her—he wanted *her*.

She knocked on the side of his trailer as she stood at his screen door. He pushed the screen door open and let her in.

"You said what I was wearin' was okay," she said, "so I didn't change."

"No, I don't *want* you to change. You're perfect."

That made her smile. He closed and locked the door, then led her down to the studio.

He went to the desk that faced the wall in a corner and opened a drawer, removed the necessary papers.

"Kendra, I need you to sign your name to some papers."

"Papers? What kinda papers?" She came over and stood beside him, looked down at the forms.

"Well, this one, for example, says that I can't take your picture unless you're eighteen. Now it's up to you what you want to do, just remember that if you *don't* sign this paper, I can't take your picture. It's up to you."

He handed her a pen, then waited, hoping he'd made the right move.

A cloud passed over the girl's face—for a second, just an instant, her eyebrows came together as her mouth curled up in a smile, and she looked like a parody of villainy—and then it was gone. Then she signed the paper.

"Very good," he said. "This next paper gives me permission to post your pictures on my websites."

"Websites? You never said nothin' about no websites."

"Oh, is that a problem?"

"Well, I ... I don't know."

"I guarantee you, your mother will never see them."

She thought about it a moment, then signed the paper.

"Why would you want pictures of me on your website?" Kendra asked.

"I'm starting a new website called Trailer Park Girls," he said. "It's going to be filled with pictures and videos of beautiful girls who live in trailer parks across the country."

"Trailer Park Girls, huh?" She got that delightfully mischievous look on her face again. "Is it a naughty website?"

A smile grew on Regent's face and he said, "Yes, as a matter of fact it is, Kendra. There's nudity on the site."

"You mean girls with no clothes on?"

"That's right."

She giggled again, then said, "Where do you want me to stand for these pictures?"

"I don't want you to stand, I want you to stretch out on the bed."

"Really?"

"Yes."

"Hm. Okay, if you say so." She kicked off her flip-flops and threw herself onto the bed like a little girl, giggling as she bounced.

Regent found himself getting an erection simply watching her. She was elemental, like a storm of silent lightning charging the air. She rolled back and forth on the bed, then stopped and stuck both legs into the air, pressed together.

It did not matter what she did, the position in which she held herself. She was always beautiful, always ripe with sexuality. And he was certain she would be just as beautiful at rest.

She said, "How do you want me to pose?" and lowered her legs.

"Just naturally," he said as he started taking pictures.

"But ... but I ..." She didn't move, just lay there.

"Here's an idea," Regent said. "Lie in the center of the bed, open your shirt all the way, and stretch your arms out at your sides, like you're flying."

She did as she was told, and Regent said, "Yeah," as he took some pictures. "Now close the shirt and put your arms down at your sides." She did that, too, and he took more pictures. "Now just relax and lie there as you would if you were relaxing at home."

But she could not relax—she remained stiff, almost rigid.

Regent got an idea, but he didn't know if it would fly with young Kendra.

"You need to relax if we're going to do this," he said. "How about some wine?"

Her eyes lit up at the mention of wine.

"No kidding?" she said.

"No kidding. I've got some very good white wine chilling in the refrigerator. Want some?"

The corners of her eyes crinkled above a generous smile as she nodded.

He went into the kitchen, took the wine from the refrigerator, and opened it with a corkscrew, poured some into two wineglasses. He returned to the studio, where she sat on the edge of the bed now. He handed her the glass.

As Regent sipped his wine, Kendra sniffed hers. Then she sipped it. Her nose wrinkled and she smacked her lips a few times. She frowned up at him.

"Tastes funny," she said.

"It's an acquired taste, I guess," he said.

"A what?"

"It's a taste you've got to get used to."

"Oh." She sipped it again. Then she drank it down in a few gulps. "Can I have some more?" she said.

"Uh, well, you know, Kendra, wine is best sipped instead of gulped. If you gulp it, you'll get drunk, and your mommy will know when she gets home. If you just sip it, you'll get a little tipsy, and it'll wear off by the time she gets back."

"Really? That's what happens when you sip it?"

"Yes, that's right. I'll get you some more, but you have to sip it, all right?"

She nodded. "All right, I will. I-I'm sorry for—"

"Oh, don't apologize, sweetheart. You didn't know. It was your first time. I'll get you some more."

Kendra felt much more relaxed than when she'd first walked into the big, beautiful trailer. The wine felt warm in her belly, and she felt a little woozy in the head.

What would Mommy think? She would be *so* angry. Kendra just had to make sure she knew nothing about it.

Mr. Regent seemed like a nice enough man. He called her "sweetheart," which was what Mommy called her sometimes, so how could he be bad? Maybe he'd even take a really good picture she could give to Mommy.

The wine loosened her up a lot. He told her to pose the way she saw models pose in magazines. So she did. She thought of advertisements she'd seen in Mommy's copies of *Cosmopolitan* and *Vanity Fair* and others. She kept moving her arms and legs into different positions. Then she sat up and removed the plaid shirt and tossed it aside, leaving only the dark bikini top.

"Very good," Regent said. "Excellent."

After awhile, Regent stopped taking pictures and turned and put the camera on the desk behind him. He went to the side of the bed and sat down, turned to face Kendra.

"Now, Kendra," he said. "I need to know if you're comfortable with what I do. If you're not, just say so, and there won't be a problem. I never force anyone. But you have to tell me, okay?"

He poured more wine into her glass, and she took it right away and sipped once, twice, a third time.

"You want to go easy with that stuff," he said. "You'll have to eat some peanut butter before you leave."

"Peanut butter?"

"It conceals the smell of alcohol on the breath."

"Oh," she said, her eyes almost as round as her mouth. "Okay."

"Look, Kendra—here, let me take that." He took her drink and set it aside on the night stand. "Like I said before, my website's naughty. It's a nudie website."

"A what?"

"A website in which women appear naked."

"Oh, yeah, that's right. That's naughty, all right," she said, smiling again.

"Well, how naughty are you willing to be this afternoon, Kendra?"

"Whatta you mean?"

"Will you take off your top?"

She gasped. "Oh, *yeah*, you want *me* to take off—oh, yeah, I see. Well." She sucked her lips between her teeth and thought about it. She smiled and muttered, "Being on the Internet," then thought about it awhile.

"You won't use your real name," Regent said. "You can make one up."

"I can make one up?" she said with a giggle.

"That's right, anything you want to be called."

"But I have to take off my top."

"Yes."

"And show my titties."

"That's right. And Kendra, I assure you, the men who look at them will never be able to get enough of them. And they'll never forget them. They'll want more of you and more of you—you'll be a sensation, Kendra, a *sensation*. I'll get tons of e-mail about you from guys who'll want to see more of you."

"A sensation?"

"You'll become *legendary* online. A star."

"Really? A star?"

"Yes."

"But ... I gotta show my titties."

"That's right."

"Well, that's okay. I don't mind, it's just that I ... I don't know ... well, see, I don't know if they're ... *good* enough for—"

"Oh, don't be ridiculous. You don't really *think* that, do you?"

"Well, I ... I don't know. Really. I don't have any idea."

"Listen, Kendra, I haven't even seen them yet, and already I know they're spectacular."

"You think so?"

"You really don't know, do you?"

Kendra said, "Really don't know what?"

"You have a boyfriend, Kendra?"

"Oh, no, Mommy'd never let me have a boyfriend. Well, not yet, anyway."

"Well, is there a boy you *like*?"

She got that look again, that delightfully menacing look, then it softened and she smiled. "Yeah, there is."

"How do you expect to get his attention?"

"His attention?"

"And once you've got it, how do you hold onto it, Kendra?"

"Hold onto it?"

"Yeah. Think about it. You ever had a boyfriend before?"

Her eyebrows pulled down at the outer ends and her eyes filled with sadness. "Nuh-no. I haven't." She bowed her head.

"Lucky you met me, Kendra," Regent said.

"How come?"

"Because I'm going to teach you what men want so you can go get this boy you like. You'll be able to get *any* guy you like."

The sadness seeped out of her eyes like invisible tears. "Will you, really?"

"Yep. And the first thing you need to know is that men are going to *love* your breasts."

"They will?"

"They'll want to look at them," he said. "They'll want to touch them, and put their mouths on them."

"Really?" Butterflies fluttered in Kendra's stomach and she felt wonderfully naughty as she smiled at Regent.

"That's right. That's why, for starters, I'd like to get some pictures of you without the bra, but with the shirt on. How's that sound. Will you do that?"

"Sure," she said. She took the shirt off and tossed it onto the bed, and reached back to unfasten the bra. She stopped and looked at him. "Um, could you … turn around?"

"Oh, sure," he said. He turned his back to her and waited.

She turned around, too. Unable to believe she was doing it, but delighting in the adrenaline burst it gave her and the delicious sense of naughtiness that crept up inside her, she unfastened the bra in back. What if Mommy saw her now, taking off her bikini bra? She would be horrified.

Kendra tossed the bra onto the bed and put the plaid shirt back on. She started to button it, then remembered that he wanted her to leave it unbuttoned. She turned around and found that his back was still to her. "How's this?" she said.

He turned and took in a little gasp and stood there and looked at her for a long time.

Thirteen

Regent stood with his mouth open, taking her in. She stood before him in the shorts, the plaid shirt hanging open in front. The inner scoops of her milky breasts were visible above her flat belly.

He wanted to tear that shirt off of her and take her on the bed right then and there. It took a great effort not to reach out and touch her, to pull her into his arms and push his mouth against hers, bury one hand in those luxurious locks of hair. He looked into her eyes—eyes that, without her even realizing it, he suspected, made promises she might not be able to keep.

She oozed sex. It glowed off her, luminescent and warm. And she didn't even know it.

Regent knew this might take some time. He'd already gotten farther than he'd expected for the first session. But he fully expected her to freeze up at some point soon. He'd need to make her more comfortable, maybe wait till the next day, or the day after that. He needed to gain her trust, that was the key.

"Why don't you lie back on the bed like that," he said.

Kendra did as she was told. She got on the bed and stretched out on her back.

"Prop yourself up on your elbows," he said.

She did. Up on her elbows, the shirt spread open a little more, but it still did not fully reveal her breasts.

It was maybe the sexiest thing he'd ever seen—Kendra lying there like that on her back, one knee cocked, the inner sides and partial undersides of her breasts visible, her skin creamy and unblemished, head back as she looked down her nose at the camera.

Regent wanted to lick those thighs, to kiss the flesh between her breasts. He wanted to feel her legs wrap around him as he slammed into her.

But that would have to wait.

He realized he had an erection, and he turned away from her. Just looking at her made him hard, made him warm and hungry for her touch. But he had to be careful with this one—she wasn't like all the others. She was different, a challenge. But God, she was incredible. He decided to go ahead and let her see his erection—let her know what she did to him, to men.

She got on all fours facing the camera and the unbuttoned shirt fell open and her breasts dangled and swayed with the slightest movement.

"Beautiful," he said as he took a few more pictures. "Now," he said, cautious, smiling. "How would you feel about taking the shirt off?"

She smiled and said, "You want to see my boobies?"

"Yes, I do, Kendra—the whole *world* is going to want to see your boobies!"

She laughed as she stood upright on her knees. She shed the shirt and tossed it onto the floor beside the bed.

She was feeling that wine, he could tell. She was a little tipsy, just happy enough to keep her going.

Kendra knelt before him wearing only the denim cutoffs. Her breasts were generous scoops of pale flesh, capped by puffy, pale-rosy nipples.

"You said ... men will ... like this?" she said. She wore an expression of uncertainty—almost childlike uncertainty.

"Men will eat it up, Kendra. This is what men love, it's what they want. They're going to be crazy about you. I'm going to use you in the preview section, and I bet you'll pull in plenty of members all by yourself."

She smiled a little. "Is that ... good?"

"That's *very* good," he said as he kept taking pictures. "Why don't you touch one of your boobies, there, and—yes, perfect, just with your fingertips like that."

Her smile grew for a moment, then began to dismantle.

"Are you wearing panties under the shorts?" he said.

"Yuh-yes. Why?"

"Let's get some panty shots, okay? Men love to see a beautiful girl in panties."

"They do?"

"Oh, yes."

She stood up on the bed and slowly lowered the cutoffs. They dropped to her ankles and she stepped out of them, kicked them off the bed.

"Great!" Regent said. "Stand right there like that." He took several pictures looking up at her, naked but for her baby-blue panties, a towering young amazon fresh out of the jungle.

Kendra lifted her hands and put them over her breasts. "I-I ... I, uh ... um, I ..." She stepped down off the bed and turned her back to him. "I'm sorry," she said.

"What's wrong?"

"I don't know, I just, um ... I just feel ... embarrassed all of a sudden. I think I want to stop now. Is that okay?"

"Sure, if you want to stop now, that's fine. But, uh … well, maybe we can do more later. Like maybe tomorrow."

"Uh … well … yeah, maybe."

She quickly began to put her clothes back on.

"What's wrong, Kendra?" he said.

"I don't know, I just … all of a sudden, I felt … naked. It's not you, Mr. Regent, and I'm real sorry, I just … I just can't right now." When she was finished, she turned to him and said, "Can I see the pictures?"

"Sure. Come over tomorrow afternoon and I'll show them to you."

"I don't know if I can. I don't know if Mommy'll be working or not."

"Oh. Then I guess we'll have to wait and see."

"Yeah. Like Mommy says, 'We'll see.'" She giggled. "I'm sorry, I hope I didn't mess anything up for you."

"No, not at all. I want you to be comfortable with what you're doing. You know, you've got money coming. A hundred dollars."

"A hundred *dollars*?" she said, putting a flat palm to her chest. "Wow. A hundred. I've never seen that many dollars in one place before. Where will I put them? Mommy'll want to know where they came from."

"You want me to keep the money here for you for now?" Regent said.

"Yes, please. Keep it here for me. And one more thing—you won't, uh, say nothin' to my mommy, will you?"

"You have absolutely nothing to worry about, Kendra," he said with his most convincing smile. "I won't tell a soul, and I recommend you do the same."

"Yeah, me, too. What you said. Well, I guess I should go home now. My doggy's home alone and I—"

She looked openly at his erection, which refused to go away.

"What's that?" she said, pointing a finger at it.

"Uh ..." Regent had never found himself faced with that particular question before. "I have an erection. My penis is hard."

"How come?"

"Because I was looking at you. You made me this way."

She grinned. "I did?"

"Yes. That's how men will always react to you, Kendra."

She stepped forward and put a hand on it, squeezed it. There was nothing sexual about the gesture—it was a gesture of curiosity.

"It's very hard," she said.

"Yes, it gets hard when I get excited."

"Yeah, I know, I read about it in an encyclopedia online. So I excited you?"

He closed his eyes a moment. "You ... excited me ... *so* ... much, Kendra." His voice was a tremulous whisper. "I want you right now. I want you here and now."

She laughed as she turned and headed out of the trailer.

Kendra returned to the trailer to find that Dexter had left another little puddle in the kitchen.

"Dexter?" she said, looking around for him. She saw him, finally—peering around the far edge of the couch looking terribly guilty. "I'm sorry, Dexter. I shouldn'a left you alone so long. C'mere, boy, c'mere, you're not in trouble."

Dexter cautiously crept from around the couch's corner and came to her with his tail between his legs. She reached down and picked him up, and he licked her face while she held him in her arms. Pretty soon, Dexter's guilt was forgotten, and he was wriggling in her arms, so she put him down.

As she cleaned up the puddle, she thought about what she had just done.

She'd had to stop taking pictures because she'd suddenly — out of nowhere, and very unexpectedly — become aware of the fact that she was naked. Well, she had panties on, but that was all. That was pretty much naked as far as Kendra was concerned. Suddenly, she was naked in this room with this total stranger, and she was ashamed of herself. It was like in one of those dreams she had sometimes where she found herself at school in her underwear, or completely naked. It was a feeling of such intense vulnerability that it had frightened Kendra for a moment. She'd *needed* to get her clothes back on, that was all, and as soon as she did, she felt okay again. Once she was outside, it was all gone, that feeling of utter helplessness, the chilling awareness of her nudity — she was fine.

"Maybe you'll be more comfortable the next time we do this, you think?" Mr. Regent said at the door of his trailer.

Kendra shrugged, then nodded. "Sure. Maybe."

"We *will* do this again, won't we? I want more pictures of you, and then I want to get some video."

"Really? Video?"

"Oh, yeah, I'm giving you the full treatment, sweetheart."

After leaving, she'd looked back as she neared her trailer, and there was Mr. Regent, smiling, watching her. He'd waved at her, and she'd smiled and waved back.

Mr. Regent was a nice man, and he was very informative. He was very handsome, too. He wasn't afraid to say *anything* in front of her, it seemed. Like talking about his erection. Kendra had read about penises and erections in what she thought of as *her* online encyclopedia. She found the very idea of them funny — imagine, living with something hanging between your legs that could, at any moment, get hard and stand up straight! It was silly. She was struck by the size of Mr. Regent's erection.

135

Of course, maybe *all* of them were that big—she had no idea, nothing to measure it against, and was only speculating.

She wondered how big Marc's got when he was excited. Heat moved up her neck to her face. She wondered what kind of things excited him. Would he be as excited as Mr. Regent if *he* saw her in a bikini bra and shorts?

Kendra felt a tickling sensation deep in her belly when she thought of Marc seeing her the way Mr. Regent had just seen her, and she giggled. Would he get hard, too? Would he want to touch her? Is *that* what he wanted?

Or would the same thing that usually happened to Kendra throughout her life happen yet again—would he point at her and laugh?

There was something about Marcus Reznick—she did not know *what*, only that she had sensed it from him while lying next to him on the roof—that told her he would not do that. Whatever it was, she could see it in his eyes. His eyes were a large part of what made him so appealing. His eyes were sad. She'd considered asking him why, but had not mustered the courage yet. She had not mustered the courage to do a lot of things, but it was about time she did.

She giggled again. It was a black little giggle that bubbled up out of her. It sounded more aggressive than simply mischievous—it sounded almost *ominous*. It sounded almost like a threat.

Then a bad thought occurred to her, a thought that struck her mind like a bolt of lightning. Big, flaming words rose up in her mind's eye: WHAT IF MOMMY FINDS OUT?

That would be bad, very bad. Kendra could not even imagine how Mommy would react if she learned she'd posed for naked pictures. But she trusted Mr. Regent not to tell her, because he'd probably be in trouble with Mommy, too. He'd promised it would be their secret—why would he lie?

But what if Mommy saw the pictures online? Would they be on a site where Mommy might go? She would have to ask Mr. Regent.

If Mommy found out … well, it would be awful, that was all. But Kendra told herself Mommy *wouldn't* find out—simple as that. And she stopped worrying about it. Simple as that.

Kendra went to the kitchen and took the jar of peanut butter from the cupboard. She got a spoon from the drawer, opened the jar, and scooped some peanut butter out with the spoon and licked some of it off slowly, wondering if it *really* hid the smell of alcohol.

Dexter went to the door and sat there with his body facing it, his head turned to look at Kendra. When she finally noticed him, she said, "Do you need to go out?"

He stood and hurried around in a tight circle.

She opened the door and screen door and let him out. She watched from the door, licking peanut butter from the spoon, smacking her lips, as Dexter went to the fruitless mulberry in the front yard and urinated on its base. Then, happy with himself, he trotted back up the steps and into the trailer. Kendra sat down Indian-style on the floor and Dexter hopped into her lap.

"Oh, Dexter, I've been *such* a *naughty* girl," she said. "If Mommy ever found out, she'd be … she'd be …" Kendra giggled. "She'd ex-*plode*."

Fourteen

Ever since lunch, since Mo Carey had left, Reznick had been toying with the idea of leaving work early. The very phrase "leaving work" hardly applied to him—he simply would be leaving an empty office.

At least he had one client, and a job to do that evening.

He decided, at three-seventeen that afternoon, to go home. His sleep had been restless last night and he could use a nap before following Mrs. Carey around.

Reznick stood behind his desk and stretched his arms above his head. He took his suit coat from the back of his chair and slipped it on, picked up his briefcase. His tie drooped and his top button was loose. He turned everything off—the coffee maker, the fan, the air conditioning—then grabbed a handful of business cards and left the office.

"How'd those ribs sit?" Leroy said as soon as Reznick entered.

"Maybe the best barbecue I've ever had, Leroy, I'm serious. Lunch was so good, I came by to get some chicken for dinner, the same sides."

"A man of discerning tastes, you are," Leroy said. He turned and went about wrapping half a chicken in aluminum foil. "Business any better this afternoon?"

"Oh, I've got one case. More than I had this morning."

"And who knows where it might lead."

"I suppose."

Leroy chuckled as he put the sides in a bag with the chicken. "I had a very optimistic momma and grandma. From them, I learned to always look at the bright side. It don't come as easy for everyone as it does for me, I know. Some find it … annoying. But sometimes, it's the only thing you can do 'sides goin' insane."

"Here are my business cards," Reznick said, putting the cards on the counter. "You show mine around, I'll show yours around."

He chuckled. "You gotcheself a deal."

The barbecue chicken's aroma filled the cab of his car on the drive home and made him feel prematurely hungry. In the trailer, he put the chicken in the refrigerator—he would heat it up later for dinner.

He quickly changed into T-shirt and shorts and flip-flops and stood underneath the swamp cooler in the hall for a while.

The heat clung to his body like honey. It seeped into his lungs like honey, too, humid and thick.

Reznick took a shower, then, with a towel wrapped around his waist, he stood in the hallway, under the air of the cooler a little longer.

When the heat was humid, the swamp cooler was little help—it just made it more humid *indoors*. Furniture became damp, once crisp and dry paper became limp. Most of the trailers in Riverside Mobile Home Park had swamp coolers— some had only fans—because it was the best they could afford.

He was still standing under the cooler when there was a knock at the door.

Reznick opened the door and looked out through the screen. Kendra stood on the other side holding a tiny tan dog.

"Hi, Marc," she said through a big smile. There was a wealth of enthusiasm in her simple greeting.

"Hello, Kendra," he said. "You have a dog?"

"Yeah! Ain't it great? Mommy took me to the Humanity Society, and—"

"The Humane Society."

"Yeah, that's it, and we picked out little Dexter, here. I couldn't *wait* to show him to you."

"Then let's get a good look at him. Step back."

As Kendra stepped back, Reznick pushed the screen door open. She stepped inside and bent down, put her little dog on the floor.

"Now, watch," Reznick said.

Conan and Dexter took turns cautiously sniffing each other's butts, then their noses. Less than thirty seconds later, they were standing on their hind legs playfully boxing at each other with their front paws.

It was a moment after he'd said, *Now, watch*, when Reznick realized she was wearing only a bikini bra and very short denim cutoffs. She stood leaning forward with her hands propped on her thighs, and his eyes passed over all that smooth, creamy flesh.

"It looks like they're gonna get along," Kendra said, standing up straight. She turned to him and he lifted his head and smiled.

"Looks that way," he said. "That's good. They'll have someone to play with besides us."

Kendra giggled. She walked into the living room and said, "How did you house-train Conan, Marc?"

"Didn't take much at all," he said. "He got the idea real fast."

"I think Dexter did, too. He let me know that he had to go out today."

"See? They're smart little things."

He watched as she sat on the couch. She tried to find a comfortable position, but seemed unable. Then she stretched her legs out on the couch and cocked one knee. And was she slightly thrusting out her breasts? God knew, they did not need any thrusting.

All that pale flesh … those pliant mounds under that dark bra … those long, full thighs … that exquisite behind …

But it was her face that really held him, her eyes, framed in all those golden locks. That face held him and made him want to reach out and touch her—gave him a palpable urge to move his hands up her body until he got to her face, then kiss her.

His breath came quick and his heart picked up its pace a little. He had to slow this down before it got carried away inside him. He turned away from her and took a few deep breaths before he got an erection.

But it still did not change one thing: He still wanted her, still craved her.

When he looked at her again, she sat with her back straight, but her legs spread wide. Her mouth hung open, and her tongue slowly, absently ran around her lips.

"Where's your mommy, Kendra?" he said.

After a moment, she closed her legs. "Mommy's at work."

"She works days *and* nights?"

"Sorta. She works with the, um … I forget what it's called. They find jobs for her in offices and—"

"A temp agency?"

"Yeah, that's it. And she dances at night."

Reznick frowned. "She dances?"

"Uh-huh. Most nights."

"What kind of, uh—" He immediately decided that any direction he took with this topic of conversation would be inappropriate, so he let it drop. But he wondered. Was Anna Dunfy an office-temping stripper? She had the looks and the body for it, that was for sure. But how much did Kendra know? She said her mother *dances*, but she didn't say what kind of dancing she did. How many different kinds were there? Redding did not have a ballet. There weren't many outlets for dancing in Shasta County. But the one place Reznick could think of where it *paid* to dance was the Mt. Shasta Gentlemen's Club.

Reznick knew a couple women who used to dance there, but no one currently working the runway and mounting the poles. He did not see it as a shameful job, not in this day and age, but some women were still ashamed of it and did their best to keep it separate from their lives. He wondered again how much Anna had told Kendra—what kind of dancing did *she* think Mommy did at night?

"I'm staying by myself for the first time ever today," Kendra said. "So I was glad when I saw your car, 'cause I wanted to come see you and show you Dexter, and … well, just … come see you."

"I'm glad you did. Looks like these two are pals."

Conan and Dexter were stretched out side by side, dozing.

While Kendra sat on the couch looking down at the dogs, Reznick looked at her. He stood before her in a towel. He wondered what she would do if he dropped it. Probably run from the house screaming. Or maybe she would laugh. Who knew what to expect? She was, after all, retarded. He had to keep telling himself that. Again and again.

She's retarded, you can't want her, she's retarded!

But it made no difference to his needs, his hungers.

Hungers *plural*—the craving for alcohol had been just at the back of his mind all day. He tried to keep his mind occupied with crossword puzzles and reading, but it was there, the whole time. That need that came from somewhere deep in his chest. Reznick often suspected that was where the soul lurked—deep in the chest—because he thought his cravings for vodka came straight from there, a soul-deep need that could be satisfied by nothing else.

And it had been with him all day. He'd hoped for a calm after the storm he'd experienced last night. And why all of a sudden were the cravings so bad? It had been a year, maybe a little more than that, and he hadn't had a drink—why were these cravings rearing up so aggressively all of a sudden?

"We'll have to make sure they get to play together often," she said.

"What?" Reznick said.

"The dogs, we'll have to make sure they get to play together often."

"Oh. Oh, yes, we will. I'll be right back, Kendra, I'm going to put something on."

He felt her eyes on him as he left the living room. In his bedroom, he put on shorts and T-shirt and flip-flops.

Reznick kept imagining resting his cheek between her breasts, feeling them on both sides of his head, so soft-skinned, so plush, so fragrant with youth.

He'd done that with Victoria when he found her. After he'd called the cops. He lay down on top of her and placed his head between her breasts, as if he were listening for the heart that would never beat again, but really just to be close to her one last time, to have one final intimate moment. That was how they'd found him, babbling and crying with his head nestled between her bloody breasts.

Kendra stood suddenly and smiled and said, "Do you think I'm pretty?"

"Pretty?" he said, his voice a hoarse whisper. "No, you're not pretty, Kendra."

Before he was halfway through the sentence, Kendra's face shattered like a reflection in a broken mirror. Her smile disappeared and the look in her eyes changed drastically, but subtly—she went from looking happy and childlike to appearing on the verge of tears, or perhaps holding back some painful cry of defeat.

"Oh, don't get upset, sweetheart, I'm not finished!" he said. "You're not *pretty*—you're *gorgeous*. You're *beautiful*. You passed up pretty a long time ago."

She gasped and slapped both hands over her mouth. Her eyes became huge. She pulled her hands away and said, "Are you—really?"

"Really. You're beautiful, Kendra, and you should never let anyone tell you any different." He spoke in a low tone, as if he did not want to be overheard.

Kendra said, "Nobody ever … said *that* to me before today."

"Then I guess it's about time someone did, huh?" He smiled, but he wasn't sure it was a successful smile because his lips trembled when he tried to move them. He sniffed and turned away from her. "Can I get you something to drink, Kendra?" he said.

"No, thank you. I should go. Never know when Mommy might come home a little early and find me outside the trailer. I'm supposed to stick to the trailer while she's gone."

"Then you'd better go."

Instead of walking around him, she squeezed between Reznick and the wall, and her body brushed against his, her breasts crushed against him. He wouldn't have been surprised if sparks had scattered from the friction between them—she felt hot to him. He felt hot, too—his face, his hands. He felt his heartbeat in his fingertips and it pounded rapidly.

She stopped, still pressed between Reznick's body and the wall, and whispered, "I'll come back over with Dexter again later." Then she kissed him.

The illusion ended there. She puckered her lips up like a child and made a smacking sound as she pressed them to his mouth. She smiled again, then slipped on by and left the trailer.

She'd kissed him the way a little girl would kiss.

But with those lips, he thought, *a little training's all it would take.*

Then he thought, *Should I feel guilty for thinking that?*

He chuckled and muttered to himself, "You've got plenty of other things to feel guilty about without bothering with that piddly shit."

Besides, he told himself, it's true—all Kendra needed was a little gentle guidance, which he suspected she would welcome, and she would probably be a passionate kisser. All the women Reznick had ever known had loved kissing—a few more than sex itself. He was sure Kendra would be no different—she would enjoy it, and she'd probably take to it quickly, just like everyone does.

He'd been haunted by the fact that she lived next door. That at the age of forty-one, Marcus Reznick had been swept away by the girl next door. Just two walls away. Thin walls—trailer walls. Never far away. His mind was like radar—it kept picking her up, showing her to him.

He wanted two things as he stretched out on the couch. He wanted an ice-cold bottle of vodka to drink from to make him numb to the aches and pains of his soul, while the lovely Kendra Dunfy did things to him she'd probably never even heard of yet. And he didn't have it in him to feel guilty for it, either, not today, when his mouth was puckering on the inside and his tastebuds imagined things like vodka martinis and vodka gimlets. It had been a year since his last drink, but his tastebuds had excellent memories, and they were feeling very nostalgic that hot afternoon.

He thought of her again. That wasn't quite true—she was always on his mind now, just off to the side a little. Then she rushed up front fast, front and center.

Everything else had been right. The look on her face, whether she'd intended it to be or not, was the look of a young woman waiting to be kissed, to be taken hard in a man's arms and kissed. Her eyes had been right—half-closed and dreamy. But her puckered lips, the little-girl peck on his mouth—they had reminded him what she was. And what he was becoming if he continued to pursue thoughts about her.

But he did not pursue them, that was the problem. They pursued him.

Fifteen

Anna Dunfy climbed the steps and entered her trailer. She found Kendra stretched out on the floor watching a game show on the Game show Network and coloring in a coloring book with felt-tip pens. Anna dropped her purse to the floor and spread her arms wide. "Congratulate me!" she said.

Kendra beamed up at her. "Congratulations, Mommy!" Then, a moment later: "For what?"

"They want me to come back."

"They do? Who does?"

"The people at the place where I worked today." Anna went to the couch and sat down, took her shoes off and rubbed her feet. "Redding Tractor and Lawn Mower. I worked in their office today. Apparently, the woman I filled in for is *always* out. She knows how to work the system, see. She comes in only as many days as she absolutely *has* to. The rest of the time, she's sick. Says she's depressed and can't work. They're getting fed up with her, though, and the way they talk, she won't be there much longer. They want me to start working there nine-to-five. Starting tomorrow."

"A full-time job?" Kendra said.

"A full-time job," Anna said, nodding. "Starting tomorrow."

"That's great, Mommy!"

"Yes, it *is* great. That means you'll have to get up early so I can take you over to Aunt Rose's before I go to—"

"Huh? *No!* No *way!*" Kendra got to her feet and faced Anna. "You haven't even asked me how *my* day went. It went just *fine.* Nothing went wrong, I'm okay, nothing bad happened. I even walked down with Dexter and got the mail and nothing bad happened. Now, if I can do that one day, why can't I do it *every* day? And it'll only be for the summer, until school starts."

Anna leaned back on the couch and thought about it. Kendra had handled herself well this afternoon. Anna had no reason to think she couldn't take care of herself while Anna was at work.

"You'll miss the rest of Vacation Bible School," Anna said.

"No, I won't. Not if Calista Hoffman's mother comes and picks me up and I go to Vacation Bible School with Calista. Then they can drop me off on their way home. They drive right down Stingy on their way to the church and back."

Kendra clearly had put some thought into it. She was determined to have her way in this, determined to have her independence for the summer. Anna saw no good reason to deny her of it.

"All right," Anna said. "I'll call Mrs. Hoffman and see if she won't mind picking you up."

Kendra's eyes widened. "Then I can?"

"I don't see why not."

Kendra slapped a hand over her yawning mouth. Then she slapped her hands together and bobbed up and down on the balls of her feet. She bent down and hugged Anna, who laughed at the joy in Kendra's reaction.

"Thank you, Mommy, thank you!"

"You're welcome. How *was* your day, by the way?"

"It was nice. Just me an' Dexter. He had a couple accidents on the kitchen floor, but I cleaned them up. Just little puddles. He lets me know when he needs to go out, though."

"He does? Already?"

"Yes."

Anna frowned. "Then why did he pee in the kitchen?"

"Uh …"

"You didn't leave him alone for awhile, did you, Kendra?"

"Uh …"

"Kendra? Are you *blushing*?"

"I, uh, I was *playing* with him," Kendra said. "And he got so excited, he piddled."

Anna still frowned. She felt strangely suspicious of her daughter—*strangely* because it was something that had never happened before. She'd never before had any reason to be suspicious of Kendra. But the stammering and the bright pink flush of her face was vaguely suspicious.

"That's all," Kendra said.

"You were playing with him."

"Yes. On the kitchen floor. He was chasing my hand in circles. He got dizzy, and—" She giggled. "—oh, you should've seen him, Mommy, he was wobbling all over the place, and all of a sudden, he just squatted and peed. It was my fault, I shouldn't have done that to him."

There seemed to be nothing suspicious about Kendra's story. Anna did not know if Kendra was even *capable* of lying to her. Kendra had never, to Anna's knowledge, lied to her. Why should she start now?

"Just don't get him so worked up indoors, okay?" Anna said. She looked down at the little dog, who was looking up at her, impatiently awaiting some attention from her. Anna patted the cushion beside her, and Dexter hopped up on the couch. She petted him, and he wagged his whole body. She rolled him on his side, then onto his back and rubbed his tummy. "You like that, you little devil?"

Dexter made a playful sound in his throat.

Anna lifted her hand and the dog struggled to get back on his feet. She petted him some more.

"Dexter seems to have made himself at home here," Anna said.

"Oh, he has," Kendra said. "He's made himself *right* at home. Haven't you, Dexter?"

The dog immediately flew from the couch and ran to Kendra. She bent down and picked him up, held him to her chest like a baby. The dog furiously licked her face.

"Are you going to keep dancing?" Kendra said.

"Good question." Anna thought about it. The job was still temporary, even though she'd be working nine-to-five for a while. She couldn't rely on it. So she would have to keep dancing. "Yeah, I guess I will. This job won't last long."

"What if they get rid of the woman and they want you to come work for them for *real*?" Kendra said.

Anna smiled—*for real* made her smile. "Then maybe I'll think about not dancing. But for now, it's not a secure job. I have to keep dancing. It's good money. I can't let that go."

"Mommy, when am I gonna get to come see you dance?"

"I've told you, they sell liquor there, so it's adults only."

"Then when are you gonna dance for me? I never seen you dance."

"It's nothin', honey. Believe me. You're not missin' a thing." She stood. "But you know what? I'm not gonna dance tonight. I'm gonna call in sick. I'll tell 'em I twisted my ankle, or something."

"Wouldn't that be a lie, Mommy?"

Anna went to the door and got her purse from the floor, took out her pack of cigarettes. She went to the kitchen table, put down her purse, and flipped up the lid on the cigarette box, took out a cigarette, and lit it. She went to the refrigerator and took out a beer. She cracked it open and sat down at the kitchen table.

"It's a white lie, honey," Anna said.

"A ... *white* lie?"

"Yep. That's something they'll never teach you about in school, or in Sunday school, or at Vacation Bible School. So don't bother asking your teachers about white lies."

"Then ... will *you* tell me what a white lie is?"

"Sure, that's what I'm gonna do. White lies are the harmless little lies you have to tell people to get through life. They don't hurt anyone. Sometimes, they even make people feel better, help them have a better day. For example, if your boss asks you if you like her new dress, and you think it's ugly, are you going to *tell* your boss you think her dress is ugly? *No.* You're going to tell her it's *lovely. That* is a white lie. Nobody's hurt, and the boss has been complimented, which is what she was expecting, anyway. A white lie isn't a sin. God understands white lies. He lets us slide on those. They're harmless. Understand?"

Kendra frowned the whole time she listened, concentrating intensely on her mother's words. "So ... that's why they're white? 'Cause they're not sins?"

"That's right," Anna said, nodding. "So, I'm going to call my boss and tell him I hurt my foot and can't come in tonight. That's gonna be a white lie. I'm gonna do that so I can stay home and you and I can go to the store and get some hamburger and some hot dogs and buns and come home and have a barbecue."

"Oh, goody!" Kendra said, clapping her hands.

"I'm gonna call Aunt Rose and see if she wants to bring the kids over. We'll make a family feast of it. Maybe we can even coax our neighbor, Mr. Reznick, to come join us, wouldn't that be nice?"

"Yeah, that would be nice," Kendra said, her voice lowering with each word until she was whispering.

Anna saw her daughter blush again.

"You're blushing," Anna said.

"Am not." Kendra turned away, then bent down and put Dexter on the floor.

"Uh-oh," Anna said, smoke billowing from her smiling mouth and nostrils. "Does my little girl have a crush?"

"Do *not*."

Anna laughed. She sipped her beer. "It's all right, you know. Nothing to be ashamed of."

"I do *not* have a *crush*." She went to the couch, sat down, and leaned forward, elbows on her knees, and watched television.

It was clear to Anna that she did—a crush on their neighbor, Marcus Reznick. She could see it. He was ruggedly handsome and had a rather craggy face with intense, deep-set eyes, and he was very interesting—a private investigator with probably a million fascinating stories to tell.

Sure, she would always have the intellect of an eleven- or twelve-year-old girl, but she had the body of a sixteen-year-old, and a crush on a handsome, much-older man was perfectly natural.

Her only concern was Mr. Reznick—how would *he* handle it? He would be exposed to it sooner or later. Would he try to take advantage of it? If he did, Anna decided she would kill him. She wasn't sure how, but she would. And no jury in the world would convict her. No woman would, anyway. No mother.

Anna stamped her cigarette out in the ashtray that had a picture of Reno on the bottom—she'd gotten it on a trip to Reno with her sister before Kendra was born — and finished her beer. Then she stood and said, "I'm going to change my clothes, then let's go to the store and do some grocery shopping, okay?"

"Okay."

"If you want to wear that bikini bra, that's fine, but there's no *way* you're wearing that shirt unbuttoned, do you hear me? Button that shirt up right now. Have you been walking around this trailer park with that shirt unbuttoned?"

Kendra bowed her head and watched her hands as she buttoned up her shirt. She did not reply.

"Did you? Because if you did, it's going to be the *last* time. I'll ask around. I *will*. And if I find out you're wandering around this park half-naked, you'll *never* be allowed to stay here by yourself, do you understand?" Anna was very firm, and even sounded a little angry. She wanted Kendra to take her seriously. She was being *very* serious. With Kendra's body, she couldn't afford to be going around scantily-clad like that. She was too innocent, too trusting of people. It was a good way to get herself raped. The very *thought* of Kendra walking down to the mailbox with that shirt unbuttoned and that bikini top on underneath — it made Anna's stomach twist into knots.

She went to her bedroom and changed into jeans, a red tank top, and red sneakers.

"Ready to go?" she said, back in the living room. She got her purse from the table.

"Yeah."

They got in the car and Anna drove them out of the trailer park.

Sixteen

He found the Carey residence. It was off Happy Valley Road, on the opposite side of the road from him, at the end of a long driveway, like so many houses on that road. They appeared to live in a pleasant-looking, medium-size, ranch-style house with a green yard and lots of trees shading the house. He found a turnout a couple hundred yards up the road and made a U-turn into it, parked, and waited.

It was six-twenty. He would not have the cover of night for another three hours, so he had to hope she didn't notice him parked down here when she left.

Carey had said she drove a white Hyundai. Reznick saw it parked in the open two-car garage at the end of the driveway. Parked in the other side was a dark pickup truck.

He waited and watched. He turned on the radio and listened to talk radio for a few minutes before it started to give him a headache. There were no jazz stations in the Redding area, but there was a "smooth jazz" station—the elevator music of jazz. He found that on FM. Couldn't take that for very long, either. Instead of putting in a CD, he chose to wait in silence. Hot, miserable silence.

He'd changed into a blue T-shirt and a pair of denim cutoffs, sneakers on his sockless feet.

He rolled down all the windows and even the hot breeze felt cool against his sweaty neck. The driveway that led to the Carey house was flanked by a field full of green shrubbery. Farther out, the shrubbery leveled out, and he saw some cows lazily grazing on the weeds and grass.

At twelve minutes before seven he heard voices. No words, just a female voice, then a male voice. Then a car door slammed and an engine started up.

Reznick wondered if that was his mark. Sure enough, several seconds later, a white Hyundai—it was a white car, he *assumed* it was a Hyundai because he knew that was the kind of car she drove, but he wouldn't have known a Hyundai from a Roman chariot—bounced and bobbed over the rough driveway on its way out.

Reznick started his car. The white car turned right and headed for Anderson. It was a long straight stretch for a while, and she had a perfect view of him behind her. He waited, hoping to be less conspicuous.

Finally, he pulled out of the turnout and headed after Alicia Carey.

———————————

Steven Regent pulled his SUV into the driveway of his partner's house in the Enterprise district of Redding at six past eight that evening. Shadows were stretched out into long, nightmarish caricatures, but the temperature did not drop. It was a muggy heat that seemed to get muggier as the evening drew on.

Regent got out of the SUV, walked into the open garage, past Josh Garner's cherry-red classic Corvette. He went to the side door of the house and went through it into the laundry room, through there into the kitchen. It felt good to step out of that miserable heat and into Regent's place—he always kept the air conditioner on high and the temperature low.

It was a nice house. Each bedroom in this house was a studio for a different website, decorated appropriately. Garner stayed here only occasionally. He had a much nicer house just north of town, out toward the lake. He and Regent both had other homes. Garner had an apartment in San Francisco, Regent had a house in Lake Tahoe, they shared a condo in Park City, Utah. The websites had been exceptionally good to them.

"Hey, anybody home?" he called.

"Be right there," Garner replied from somewhere in the house.

There was an open bag of Laura Scudders Maui Sweet Onion Potato Chips on the counter, and Regent went to it, picked it up, plunged a hand in. He leaned his hips back on the edge of the tile counter, put one of the chips in his mouth, tasted it, and nodded with approval.

Garner walked in wearing a bathrobe, his hair wet.

"Where do you get all these weird potato chips?" Regent said. "I come over here and you've always got these weird, exotic potato chips. You shop someplace funny?"

"You just have to look for them, they're everywhere," Garner said.

"Have you seen the pictures of Kendra I sent you?"

Garner rolled his eyes and whistled. "I've seen them. She's … fanfuckingtastic. There's only one problem, and it's a big one."

Regent frowned. A problem? A *big* one?

"How are you gonna top that?" Garner said as he opened the refrigerator. He took a bottle of beer from it and twisted the cap off, took a swig. "She's untoppable. After her, it's all downhill. You're gonna *open* the site with her, and then everything after her is anticlimactic." He searched the shelves for something.

"You think she's that good?"

Garner turned to him with wide eyes. "She's incredible. I got wood before she even took her clothes off. But you need more of her, Steven, *more*, a *lot* more."

"Yeah, yeah, I know."

"You want one of these?" Garner said.

"Yeah."

He handed a beer to Regent, then closed the refrigerator door.

"What were you looking for?" Regent said.

"I don't know. Something to eat. I'm kinda hungry. Ish. But nothing sounds good."

"Want me to order pizza?"

"Hm, pizza. Sure, go ahead."

"What's up tonight, anyway?" Regent said as he went to the phone.

"Change that. I don't want pizza. I want Chinese food. Where's the menu from Oriental Express?"

"You're asking me? You live here."

"Yeah, yeah, I know." Garner got up and went to the pockets of old mail and scribbled messages and jotted phone numbers that hung on the wall beside the phone, three of them in a vertical row. He rifled through them and found the pink menu folded up in the second pocket. He opened it up and looked it over. "What do you like, Steven?"

"Chow mein, sweet-and-sour prawns, broccoli beef, I'm easy to please," Regent said.

Garner called the number at the top of the menu and ordered several different dishes, along with some rice and an order of crab puffs.

"That's a big order," Regent said. "I take it we've got company coming?"

"Yep. Alicia."

Regent nearly spit up his beer. He gulped it down, then wiped his mouth with the back of his hand as he laughed. "You're kidding. She has *got* to like it, man. I mean, she must really *want* it, she keeps coming *back* so much."

"You're just figuring that out? She gets off on it—on doing it, and on people seeing it on the Internet. *Especially* on people seeing it. It gets her off. Which is why she keeps coming back for more. The money's gravy, far as she's concerned. She'd probably do it if there was no money involved."

"What'd you need me for?" Regent said.

"She's bringing a friend."

"A *friend*?"

"Yep."

"Have you seen this friend?"

"Not yet." Garner took a few more gulps of beer, and the bottle was empty. He turned and put it on the counter behind him. "And there's no guarantee with the friend."

"What do you mean, there's no guarantee? You mean she might be ugly as a jar of warts?"

"No, Alicia says she's a real looker. But she's *curious*."

"Oh. *Curious*."

"Yep." He opened the refrigerator, took out another beer, twisted it open with a *phut* sound. "She doesn't know if she'll do anything, or if she does, how far she'll go with it. So she may just end up watching."

"I hope not. You got some good weed?"

"Good weed and good whisky. We'll get them well-lubricated."

"What time are they coming?"

"Should be here any time."

Regent opened his second beer a few seconds before the doorbell rang.

"The ladies have arrived," Garner said as he left the kitchen.

"Either that or some really fast Chinese food," Regent said as he followed him.

Alicia was a busty, blowsy dark-blonde with a lot of freckles all over her body, but oddly none on her face, who liked to laugh and drink. She wasn't a great looker—in fact, she was quite plain with a chubby face to match her plump body—but she was an animal in front of the camera, and the members of MILFParade.com loved her. She had loyal fans who sent her money and gifts. She wasn't much to look at, but there was little, if anything, she wouldn't do in front of the cameras. Her friend Beverly was a short, slender brunette with a beautiful face and a body that filled her green tank top and blue shorts quite nicely. She had a great tan and shapely legs, a tight ass, and nice round breasts that weren't too big and weren't too small. She had a long slender neck and an exotic face, with almond-shaped eyes—she *almost* looked Asian. Unlike Alicia, Beverly *was* a looker.

Garner poured drinks and said the food was on the way, but in the meantime, "Drink up!"

Reznick parked across the street and wished the sun would go down faster. After dark, he was just another car parked at the curb, but in daylight, he was plainly visible sitting there staring at the house to his left across the street.

First, he'd followed Alicia Carey to an apartment complex on Hilltop where she had picked up a woman. She'd stayed there for a while. Then he'd followed her and her friend here, to this house on Jupiter Street in a subdivision of streets named after planets.

He turned his head to the right. He was parked in front of a house not unlike the one he was watching. Ranch-style, a semicircular driveway with an entrance and an exit, double doors with beveled glass in the rectangular windows. A landscaped yard with an old-fashioned tire swing hanging from a branch of a big old oak in the front yard.

The yard across the street looked much the same, but without the swing. The double doors didn't have any glass in them. The drapes were drawn on the large window in front. But Reznick had learned a great deal could be seen through the narrow slit between closed drapes.

Of course, he couldn't walk over there and start peering into windows in the light of the late day. So he waited.

———————

Regent worked on Alicia's friend, Beverly.

"You look like you could use some more whisky," Regent said.

"Oh, no, really, I probably shouldn't," she said as he poured more into her glass on the coffee table.

"More ice?" he said.

She laughed and shook her head. "I really shouldn't, but … yeah, more ice."

He scooped his hand into the ice bucket Garner had brought out and dropped a few cubes into her glass.

"I understand you're curious about what we do," he said as he handed her the glass.

"Oh, yeah, well … yes, I am." She laughed. She was clearly nervous. Her second drink should relax her.

"You married, Bev?"

"Oh, no. Not the marrying type. I enjoy being single." She sipped her drink, then sipped it again, a little more fully the second time.

"Good for you. Kind of frees you up to ... well, to experiment."

She grinned and leaned toward him and said, "Yes, that's right." The whisky was kicking in. She put a hand on his arm and said, "I don't mind a little experimentation now and then."

"You ever been with another woman?"

"I tried it once," she said. "It wasn't bad, really. But I've never gotten around to doing it again."

"Ever been with her?" he said, nodding to Alicia, who was standing across the room looking at a large painting on the wall, talking with Garner.

"No."

"Would you like to be?"

"Well ... I dunno." She smirked. It was a flirtatious smirk. Another sip from her glass, followed by a couple gulps.

Regent smiled.

She said, "Do I get to experiment with *you* a little?"

"I think that could be arranged," he said.

She put her drink on the end table. They kissed, and she was aggressive—her tongue plunged into his mouth and she sucked his tongue into hers. Her hands moved all over him as they kissed, all over his back, his chest, his face and hair.

Suddenly, she was on him, straddling his lap and pulling at his pants.

"Whoa," he said, pulling his head back. "Let's save it for the cameras."

"Really?" she said. Her eyes got big for a moment, then narrowed and crinkled up. She curled up against him, her head on his chest. "I don't know if I can do that."

"Oh, sure you can. Easiest thing in the world. Now, why don't you finish that drink so I can pour you some more."

Reznick waited for the dark, then got out of his car. He was parked between street lights, so he was hidden by darkness between them when he crossed the silent, empty street. He stepped up on the sidewalk in front of the house, then turned right, his sneakers quiet on the concrete. He turned left, walked up the driveway, on the far side of the cars parked there.

Crickets chirped somewhere, and a frog croaked nearby. There were gardenias growing in front of the house, and the hot, humid night air was thick with their sweet fragrance.

The garage and the house were attached, but the garage was set back from the front of the house. There was a side window on the house that appeared to look into the same room as the large front window, and Reznick went to it. He peered through the sliver of space between the drapes. Couch, coffee table, chairs, fireplace, television—it was a living room. An *empty* living room—there was no one there.

Reznick cocked his head and listened closely for something, anything.

Was that the hint of voices he heard? Laughter?

They had gone to the rear of the house.

He doubled back and crossed the front of the garage, then turned left around its corner. He walked down a narrow passageway between the side of the garage on his left, and a six-foot-tall wooden fence on his right. The fence divided this yard from the neighbor's. He came to a gate that matched the fence in height. He fumbled around in the dark for a latch. He found it a moment later and flipped it up, pushed the gate open and went through. He closed the gate behind him, latched it, then walked on until he came to the end of the garage.

He stopped at the garage's back corner and very carefully, slowly, peeked around the edge. There was no one there, but he saw a window with light in it. He stepped around the corner and saw that the window's drapes were open, and there were people on the other side of the window moving around, and Reznick quickly stepped back behind the cover of the garage's corner.

Once again, he moved forward slowly, peered around that edge.

A naked man stood by the window. A moment later, he was joined by a naked woman who threw her arms around him and lifted her knee up high on his hip. Then she pulled back, took his hand, and pulled him away from the window.

The light came through the window and spread over the ground in a widening rectangle. Reznick neared the window but stayed out of the light. He walked around it and along the other side to the edge of the window. He pressed his back to the wall beside the window.

The window was to his right, and to his left was another corner, the corner of the house. Beyond it was a swimming pool, a small pool house to the right, and what appeared, in the dark of night, to be a sprawling, gently down sloping back yard beyond that.

He looked to his right again, at the window. From where he stood, he could see down a hallway. The window was at the end of that hallway, facing an open doorway across the hall.

Reznick turned around and faced the wall of the house, and slowly eased his head around the edge of the window. No one was looking his way.

The window looked across the hall at an open doorway, into a room. Naked people stepped in and out of view. Across the

163

room from the open door was a bed with the covers in a tangle at the foot. On the wall above the bed was a large colorful banner that read MILFPARADE.COM—HOT MAMAS ONLINE!

Someone brought a light into view and set it up in front of the bed. As far as Reznick could tell, it was the kind of light used in photography or video sessions.

Alicia Carey got on the bed.

Reznick quickly removed his phone from his pocket, opened it up, and began taking pictures.

Alicia jumped up and down on the bed like a teenage girl at a slumber party. Another naked woman got on the bed and joined her.

A naked man approached the bed and waved his arms back and forth, shaking his head at the same time, like a disapproving adult. They stopped jumping and sat down. The woman who had joined Alicia got up and left. A man joined Alicia.

Reznick kept taking pictures.

Seventeen

When Reznick got home, he printed the pictures up and looked them over.

There was Mrs. Carey, plain as day, going at it with a handsome fellow who seemed to be enjoying himself.

There was that banner: MILFPARADE.COM—HOT MAMAS ONLINE!

He went to his computer and typed in the address. The page popped up on his screen. On the left was a beautiful naked woman in her late thirties, standing in an alluring but unrevealing pose, and on the right was a column of text:

Hi, kids! Wait till you see the new MILFs who've joined us here at MILFPARADE! It's amazing what a little cash'll get some people to do. They might say no at first, but when you flash some of that green stuff, they get mighty cooperative. And it doesn't even have to be that much, either! Next thing you know, they're naked and fuckin'! Which is why you're here. So, if you're a member, come on in and see what's new. If you're not a member, then what the hell are you waiting for? Join now by clicking on the Join Now button!

Reznick clicked on the Join Now button. He took his wallet from his back pocket, took out a credit card, typed the number into the correct window, filled out all the information requested, then clicked on the button at the bottom of the page.

Seconds later, he was a member of MILFParade.com.

Someone knocked at his screen door.

Reznick left his bedroom, went down the hall, and stepped up to the open door. He smiled down at Anna Dunfy. "Hi," he said.

"Hello there," she said. "I hope I'm not bothering you."

"Not at all." It was then that he noticed the smell of something being cooked outdoors, and he realized how hungry he was.

"We're having a barbecue, and I thought you might like to join us. We're about ready to wrap it up, but I'll gladly hold it open for you, if you're interested."

He thought of the barbecued chicken in his refrigerator, but that would keep until tomorrow night. "You know what?" he said. "That sounds delicious." He slipped his bare feet into the flip-flops beside the door, grabbed his keys, and opened the screen door. He pulled the front door closed as he came out, locked it. "I'm glad you invited me, because it smells delicious."

They started walking toward Anna's trailer.

"It's nothing special, just hamburgers and hot dogs, macaroni salad, some chips, some dip."

"All of my favorite foods."

"The macaroni salad *is* special. I went all the way to Kent's Market for it, way up on Airport Road."

"I'm familiar with Kent's Market. He has a great deli. And he makes the best macaroni salad in the world."

"Then you've *had* it."

"Oh, yes."

"Then you know what I mean."

"I do."

Anna had a small Webber Kettle barbecue. There were hamburger patties and hot dogs on the grill just waiting for him. He got a paper plate, put buns on it, then went to the Webber.

He saw Kendra, smiled and nodded once at her, then vowed to pay her no more attention for the rest of the evening. There were other people there, too, but he did not know them. He would wait for Anna to introduce them.

Anna lifted the lid and speared a hamburger patty with the long, two-pronged fork she held. She put the patty on a bun, then speared a hot dog and put it on the hot dog bun on his plate. A TV tray had been set up and condiments were arranged on it. He went to the tray and dressed his burger and dog. Another TV tray held the macaroni salad, chips, and dip. Reznick loaded up.

He held the plate on his left hand and ate with his right as he walked back to Anna. There was a round table under the trailer's awning, and at that table sat a woman Reznick did not know. There were two kids playing catch with a ball in the small yard.

"Come here," Anna said. "Let's sit down at the table."

Once they were seated, Anna said, "Marcus Reznick, this is my sister Rose Pasternak, and her children, Ramona and Bobby, playing catch over there."

"Nice to meet you," Reznick said with a smile.

"Good to meet you, too, Mr. Reznick."

"Please, call me Marc."

"Anna tells us you're a private investigator."

"That's right."

"I think that's very exciting."

"Well, it's probably not as exciting as you think it is. Mostly it's following people around and taking pictures. Kind of sleazy, if you ask me."

"Is that what you do?" she said, tilting her head to one side. "You follow people around and take pictures?"

"In divorce cases, yes. When one spouse is looking to catch the other in an adulterous affair, yes, that's what I do. And that's mostly what I get these days, divorce cases."

"Oh. So … it's not like *Magnum P.I.*, then, huh?"

He laughed. "No, I'm afraid not."

Rose was older than her sister and not as attractive. She had a round face and was developing a double chin. Her dark hair was short and appeared coarse. Her eyes were set too close together, and her nose was too narrow and blade-like. And yet she was the one married to a husband who was providing for her while Anna, who was gorgeous, had to struggle on her own to support herself and her daughter. Why wasn't Anna married? It didn't make sense.

Reznick bit into his hamburger and made sounds of great satisfaction. He chewed for a while, then said, "Delicious. Really. Delicious. S'been a long time since I've had outdoor cooking like this. I've missed it."

"I like to do it once in awhile," Anna said. "Tonight, we're celebrating."

"What are we celebrating?" Reznick said.

"I've been working with this temp agency for months, now," she said. "I did this job today, and they really like me there, so they want me to come in nine-to-five for a while, and it might—fingers crossed—it *might* turn into a permanent job."

"Well, congratulations, Anna," he said. "I'd toast your new job, but I—"

"Oh, you want a beer?" Anna said. "I'm sorry, I completely—how about you, Rose, you need another beer?"

"Uh, no beer for me, thanks," Reznick said. "But I'll take a soft drink, if you have one."

She went inside and came back with a beer for herself, one for her sister, and a Pepsi for Reznick.

He cracked his can of Pepsi open and raised it in a toast. "To your new job, may it be permanent for as long as you want it."

Anna and Rose touched their beer cans to his, and then they drank.

Reznick was glad she wasn't wearing that perfume again tonight. He wouldn't be able to stick around if she were. He ate and chatted with Anna and Rose. But he glanced now and then at Kendra, who stood over by the porch. She was always watching him, every time he glanced at her. And when he caught her at it, she did not look away. Even when he didn't look at her, he could feel her eyes on him.

He thought of her in his trailer earlier that day—all that smooth, milky flesh exposed ... that beautiful long blonde hair ... that sultry face above those breasts like small melons. When was the last time he'd wanted a woman so much? He had to divert his thoughts before he got an erection.

"How would you like to do me a favor?" Anna said.

"What's that?" Reznick said.

"I'm going to be leaving Kendra alone while I'm at work during the day. I don't know what your schedule is like—if you come home for lunch, or how often you come home, if at all. But if you *are* at home, maybe you could look in on her and just make sure everything's okay?"

"Oh, sure, I'd be glad to."

"One more thing." She leaned close and whispered, "In case you haven't noticed, Kendra has quite a crush on you. I hope you'd never consider taking advantage of that. Because if you did, I'd kill you, understand?" She smiled. "And you wouldn't even see it coming." Then she backed up again, still smiling.

A smile slowly grew on Reznick's face, then he laughed quietly. "Okay. That's good to know. But I assure you, it never crossed my mind."

She nodded. "Just so you know."

Back in his trailer, he sat down at the computer again. He browsed through MILFParade.com. Lots of pictures and videos of women in their thirties and early forties, some simply posing nude, others having sex with the same two men over and over again—the same two men who were in the pictures he'd taken through the window in the backyard of the house on Jupiter Street.

As he browsed through the site, he found several pictures of Alicia Carey. She seemed to be quite popular on MILFParade.com. Sometimes she was nude and masturbating, and sometimes she was having sex with one of the two men who ran the site. There were even videos of Alicia, a few of which Reznick watched. She seemed to enjoy herself, to say the least. Reznick did not look forward to it, but he would have to show some of this to Mo Carey.

Throughout the site, there were ads for other sites— LovingCouples.com, YoungandLovely.com, and LustyLesbians.com, all apparently owned by the same company, Burning Lizard Amusements. He visited the other sites and went to their preview pages.

Then he saw it. The words "And coming soon" next to a link to something called Trailer Park Girls. Reznick clicked on the link.

A page opened up with a cartoon showing a buxom girl in a too-small halter top and short-shorts standing in front of a trailer. Below the picture were the words, "Real trailer parks. Real girls. Coming soon."

Trailer parks, Reznick thought. Something about it set off an alarm in his head. He wasn't sure why, but it did.

He clicked his mouse, then his fingers clattered over the keyboard. He had more work to do to prepare for tomorrow.

Anna called Calista Hoffman's mother and explained her problem, asked if she'd be willing to pick Kendra up and take her to Vacation Bible School with Calista each day.

"You know, I wouldn't mind at all," Mrs. Hoffman said, "but Calista won't be going anymore. As of tomorrow, she's going down to Sacramento to spend the rest of the summer with her father. I'm really sorry."

After ending the conversation, Anna told Kendra.

"Do you know of anyone else who might be able to come pick you up?" Anna said.

Kendra shook her head. "Nobody who drives by this way. And nobody who'd do it, probably. Calista's really my only friend there."

"Well, then, what do you want to do?"

Kendra thought for a while. Then she sighed and said, "Well, I guess I'll just miss the rest of Vacation Bible School this summer."

"Really? Are you sure?"

"Unless maybe Aunt Rose could do it."

"Yeah, I suppose I could call her and ask. But it would be kind of a pain for her to come all the way over here and pick you up, take you to the church, then go home, come back to the church two hours later, pick you up and bring you back over here."

"That's okay, Mommy. I don't mind missing it. Really."

"You're sure, now."

"I'm sure." She gave Anna a big smile. "Don't worry. Jesus will understand."

Sherry sat bolt upright in bed, sweat dripping from her.

She'd heard a sound somewhere in the night.

Andy snored beside her.

Sherry listened hard, wondering what she'd heard.

"Andy?" she whispered. "Andy? I *heard* something."

He did not stir, did not even budge.

She got up and stood beside the bed and realized she was shaking. It was hot in the trailer, but she was shivering as if she were freezing cold, sweating as if she were sweltering. She felt sick to her stomach.

She listened, but heard nothing.

Sherry walked down the hall, her body quaking, and went to the bathroom, where she hunkered down at the toilet and vomited. Afterward, she rinsed out her mouth, brushed her teeth, and left the bathroom. She went down the hall, then through the dark kitchen to the dark living room, where she turned on the light on the end table by the couch. She turned on the swamp cooler then. The VCR clock read 3:22. She found her kit on the couch. She fumbled with it, unzipped it, and removed the contents. Her hands were shaking so bad that it was difficult to prepare the stuff, but she somehow managed. She used her teeth as well as her right hand to tie on the tourniquet.

The needle trembled in her hand and she cried a little as she tried to steady her hand enough to inject herself. She sniffled and whimpered and finally drove the spike home. Then she sat back and let it flow through her.

The shakes subsided. The sweating stopped. She moaned a little as she melted into the couch, became a part of it.

"What'd I tell you about that shit, huh?"

She opened her eyes halfway. Andy stood before her, frowning down at her. He wore his boxers and had his hands on his hips, elbows out at his sides.

"I told you it would be a problem once you started that shit," he said. "It's one thing to do it for a day, but two, three days—that shit gets under your skin."

She realized the needle was still in her arm, the tourniquet still on. She removed the needle, undid the tourniquet, put them back in her kit.

"I-I, I thought I heard something," she said.

"You were having withdrawals, weren't you?" he said. "Your side of the bed is soaking wet."

"No, really, Andy, I *heard* something."

"What? *What* did you hear?"

"I don't know. But it scared me. I thought it might be those men … coming back for us."

Andy rolled his eyes. "Nobody's coming back for us, okay? So just quit worryin' about it. You wanna worry about somethin', worry about how you're gonna get off that shit, 'cause I'm not gonna support your habit, and I'm not gonna hang around with a junky. I'm goin' back to bed."

He turned and left the living room.

Sherry stretched out on the couch and turned on the TV. She watched an old movie without comprehending it. She wallowed in how good she felt until she drifted off on a cloud.

173

Eighteen

The next morning, Kendra ate her breakfast while Mommy hurried around getting ready for work. Mommy had gotten up early enough to fix her a delicious breakfast of eggs, bacon, and toast. Dexter sat beside her chair staring up at her with big, pleading eyes.

"Here, Dex," Kendra said, breaking off a piece of bacon. She held it down for the dog and he plucked it from her fingers with his teeth and chomped it down quickly.

"Don't get him into the habit of eating at the table," Mommy said as she hurried by on her way back to the bathroom.

"We won't tell, Dexter," Kendra whispered as she gave him another piece of bacon.

When she was finally ready, Mommy stood before her and said, "How do I look?"

She wore a grey-and-black suit and black shoes with heels.

"You look very nice, Mommy," Kendra said.

"You sure?"

"Yes, I'm sure. I'd tell you if something was wrong."

"Okay."

"Breakfast was real good, too, Mommy."

"Good, I'm glad."

"Aren't you gonna eat?"

"I'm too nervous to eat. In fact, I'm sick to my stomach."

"You should take a lunch with you."

"I'm going to. I'll do that next."

She quickly made a peanut butter and jelly sandwich and cut up some celery sticks, put them in plastic baggies, then put them in a small brown paper bag.

"Well, it's about time for me to leave," Mommy said. She turned to Kendra and looked serious. "Now, you're going to be good today, right?"

"Yes, Mommy."

"You can go get the mail if you want, but that's all. I don't want you wandering around all day. And do *not* go down by the river, don't even *think* about it. Okay? And keep your clothes on, little girl, I'm *serious*."

"Okay."

"I've put the number of my office on the refrigerator door, but only for emergencies, okay?"

"Okay."

"Now, stand up and give me a hug and kiss."

Kendra stood and hugged her, then Mommy gave her a wet kiss on the cheek.

"I'll see you later this afternoon, okay?" Mommy said.

"Okay. Have a good day."

"I'll try."

And then she was gone.

Kendra sat at the table and listened as Mommy started the car, then backed it out and drove it away.

She went on eating her breakfast, planning her day. She felt a tingle of excitement as she thought about what she was going to do later in the morning. She was going to go over to unit five and take some more pictures. And this time she wasn't going to chicken out. She was going to do whatever Mr. Regent wanted her to do.

She smiled as she ate her eggs.

———————

Mo Carey showed up at a few minutes before eleven and seated himself before Reznick's desk.

"Mr. Carey," Reznick said.

"Call me Mo."

"Okay, Mo. Look, Mo, I hate to be the bearer of such bad news."

Carey frowned and leaned forward in the chair. "What bad news?"

"I'm getting to that. I followed your wife last night. She went to a friend's apartment to pick her up, and together, they went to a house in a Redding subdivision. There, they met with two men. I got some pictures." Reznick opened the folder in front of him on the desk. "Like I said, I hate to give you bad news, but that's the job." He handed over the pictures he'd taken through the window.

Carey slowly looked through them. His face collapsed gradually as he examined the pictures.

"What … what is this?" Carey said. He turned his head back and forth very slowly. "I don't understand."

"Apparently, Mo, your wife has been meeting with these two men and posing nude for their cameras and having sex with them in front of those cameras." He took from the folder more pictures, these from the website. "And those pictures and videos have been posted on a website called MILFParade.com."

"MILF? What … this can't …" He squinted at Reznick, mouth open, head tilted to one side. "I don't understand. This

... this don't even *look* like Alicia. I mean ... I mean, *look* at her, she's *smilin'* and *laughin'*. She don't even *like* sex."

"Your wife is in her thirties, correct?"

Carey nodded.

"MILF stands for Moms I'd Like to Fuck," Reznick said. "She took a friend with her last night, someone about the same age as your wife, and she, too, posed for pictures and videos and had sex with one of the men."

As he went through the pictures, Carey's face gradually changed. The squint slowly went away. He set his jaw and his eyebrows came together above the bridge of his nose. His eyes slowly widened, and he finally lifted them from the pictures and met Reznick's. "Who are these men?" he said through his teeth.

"I don't know yet. They run something called Burning Lizard Amusements, a company based in Redding. I'm going to look into it further. They run some other websites, too. Apparently, your wife has been working with them for a while because they have a *lot* of pictures and videos of her on MILFParade.com."

"MILFParade.com—is that a pay site?"

"Oh, yeah. Not cheap, either. It's thirty-nine bucks a month. I had to buy a membership to check it out, which will go on your bill, by the way. I can give you the password I used, if you'd like, and you can take over the membership. Might as well, since you paid for it."

"Will you find out who those men are for me?"

"Look, I don't want you to do anything that's going to land you in jail. If you're angry, you should focus that anger on your wife. I'm not saying you should beat her up, for crying out loud, but you've got plenty of reason to be angry with *her*. Confront her with these pictures."

The pictures in his hand trembled because his hand was trembling. He stared at them for a long moment. "These pictures ... I can't believe 'em. She looks so ... *happy*. Like she's havin' the time of her life. She never looked like that with me, not once. Not even before we were married. What ... what *is* it? I don't get it."

"Maybe your wife is an exhibitionist," Reznick said. "Maybe she can't really get off unless she knows people are watching, or are *going* to be watching. When she's with these men, she knows her pictures and videos are going to be seen by a lot of men on this website."

Carey lowered the pictures, closed his eyes, and tipped his head back. "They must be payin' her. That's how she's able to buy stuff."

"They are paying her," Reznick said. "But I don't think it's much. I read her bio on the website. She's one of the site's most popular models. She has a lot of fans, and they send her gifts regularly."

Carey slowly pulled his head back down and looked at Reznick with a flat expression. "Gifts. From fans."

Reznick nodded. "That's right."

Carey's shoulders lifted as he inhaled and he moved his head back and forth as he sighed.

"What do you want me to do now, Mo?"

"Find out who those guys are."

"You're sure you don't want me to just close this case? You've got more than enough to confront your wife. What good will it do you to know who these guys are?"

"Because I'm gonna—" He stopped abruptly and ground his teeth together noisily.

"No. I'm not going to do it. You're going to get yourself in trouble. If I tell you who these guys are, you'll go after them, and I can't have that on my conscience. You'll end up in jail. You might even end up hurt."

"If anybody gets hurt, it won't be me."

"See? That's what I'm talking about. You'll go after them. I won't find out who they are, Mo. I won't do it. You'll have to find somebody else to do it, because I won't."

"Fine, then. Maybe I will."

Reznick nodded once. "Fine."

"How much do I owe you?"

Reznick took the bill from the folder and handed it across the desk to him.

Carey produced a checkbook and wrote a check. He ripped it from the book and put it on the desk.

"Can I keep these pictures?" Carey said.

"They're all yours. The whole file is yours. Here." Reznick picked up a pen and on the bottom of the manila folder, he wrote the password he'd used to get into MILFParade.com. "That's the password you can use to get into the website."

"Thank you."

Carey took the folder and stood. "Burning Lizard Amusements, you say?"

"That's right. It's in the file."

"Okay. Thanks for your help."

"Not at all. You paid for it."

Carey left the office.

Reznick sighed. Another job done.

He sat back in his chair and locked his hands together behind his head. He was tempted to go home, and it wasn't even noon yet. He remembered that Kendra was home alone all day. Home alone, all by herself.

In case you haven't noticed, Kendra has a crush on you, Anna had said with a smile. *I hope you'd never consider taking advantage of that, understand? Because if you did, I'd kill you. And you wouldn't even see it coming.*

Reznick chuckled a little. But it wasn't funny. He knew she'd meant it.

But when he thought of Kendra in those short shorts and that bikini bra … all that bare creamy flesh … that sultry face and all that luxurious blonde hair …

He started getting an erection just *thinking* about her while sitting there in his office.

He decided not to go home. Not just yet.

He took out a book and started reading, hoping the door would open again soon and another client would come in with another case.

———————

Steven Regent was fixing himself a sandwich in the luxurious cool of the air conditioner when someone knocked at his door. When he opened it, he looked down at Kendra and returned her big smile. She wore a baggy white T-shirt with the Three Stooges on the front, a pair of black shorts, and flip-flops on her feet. The T-shirt could not conceal her generous breasts.

"Well, hello there," Regent said.

"Hi, Mr. Regent."

"I thought I told you to call me Steven."

"Did you?"

"I think I did. Didn't I?"

"Well, I will if you want me to."

"Good. Come on in."

He opened the screen door and she climbed the steps and came inside.

"I was just fixing myself some lunch," he said. "You hungry?"

"No. I thought maybe you'd like to take more pictures."

"Oh. Okay. Sure. Lunch can wait. I'm not that hungry, anyway." Regent put the mayonnaise and mustard away, then picked up the plate with the unfinished sandwich on it and put it in the refrigerator. "Come on back to the studio."

Regent wore a grey UCLA T-shirt and a pair of blue shorts, with sandals on his feet. "Where did we end up last time?"

"Well, you were about to take some pictures of me in my panties, but I chickened out," she said.

"That's right. You feeling braver today? You feeling *naughtier*?"

She giggled. "Yeah, I am. I'm feelin' real naughty."

"That's my girl."

In the bedroom studio, he turned on a couple lights, picked up his camera, and when he turned around, she already had her flip-flops and T-shirt off. He sucked in a little gasp of air at the sight of those glorious breasts. She dropped the black shorts and wore lavender panties underneath.

"How's this?" she said.

He swallowed—it was more of a gulp—and nodded. "That's … just … fine. You want to get on the bed and pose for me?"

"Sure. You want me to pose like the ladies in the magazines again?"

"Yeah, that would be good."

She began to pose and he took pictures. As she moved around on the bed, her breasts swaying from side to side, Regent stiffened in those blue shorts.

Suddenly, Kendra sat up.

"You're hard again," she said, staring at the bulge in his shorts.

"Uh, yeah," he said with a smile. "You don't mind, do you? I mean, I can't help it. You do it to me every time. And you're gonna do it to every man who looks at your pictures."

"Can I see it?" she said.

"Whuh ... what?"

"Your hard penis. Can I see it? I've never seen one before."

Regent felt a tingle of excitement. "You want me to ... *show* it to you?"

"Yes. You told me you wanted to teach me everything I needed to know to get that man I was attracted to, remember? Well, how am I gonna get him if I've never even seen a hard penis before?"

He grinned. "Okay."

She came to the foot of the bed and sat on the edge, folded her arms across her lap, and leaned forward, staring at the bulge.

Regent lowered his shorts and it sprang free.

Kendra's eyes widened a little. "It's big," she said. "Are they all that big?"

"Well, they come in different shapes and sizes."

"Oh." She looked awhile longer, then said, "Can I touch it?"

Oh, God, Regent thought. If she touched it, he wasn't sure he was going to be able to control himself.

"Well, uh ..." He took a deep breath, let it out slowly.

"What do men like girls to do to their hard penises?"

"Are you serious?"

She smiled. "How'm I gonna know how to please the man I'm after if somebody don't tell me?"

Regent thought fast. "If I tell you what to do and you do it, can I get it on video for the website?"

"Sure, I guess so."

Regent quickly pulled up his shorts, turned around, and readied the video cam. "Okay," he said, "sit over here on the side of the bed." She did. "Now, what a man likes more than anything is for his girlfriend to take his penis into her mouth and suck on it."

Her face screwed up and she said, "In her *mouth*?"

"Yeah," he said. "Don't worry, the penis is clean. There's nothing dirty about it."

"But ... in the *mouth*?"

"Just you wait. When you see what it does to *me* when you do it, you'll *like* it."

"I will?"

He grinned down at her as he pulled his shorts down again. "Just you wait."

Nineteen

Lunchtime came and went, and Reznick's stomach growled. He'd eaten only an apple for breakfast. At one thirty-five, he decided to go home, if only long enough to eat lunch. He thought of that barbecue chicken in his refrigerator, waiting to be heated up and eaten.

He turned everything off and locked up his office on the way out, got into his Toyota, and drove home.

———

Kendra returned to the trailer, hoping Dexter hadn't piddled on the floor again in her absence. When she went inside, she found no puddle on the kitchen floor. Dexter was curled up on the couch, but when she came in, he immediately dove off the couch and came to her. He went to the screen door, hopped up on his hind legs and pawed at the screen.

"You need to go out?" she said. She opened the screen door and Dexter hurried out and piddled at the base of the tree outside. He walked a few feet away and squatted to move his bowels on the grass. Then he came back in and pawed at her leg. She picked him up and he licked her face.

Kendra could not get the smile off her face. She could not *believe* just how *naughty* she had been today. Not only had she taken Steven's hard penis into her mouth and stroked it up and down with her hands, she had made it ejaculate all over her face.

"That's the technical term, *ejaculate*," Steven had told her. "But most people call it *coming*."

Then, after he had wiped it all away with a wet washcloth, she had posed totally naked for his camera, and she'd even touched herself for him. It was a little embarrassing, but it was about as naughty as she'd ever been and it tickled her inside. She thought about the men who would be looking at her pictures on the website, and at the video of her sucking on Steven's penis. How many, she wondered, would see her? Steven said they would all fall in love with her. That made her feel like butterflies were fluttering inside her belly, the thought of all those men looking at her and falling in love with her online.

But she did not really care about them. The only one she cared about was Marc Reznick. She wondered what he would say if she sucked on *his* penis. Had he already imagined her doing that in his mind? Is that what was going through his head when he looked at her? She wondered. She also wondered what his hard penis looked like. Was it as big as Steven's? It didn't really matter. Did it?

The thought of touching his hard penis through his pants excited her, made her tingle inside her stomach.

Something else was going on inside her stomach—hunger. It was five minutes after two, past lunchtime. Kendra thought about what she wanted for lunch. She looked in the cupboard and found three stacked cans of tuna. A tuna salad sandwich sounded good. She took a can out, took the can opener from the drawer, and opened it, drained the water out of the can, and scooped the tuna into a bowl with a fork. She mixed in mayonnaise. Mommy always put chopped celery and onions in tuna fish salad. Kendra put the mayonnaise back in the refrigerator, then opened the crisper drawer and removed celery and green onions. She got a big knife from the drawer and broke off a celery stick, washed it in the sink, then began cutting off small pieces on the cutting board.

She did not feel it when it happened. She did not even know she had cut herself until she saw the blood. It came from a long, deep cut down the side of her index finger on her left hand. It bled furiously. Blood dribbled on the cutting board and counter, splashing in deep-red spots on the surfaces.

Kendra felt light-headed at the sight of all the blood and she had to grip the edge of the counter with her right hand. She went to the sink and held the finger under cold water. The water washed the blood away for a moment and she saw how deep and long the cut was. She wasn't even sure how she'd done it. She hadn't been cutting *that* fast, had she? Or had she been cutting at all? She could not remember. One minute, everything was fine, and the next, blood was everywhere.

The next thing she knew, she was sitting on her ass on the floor, holding her hand out before her, dripping water and blood, her head spinning dizzily. The blood was getting everywhere and her finger began to throb with pain. It felt twice, maybe three times its actual size, and when she looked at the finger, she was surprised to find that it was the same size as all the others.

Dexter came to her side and looked at her with puzzlement.

Blood was getting all over the floor, over her legs, but all she could do was sit there and stare at it.

Someone knocked on the screen door.

"Kendra?" Marc called. "Hello? Your mom told me to look in on you. You around?"

"Cuh-come in, please," she said, her voice broken and hoarse.

He pulled the screen door open and stepped up into the trailer smiling—until he saw her sitting on the kitchen floor with blood everywhere.

"Oh, my God," he said, rushing to her, "what *happened*?"

"I-I-I … cut myself."

He hunkered down beside her and held her left wrist as he examined her finger.

"Oh, boy," he said. "That's going to need stitches."

"Stitches?" she said weakly, her eyes wide.

"Yes. Come on, let's go. I'm taking you to the Emergency Room to have that stitched up. Do you have something we can wrap it up in 'til we get there? Do you have any gauze?"

"I … I think there's some in the bathroom."

Marc stood and went down the hall to the bathroom. She heard him fumbling around in there, searching.

Her head spun and she had to look away from the blood.

Marc finally returned with a roll of gauze, a small pair of scissors, and some white tape. He wrapped the finger snugly, taped it, then cut the tape.

"Okay, can you stand up and walk?" he said.

"I … I think so."

He took her elbow and helped her to her feet. "Let's go, now. Out to my car. I'm taking you to the hospital. Get the keys to the trailer so we can lock it up on our way out."

Kendra took the key Mommy had left her on the table and put it in her pocket. She locked the trailer door on the way out and said, "Bye-bye, Dexter."

They sat for what seemed like hours in the waiting room of the Shasta Regional Medical Center Emergency Room. When Kendra's name was finally called, Reznick went with her through the double doors and into the back.

The doctor unwrapped the bloody bandage from her finger and cleaned the wound, then he gave her a shot in the finger to numb the area. The shot hurt a *lot* and made Kendra cry. Reznick held her right hand and squeezed it as the doctor gave her the shot, but it didn't help.

Then the doctor stitched up the cut. Kendra could not watch, had to look away, or she knew she would pass out. Reznick squeezed her right hand the whole time and whispered to her that everything was going to be fine, that it would all be over soon. Once he was done stitching the cut, the doctor wrapped the finger lightly.

When he was finished, the doctor said, "I'm going to give you a prescription for a mild dose of codeine, because that finger is going to hurt pretty bad once the shot wears off." He disappeared for a moment, then returned with a pad and pen. He scribbled on the pad, tore off the page, and handed it to Reznick. "You can take that to any pharmacy."

When they left the Emergency Room, Reznick walked with his arm across her shoulders. Kendra walked unsteadily, holding her left hand in her right, her cheeks glistening with spilled tears. She leaned against him as they walked out into the stifling heat and crossed the parking lot to his Toyota.

In the car as they drove back to Anderson, Kendra said, "Thank you."

She spoke very quietly and Reznick did not hear what she said. "What?" he said.

"Thank you. For taking me to the hospital."

"Oh, no problem. I'm not sure if your mom is going to be too crazy about the bill, but it was no problem, really. Let's go to the drugstore and get those pills."

Reznick drove to Owen's Pharmacy in Anderson, which was just down the street from his office. They waited while the prescription was filled, then Reznick paid for it, and they got back in the car and he drove them to the trailer park.

In the trailer, Kendra saw a turd on the kitchen floor. "Oh, Dexter, I'm sorry I wasn't here to let you out."

"Don't worry about it," Reznick said. "I'll clean it up." He got a paper towel and cleaned up the mess.

Kendra stretched out on the couch, and Dexter hopped up and joined her, curled up on her tummy. He seemed to know something was wrong and he stared at her with big sad eyes.

Reznick got a couple pills from the bottle, got a glass of water, and a banana, and took them to Kendra on the couch.

"Here," he said. "Take a couple of these with water. Then eat the banana. If you don't take them with food, they'll make you sick. I'll go clean up the blood in the kitchen."

"You don't have to do that," she said.

"Don't worry, I don't mind."

Kendra's finger began to throb again. She had taken the pills just in time. She rested her head on a throw pillow and closed her eyes, frowning at the pain.

As time passed and Reznick cleaned up the blood in the kitchen, the codeine pills kicked in. Kendra experienced a giddy feeling that made her smile, and a tiredness washed over her. By the time she heard Mommy drive up, she was feeling no pain.

———

Anna Dunfy pulled in under the carport beside her trailer, and she was smiling. Her day had gone so well, she still couldn't believe it. It was a good job, a job she could do well, and a job where she felt welcome. It was such a good job that by the end of the day, she was praying she could stay on full-time.

She got out of the car, looking forward to putting on a T-shirt and shorts and relaxing with Kendra. She put her purse strap over her shoulder, went up the steps, opened the screen door, and went inside.

Kendra was stretched out on the couch, and Marc Reznick was in the kitchen wiping down the floor with a rag.

"Hello," Anna said, frowning a little. Something wasn't right. "Kendra?"

Kendra opened her eyes and turned to her with a drunken smile. "Hi, Mommy. How'd your job go?" She sounded groggy. The index finger of her left hand was bandaged.

"Hi," Reznick said. He stood up straight, tossed the rag into the sink, and washed his hands. He dried them on a hand towel. "We had a bit of an accident today."

"An accident?" Anna said, alarm coming into her voice. Her purse dropped to the floor. "What happened?" She went to her daughter's side. "Honey? What's wrong?"

"I cut my finger real bad," Kendra said. "Marc took me to the hospital."

"The *hospital*?" Anna said, her eyes widening as she turned to Reznick.

"It was a pretty bad cut," he said. "Long and deep cut. I knew right away it needed stitches, so I took her to the ER."

"The ER?" she said, her voice becoming high and squeaky. "You couldn't have taken her to a walk-in clinic?"

"Oh, well … it didn't occur to me to take her to a walk-in clinic. The doctor stitched her finger up and gave us a

190

prescription for codeine, because he said the finger was going to hurt really bad once the shot he gave her wore off."

Anna knelt down beside the couch and took Kendra's hand between both of hers. "How'd you cut your finger, honey?"

"I was tryin' to make tuna fish salad like you do, and I was cutting up celery. I don't know how I did it. One minute, everything was fine, and the next, I was bleedin' all over the place."

She looked over her shoulder at Reznick. "You paid for all this?"

"Yeah. I've got the receipts." He reached into his right pocket and took out two slips of paper. He walked over to Anna and handed them to her. "One for the hospital, one for the pills."

She unfolded the receipts and looked at the totals. "Oh, God," she whispered. "Over five hundred dollars." She closed her eyes as she took a deep, steadying breath. She didn't want Kendra to see her get upset, but inside, she was. How could she pay for it?

Anna slowly got to her feet and turned to Reznick. "Thank you for taking care of her," she said. "And for cleaning up in here. I can't tell you, I really appreciate it."

"Hey, it was no problem at all," he said. "I'm just glad I was around when she needed me. Well, if you don't need me for anything else, I think I'll be going."

"Thanks again," Anna said. She went to her purse and took out her checkbook, then put the purse on the kitchen table. She wrote the check and tore it from the book, then handed it to Reznick. "Do me a favor and don't cash this for a couple days, okay? I've gotta figure out some way to cover it."

"Sure," he said. "No problem."

Reznick went to the couch and looked down at Kendra, smiled. "You take care of yourself, okay?" he said.

She smiled back at him, her eyes half-closed. "Thanks, Marc."

After he was gone, Anna looked at the receipts again. Five hundred and eighty-four dollars and eighty-eight cents with the hospital and pharmacy bills combined. She had no idea how she was going to cover the check she'd written for Reznick.

She looked at Kendra, who was snoring gently on the couch, with Dexter curled up and asleep on her stomach. Anna went to the kitchen table and sat down, put her face in her hands, and exhaled heavily into her palms.

She lifted her head when she remembered the business card the man had given her at the club night before last. He'd said he would pay her to pose for pictures for his website. She wondered how *much* he would pay her.

Anna reached over and pulled her purse toward her and began to prod her hand around in it. She was pretty sure she'd put the card in her purse. She could not find it, so she overturned the purse and dumped its contents on the table. She sorted through all the stuff until she found the small white card.

Burning Lizard Amusements. She looked over at Kendra to make sure she was still asleep. She took the phone from its base and punched in the number that was on the card. It purred a few times, then a man said, "Burning Lizard."

"Hello," she said. "Uh, I'm not sure if you're the man who gave me your business card, but—"

"Who's this?" he said.

"I'm Kitten. The dancer from the Mt. Shasta Gentleman's Club. You gave me your business card the night before last, and you—"

"Oh, yes, I remember you well, Kitten. What can I do for you?"

"Well, I was wondering if the invitation was still open. To pose for pictures, I mean."

"For you? You *bet* it is!"

"Could we do it soon? I mean, like *today*?"

"I don't see why not."

"Where are you? I'll come over."

"Do you know where the Riverside Mobile Home Park is?"

Anna frowned and paused a moment. "Are you joking?"

"Why would I joke? Do you know where it is?"

"I *live* in the Riverside Mobile Home Park."

"*Really*? Well, then, we're neighbors, aren't we?" He laughed a big, bellowing laugh. "What are you doing right now? I'm in unit five."

"I'll be there in awhile." She hung up.

Anna stood and went to her bedroom, where she changed into a yellow T-shirt and a pair of green shorts. She put flip-flops on her feet, checked on Kendra again—she was sound asleep on the couch—then left the trailer. She walked down to unit five and knocked on the door.

———————

Regent smiled as he let her in the trailer. She was just as gorgeous as he remembered. He guessed she was in her early thirties—since she lived in the trailer park, he could use her on TrailerParkGirls.com.

"What a coincidence, huh?" he said, still smiling. "We both live in the same trailer park."

"Yes. It's a coincidence, all right. So, tell me about what you want."

He outlined the pay scale to her, told her everything.

When he was done, she thought about it awhile, chewed on a thumbnail, frowned. Then she said, "I'll do the whole thing for twelve hundred dollars, but it has to be done right now, and only for cash."

"No problem there. I'll have to call a buddy of mine over to help me—"

"Oh, no. I'll only do it with you. You bring somebody else in, and I'm outta here."

He stopped and thought about that. He could do it himself, but he preferred to have an extra hand. Oh, well. He'd do it her way.

"All right," he said with a nod. "Well, then. Let's get started."

———————

Kendra awoke when she heard the door open. Her eyes felt sticky and puffy, and she still had that giddy feeling, but it was diminished, and mixed with a heavy grogginess. Her finger throbbed, but it was a faraway kind of feeling, distant. She turned to see Mommy coming into the trailer. She watched Mommy pull the screen door closed, then walk slowly to the kitchen table. She sat down and reached into a pocket, pulled something out, and put it on the table. Then she leaned her elbows on the tabletop and put her face in her hands. Her shoulders shook with quiet sobs.

Dexter was still curled up on Kendra's stomach, and she gently picked him up as she sat up and swung her legs off the couch. She put him down on the floor and carefully stood. She felt a little light-headed, but she managed to keep her balance. She walked carefully over to Mommy. A stack of cash lay on the table before her. Kendra put her hand on Mommy's back.

Mommy jerked with surprise and gasped as she turned her head and looked up at Kendra. Her eyes were puffy and wet.

"What's the matter, Mommy?" Kendra said.

"Oh, sweetheart." Mommy turned toward her and wrapped her arms around Kendra's waist. "It's nothing. I just felt like having a good cry, that's all." She pulled back and looked up at Kendra. "How's your finger?"

"It hurts a little, but not bad. The pills helped a lot."

"When did you take them last?"

"I don't know."

"Well, we need to keep track. You can only take them every four to six hours." She sniffed and rubbed a hand down her face, then wiped her eyes with her knuckles. She sighed heavily. "You didn't fix your lunch, did you? You must be hungry. Want me to fix you some tuna fish salad?"

"That would be good."

"You go back to the couch and sit down. Watch some TV. I'll fix you some tuna fish salad for a big sandwich."

"What's the money for?" Kendra said.

"That's got to go into the bank to cover the check I wrote Marc for the hospital and pharmacy bills."

"I'm sorry I cost you so much money, Mommy."

"Oh, huh-honey, it's not your fuh-fault," she said, her voice cracking. "Don't you worry about it. Now, go back to the couch and turn on the Game Show Network and watch your game shows. I'm gonna fix something good to eat."

Kendra bent down and kissed Mommy's wet cheek, then returned to the couch.

Twenty

Reznick left his trailer around eight-thirty and walked through the sweltering shadows of dusk to Anna's and knocked on the screen door. Anna came to the door.

"Hi, Marc," she said as she opened the screen.

He went inside. "I just wanted to check on Kendra, see how she was doing this evening."

"She's been sleeping a lot because of the codeine."

"Hi, Marc," Kendra said from the couch. She was lying there with Dexter on her flat belly. Lying there with the dog, she looked more like a child than he'd ever seen her look before. It almost made him feel guilty for all the thoughts he'd had about her. Almost.

"How's the finger?" he said.

"It hurt really bad for a while, but I took a couple more pills."

"That's good, I'm glad they're helping." He turned to Anna. Her face looked puffy and she looked worn out. "You okay?"

"Oh, I'm fine."

"Look," he said, lowering his voice, "I want to apologize for taking her to the hospital. It never occurred to me to take her to a walk-in clinic, and I know it would've been a lot cheaper. I'd like to help you out with that bill."

"No, don't worry about it, Marc, really. I've got the money to cover it now, and it'll go in the bank first thing tomorrow morning."

"You're sure?"

"Positive. But thanks for the offer. It's very good of you."

"Is there anything I can do? You need anything from the store, anything at all?"

Anna shook her head. "No, I think we're fine. But thanks a lot for the offer, Marc, I appreciate it."

"Okay. Well, you know where to find me if you need anything."

He left their trailer and walked slowly back to his own, thinking of Kendra stretched out on the couch like that, one bare knee bent upward, belly flat, breasts at rest, but still quite visible under her shirt, her blonde hair in a pool around her head on the throw pillow.

He felt ashamed of himself—but only a little—because he still wanted her. He still wanted her bad.

———————————

Anna could not very well leave Kendra home alone in the shape she was in, so she called the Gentlemen's Club and told Paul her foot was still hurting and she needed to stay off of it one more night. She'd go back to work tomorrow—Kendra should be feeling better then. If necessary, she would take her over to Rose's.

Anna had taken a long hot shower after her experience with Steven Regent in unit five. She'd felt filthy afterward and stayed under the stream of water until she didn't feel that way anymore. But it never went away, not entirely. She left the shower feeling heavy as lead.

Kendra was asleep again on the couch. Another game show was running on TV. Kendra loved her game shows.

Anna lit a cigarette and went into Kendra's bedroom and sat down at the computer. She checked for e-mail but there was none.

What was the website Steven had said she would be featured on? Something about trailer parks ... Trailer Park Girls, that was it, TrailerParkGirls.com. Anna typed that in, and after a moment, the site opened up.

She looked at the cartoon of the busty young woman standing in front of a trailer. At the bottom of the screen, she read, "Real Trailer Parks. Real Girls. Coming Soon." Then, below that, "NEW! Preview."

Surely he didn't have her pictures up already. She clicked on the hyperlink word "Preview."

A moment later, another page opened with several small pictures on it. Anna looked at the pictures for a long time without fully realizing what she was seeing at first. As she looked at the photos, a numbness crept through her entire body, until she felt as if her whole body had been shot up with Novocain. It was the same blonde girl in all the pictures, first clothed, then topless, then in panties, then naked. Then she had Steven's filthy cock in her mouth, then his filthy fluids all over her face.

It couldn't be. It was impossible. Just a strong resemblance, that was all.

She clicked on one of the pictures and it became enlarged.

It was no mistake. It was not just some blonde girl. It was her daughter. It was Kendra. Kneeling naked on a bed, her legs spread, her arms together to press her large breasts close. And she was smiling. *Smiling.*

What had he done? Had he *drugged* her? Had he—had he—had he *hypnotized* her?

Anna heard a strange growling sound. For a while, she could not figure out where it was coming from—then she realized it was coming from deep in her chest. *She* was growling. Like some kind of animal. Her fingernails clawed at the top of Kendra's desk. Everything turned a dark shade of red, as if blood had run into her eyes. Her teeth ground together, sounding like thunder in her skull.

She enlarged each picture and looked at it, starting with the first and through to the last. The final picture was the most sickening—Kendra grinning up at the camera with Steven's semen spattered all over her face. She knew Kendra's face, knew her expressions—that was a real smile, a real, genuine grin on Kendra's face. Anna could not understand, how could it *be*? He must have gotten her drunk. But when? How could Anna not have *known*?

Her stomach tightened, then turned over and over inside her.

Her lungs felt filled with ice water.

Her hands curled into fists and her fingernails dug hard into her palms until they nearly broke through the flesh.

Her brain felt on fire inside her head, as if the flames might be shooting out her ears, as if her smoking hair might be singed from the roots up.

She returned to Kendra's homepage with a click of the mouse.

She pressed her hands flat on the desktop and stood gradually. She walked very slowly out of the bedroom and down the hall to the kitchen. She went to the living room and looked at Kendra. She was still asleep on the couch. Anna turned back and went into the kitchen. She took the large knife from the counter, the knife with which Kendra had cut herself.

She slid the blade down into her shorts on her hip, pulled her T-shirt down over the handle that stuck up from the shorts' elastic band. She slipped her bare feet into flip-flops and left the trailer.

Anna walked slowly down the road to unit five, the flip-flops slapping against her heels. She knocked on the door. It opened a moment later and Steven Regent smiled widely down at her.

"Hey, baby, how's it going?" he said. He pushed the screen door open and she went up the steps, into his trailer.

Behind her, he closed the screen, then the door, and turned to her. "You come back for some more, honey?" he said.

She stepped up to him and put her left hand to the back of his neck, pressed her body to his, and gave him a long, deep kiss. When she pulled back, just a little, he said breathlessly, "Whoa, you really *did* come back for some more, huh, Kitten?"

She did not smile as she looked at him. When she spoke, her voice was low, but clear and crisp. "How did my daughter get on your fucking website?"

His smile faltered a little. "Wha ... *what*?"

As she replied, she reached down with her right hand and removed the knife from her shorts. "I *said*, how ... did my *daughter* ... get on your fucking *website*?"

"Your ... daughter? I don't understand, Kitten, whatta you mean, your—"

She plunged the blade into his stomach. It made a wet sound going in.

Steven gagged and gurgled and his tongue jutted from his mouth as his eyes bulged.

"You filthy fucking bastard," Anna growled as she pulled the knife out.

Blood gushed from the wound.

Steven's mouth hung open and his eyes rolled around in their sockets.

She sent the knife in again, to the hilt, her teeth clenched. This time, she twisted the blade inside him.

Steven released a pathetic gurgle and went down. He fell backward, pulled away from the blade, and hit the floor heavily.

"How dare you," Anna said. "How *dare* you!"

She knelt beside him, and with Kendra on her mind—her innocent, retarded daughter, her little blonde baby girl—she stabbed him again, and again, and again. She held the knife in both hands and brought her arms up and down, up and down. She did not notice the blood splashing up from Steven's body, getting on her arms and the front of her T-shirt and shorts, even spattering her face. She kept stabbing him long after the final death rattle escaped his lungs and he lay dead and staring up at the ceiling with wide milky eyes. After awhile, her hands appeared to be wearing wet, red gloves up to her elbows.

She stopped, sat back on her lower legs, dropped the knife, and heaved with sobs. They shook her entire body. She lifted her hands and held them at each side of her face without touching it. She looked at them—first the left, then the right— and saw all the blood on her, and only sobbed harder. Blood dribbled down her cheeks, down her arms. It was everywhere, all over her. Steven was a mass of blood before her. She could smell it, and it was sickening. She could smell the blood and shit from his dead body.

Anna sobbed until she could sob no more, until she was empty, exhausted, blasted out inside. Her sobs subsided and became small whimpering sounds. At first, she didn't realize the sounds were coming from her and she looked around for their source.

She almost collapsed. She wanted to lie down beside him and sleep. But she couldn't do that. She did not know *what* to do next. All she knew was that she had committed murder.

She had killed a man.

And she did not know what to do next.

Kendra straddled Reznick in his recliner. She was naked.

"You're hard," she said as she massaged the bulge in his pants. She smiled as she moved forward and kissed him. Her hair fell forward in drapes on either side of them.

He felt her breasts press against him, warm and pliant.

Then she pulled back and began to unbutton his shirt.

He lifted his hands and put them on her breasts. He squeezed them gently, ran his thumbs over the nipples until they became hard and puckered.

"Kendra," he whispered, just to say her name.

She smiled as she ran her hands over his bare chest, dragged her fingernails lightly over his skin, over his nipples.

She moved back a little, reached down and unbuttoned his shorts.

Someone knocked on the door.

Kendra unzipped his shorts and reached in to find his erection.

"Wait," Reznick said when the knock came again.

But Kendra ignored the knocking and wrapped her fingers around him.

"No, wait, there's somebody at—"

The knock at the door sounded again.

When he looked at Kendra again, she was Victoria. She held a gun in her right hand. She put the gun to her temple as her left hand fondled Reznick's erection.

He heard the gun explode as he jerked awake with a small cry.

"Marc?" someone said. "Marc? I need some help."

He recognized Anna's voice.

Reznick's hands trembled and his heart hammered as if he had just gone for a long run, something he hadn't done in ages. He straightened up in the recliner, wide awake now, and stood unsteadily. He felt weak and shaky all over.

"Marc, please."

"Anna?" he said as he turned to the door. He walked over and opened the screen. "What's up?" He flipped on the porch light, and what he saw made him gasp.

"I don't know if I should come inside," she said. "I'm kind of a mess." She laughed, then—a high, abrupt, breathy laugh that sounded on the verge of hysteria. He'd heard it before, that laugh, and it caused him great concern.

"Are you hurt?" Reznick asked as he came down the front steps.

"No, no, not me, not me, it was someone else who was hurt, and I hurt him." Another of those spooky laughs. She held her hands out before her, fingers apart.

"Is that *blood* that's all over you?"

"Yes, yes, it's blood."

"You must be dripping it all over the place. Where did you come from?"

"Unit five."

"The new trailer?"

"Yeah."

"What happened?"

"I killed him, Marc, I killed him, stabbed him to death for what he did to my little girl."

"You ... you just killed someone?"

"Uh-huh."

"Here in the park?"

"Yes."

"And you came straight over here?"

"Yeah."

Dripping blood like that, he thought, looking around to see if anyone was watching, seeing. He saw no one.

Reznick thought fast. "Okay, look, here's what I want you to do. Walk across the road to that trailer over there, okay? Right through the trees to that trailer over there."

"What for?"

"I'll explain later. Then I want you to walk diagonally over to this trailer over here," he said pointing. "Can you do that? Just do it quickly, and we'll get it over with."

Reznick's heart was still pounding, but now for a different reason. His erotic dream was forgotten, as if he'd never had it.

Anna zigzagged like a drunk over the narrow trailer-park road, crossed the divider, then crossed back again, then stopped, turned to him, and said in a stage whisper, "What now?"

He walked over to her and stood beside her for a moment, looking at her.

"What'd you have me do that for?"

"You're trailing blood all over the place. You came straight to my trailer. I'd rather not be involved once the police are pulled into this tomorrow, *if* they're pulled in tomorrow. Now it looks like you wandered all over the place and didn't just come over here." He pointed to another trailer. "Go over there, under the carport, and stand there for a few seconds and just drip for a while."

As she did as she was told, Reznick walked down to unit five. The door was open, the screen door closed. He approached the door and looked in through the screen.

"Oh, my God," he whispered.

It was a slaughterhouse. There was blood everywhere. The corpse was bathed in it and it covered the carpet and some of the furniture. Through the screen, the blood looked black, like motor oil.

He heard her approaching behind him, her flip-flops slapping her heels.

"What happened?" he whispered.

They stood close, and in the glow of the porch light, he could see her face, see the expression on it, see her eyes, her lips.

"He runs a website," she said, her voice quavering. She sounded unlike herself, as if she were about to snap. But obviously, she had already done that.

"A website?"

"Trailer Park Girls. He has her pictures on it. Naked. Pictures of her touching herself. Pictures of her … of her … sucking on his *filthy cock*." She said the last two words through clenched teeth.

"What? Who?"

"Kuh-Kendra. My Kendra."

"TrailerParkGirls.com?"

"Yeah, that's it."

Reznick frowned. That was one of the websites owned by Burning Lizard Amusements. That meant the dead man lying on the floor in the trailer was probably one of the two men he'd seen frolicking with Alicia Carey and her friend on Jupiter Lane. And he lived here in the Riverside Mobile Home Park.

"I think he drugged her," Anna whispered.

"What?"

"Kendra." Her lips were a tight straight line. "I think he drugged Kendra. Or he got her drunk. Or something. I mean … *my* Kendra." Her voice was merely a breath now as her face softened. "How could she do such a thing? How did he make her do it?"

205

"He was probably very good at it," Reznick said. "Very manipulative. He's talked a *lot* of women into taking their clothes off. I've seen his other websites. They're filled with women who've done it. I wouldn't worry too much about it. I don't think it's scarred Kendra, or anything like that."

"How do *you* know? How will we *ever* know? Until later, I mean? It might not show itself for years."

"Look, I'd love to stand here and talk about this with you, but, uh … what exactly do you want me to do?"

"I … I don't … I don't know. I don't know what to do. You were the first person I thought of. I didn't know who else to go to. I … I just, I lost it, something inside me, it snapped, and I couldn't stop, I couldn't stop stabbing him, I've never felt that way before in my life."

Reznick thought of what she'd told him earlier that night, the threat she'd made if he ever took advantage of the crush Kendra had on him. He'd had no idea then that she was so capable of actually going through with it.

"I can't go to prison," Anna whispered. "Who will take care of my Kendra?" Her hoarse voice trembled and she interlocked her bloody fingers just below her chin, her eyes wide and glistening. "I can't leave her all alone. I-I can't, I can't *abandon* her."

"You want me to help you dispose of the body?"

Her eyes widened more, even though it didn't seem possible. She put a bloody hand on each side of her head, curling her fingers into her auburn hair. "I-I-I don't knuh-*know*. I cuh-can't *think*."

Reznick began to pace. "Let me think," he said. "Let me think."

And for a while, Reznick thought.

Twenty-One

"Can you wait right here?" Reznick said.

Anna stood nearby crying quietly. "What-huh?"

"Wait right here. I have to go to my trailer and get some stuff. I'll be back in just a few minutes."

"Oh. Okay. Okay."

He broke into a jog and returned to his own trailer. At the rear of his carport was a small metal shed he'd had since he'd lived in the smaller trailer park over on River Valley Drive. He went into the trailer to get his keys and a flashlight and, from a bedroom dresser drawer, a pair of work gloves, which he put on. From the top shelf of his closet, he took a roll of duct tape. Then he went back outside and unlocked the padlock on the shed. He turned on the flashlight and looked around. There were a few boxes of junk stored in there. On top of one stack of boxes was an old duffle bag he hadn't used in many years. He picked up the duffle bag and opened it wide, and put the duct tape in. He put the bag on a box, then looked around for something else.

There they were—weights he hadn't used in ages, dumbbells that had been tucked away in this shed over in the other trailer park for years. He removed the weights from the bars and put them in the duffle bag. He put *all* of them in the bag and tried lifting it. It wasn't easy, but he could manage.

Standing in the back corner of the shed was an old rolled-up canvas he'd had so long that he'd forgotten *why* he had it. He stepped over a box and wrapped an arm around the rolled-up canvas and carried it clumsily to the door.

It wouldn't work. He couldn't carry it all at once. Using both hands, he carried the bag of weights down to unit five, then came back and hauled the rolled-up canvas over, with the flashlight in his right back pocket. On his way to unit five with the canvas, he thought, *Why am I doing this?*

The response was a long time coming. But when it came, it was strong, and it was enough.

I'm doing it for Kendra, he thought.

When he reached the attractive new trailer, he exhaled loudly as he leaned the canvas up against the side of it. He blew air out through puffed cheeks. Stinging sweat had sprung up on his neck and forehead and trickled down his back.

"Whew," he said, "didn't think I was gonna make it over here with that load."

"What's in the bag?"

"You'll see. Take off your flip-flops," he said, slipping out of his own.

"What?"

"Take off your flip-flops. I want to wear them in there, so it won't look like there were two different people walking around in all that blood."

"Oh. Okay." She pulled her feet out of the flip-flops and stepped away from them.

Reznick put his feet into the flip-flops, which were much too small for him, but he would make do. He wrapped an arm around the canvas, picked it up, opened the screen door, and climbed the steps, hefting the canvas into the trailer.

"Oh, God," he whispered.

It was even worse than it had looked through the screen. A large butcher knife lay on the floor beside the dead body. He could not tell the color of the shirt the man was wearing—it was too soaked in blood. It was torn and tattered, and Reznick assumed the man was just as torn and tattered beneath it. He might not have to puncture the lungs and stomach after all—it looked like she'd probably done that already.

The air conditioner was running on high in the trailer, but the smells of blood and feces were still heavy in the room.

Inside the trailer, Reznick walked on the balls of his feet so his heels wouldn't sink into the bloody carpet over the ends of the short flip-flops.

Reznick took a good look at the face. Sure enough, it was one of the two men he'd seen in that house with Alicia Carey. It seemed that Anna Dunfy had done half of Mo Carey's job for him. Mo would no doubt be happy to hear about it. Then again, he might be angry that he was robbed of the pleasure of doing it himself.

He put the rolled-up canvas down on the floor beside the body. He picked up the knife, went to the door, and opened the screen. "Here," he said, holding the knife out to her. "Hold onto this for me."

She took the knife without saying anything.

Reznick unrolled the canvas, then rolled the body onto it, rolled the canvas out some more, until it was all the way open. He rolled the body onto it further, then rolled the canvas up over the body. He went to the door and opened the screen.

"Anna," he whispered. "Hold this screen door open for me."

She went to the door, held it open with her left hand.

He went back to the rolled-up corpse, bent down, and took the foot-end. He pulled the body around and dragged it feet-first toward the door. He dragged it out the door and down the steps. The head thunked against the steps on its way down. On the concrete below, he turned the body until it was parallel with the Porsche SUV parked in the carport, then dropped the feet to the concrete.

Another long exhale through puffed cheeks. He felt itchy as sweat trickled all over his body.

"Okay," he whispered. He kicked off the flip-flops, walked over to his own, and put them back on. "You can put your flip-flops back on now," he whispered.

She did.

"Put down the knife by my duffle bag."

She did that, too.

"Now," he said, "this is going to be a lot easier if you can lift up one end of this thing and carry it."

"Where are we taking it?"

"To the pier."

"Oh. Well, I can try."

"Take the feet, I'll take the head."

Reznick went to the head and lifted it off the concrete. Anna went to the other end, and with a grunt, lifted the feet.

"No," Reznick said. "Turn around and lift it from behind so you don't have to walk backwards."

Anna dropped it, turned around, then bent at the knees and reached behind her, picked it up again. She straightened up with another grunt and started moving forward.

They passed through the rear of the carport and went through tall pale weeds, between two tall, fat oaks. It was dark back here and Reznick wished he could use his flashlight.

"I can't see," Anna said.

"Yes, you can," he said. "Just go slowly."

They went slowly down a gentle slope that led to the riverside and moved to the left, toward the pier. It was white and stood out, even in the dark, but it was another thirty or forty yards away.

The night was hot and muggy. Reznick felt sweat running down beneath his shirt. It trickled down his temples and forehead and dripped into his eyes and stung. He stopped a moment and wiped the back of his hand over his eyes, tried to get the sweat out.

"Want to stop and rest?" Reznick said.

"Yeah," Anna said, panting.

They put the body down.

"What're we gonna do with it?" she said.

He walked over to her and stood close, whispered, "Be quiet. We don't want anyone to hear us. We're right behind these trailers, and most of the bedrooms are in the back. Some people are already in bed. Whisper only, okay? And only when absolutely necessary."

"Okay," she whispered. "What're we gonna do with it? Throw it in the river?"

"We're gonna weigh it down first."

"Oh. Okay."

"Wanna try again?"

She took a deep, steadying breath. "I feel so … numb."

"Yeah. It happens. Let's go."

They returned to their positions, lifted the body again, and carried it the rest of the way over uneven ground thick with weeds and stickers that tore at their bare legs. They came to the sandy shore of the river, then to the pier.

"Take him all the way out," Reznick said in a loud whisper.

Anna was panting heavily, grunting between breaths.

They reached the end of the pier and Reznick said, "Okay."

Anna dropped her end with a heavy *thunk*. Reznick put his end down and went to her.

"Now stay right here," he whispered.

Reznick took the flashlight from his back pocket and turned it on. He hurried back up the slope at an angle. Halfway up, he stopped. He looked at the back ends of the trailers that were visible from there. Only one had light in the windows, the others were dark. But no one appeared to be looking out their windows, thank God. He returned to the trailer. He grabbed the knife and the duffle bag, then turned around, heavily weighed down now, carrying the bag with both hands, and hurried back to the pier, but not as fast as before.

At the corpse's head, he put down the bag and the knife, then went to the side of the rolled up body and unrolled it just enough for the body to be exposed. He gingerly pulled up the corpse's shirt to expose the torn and tattered abdomen and chest.

"What're you doing?" Anna whispered.

"Just watch and see." Reznick looked the body over. "You really did a good job on this guy." He handed her the flashlight and said, "Hold this on him for me, okay?" Still wearing the work gloves, he picked up the knife. Starting at the sternum, he cut straight downward through the abdomen.

"Oh, Christ, what're you *doing*?" Anna rasped.

At the top of the incision, he made another, this one horizontal.

Reznick whispered, "The biggest mistake people make when they get rid of a body by throwing it in the drink is that they don't puncture the most buoyant parts of the body—the lungs and the stomach, and with a woman, the womb. Then the body bobs to the surface and the cops have something to go on. Before you know it, the killer's arrested and the game's over."

Reznick pulled the incision open wide with his gloved hands, making an ugly wet sound. He winced, disgusted by what he was doing.

"Yeah, looks like you did plenty of puncturing," he whispered. "But we're going to make sure."

He stuck the knife up under the rib cage on the right side and sliced, then the left side and sliced. He then cut the stomach open. The sounds it made were awful, the wet smacking sounds, a small farting sound. The smell of fecal matter rose from the body's opening.

"That oughtta do it," he breathed.

Anna made disgusted noises.

Reznick opened the duffle bag. He removed the first round, disk-shaped weight with his right hand, used his left to hold the incision open, and stuffed the weight as deeply as he could into the cavity. He did the same with the next weight, and the next, and the next, until the duffle bag was empty except for the roll of duct tape.

Then Reznick removed the duct tape. He pulled a strip off the roll and stretched it taut across the corpse's abdomen. He covered the opening with duct-tape, until the body looked like a duct-tape mummy. He wrapped the body up in the canvas again, then used the duct tape to wrap up the canvas.

"*Whew,*" he said, standing when he was finished. He scrubbed a hand down his sweaty face a couple times.

"What now?" Anna whispered.

"Now, we throw him in. You think you can manage with all those weights in him?"

"I'll try." She turned off the flashlight and put it down on the pier.

"You pick up his feet." Reznick went to the head and scooted the rolled-up body around so it was lying across the pier. "Okay, you ready?"

Anna went to the foot of the bundle. She bent her knees, clutched the canvas, tried to lift it. With a big grunt, she tried again. She could only raise the legs. Reznick raised his end. The middle sagged.

"C'mon," he said, "we've gotta be able to give it a little swing."

They both tried harder and managed to raise the middle just a bit, just enough to swing it back and forth a couple times before tossing it in. They did not toss it far.

Reznick quickly swept up the flashlight and turned it on, sent the beam searching for the bundle, found it.

The current of the Sacramento River swept the rolled-up body away and twirled it around for a long moment. For just that moment, it danced on the water's surface, bobbing up and down and spinning around like a wobbly top.

Reznick's gut became icy and frozen. For a moment, he was afraid the body was not going to go down.

Then, as if suddenly realizing it was too heavy to float, it sank out of sight and disappeared as if it had never been there.

Reznick bent down, picked up the knife, and threw it hard out into the river.

———

They returned to the trailer in unit five and Reznick locked the door and pulled it closed, then closed the screen. He carried the duffle bag in which he'd put the flashlight and the wet, bloody gloves, and duct tape.

"I hope Kendra's not awake," she whispered.

"What are you going to tell her if she is?" Reznick said. "How are you going to explain the fact that you're covered with caked blood?"

She sighed. "I have no idea." She turned to him, fidgeting nervously and wearing a deep frown. "Look, Marc … I-I can't thank you enough. What you've done … you've saved my life."

"We'll see. You've got one thing in your favor. He runs a bunch of porn websites, and he takes pictures and videos of a lot of women. Porn pictures and videos. He could have been the victim of any angry husband or boyfriend, or even an angry woman. The field of possible killers is big. They're liable to talk to you, the cops. They'll talk to everyone in the park. You'll just have to keep your cool when they do."

"Yeah. I … hope I can."

"Well, I think we're through for the night, Anna."

She released a long, trembling sigh. She reached out and squeezed his hand. "Thank you so much."

"You're welcome. But don't forget, Anna—you owe me. You owe me big-time after this. And one day soon, I'll collect."

Reznick could not tell for sure in the dark, but it seemed a curious frown passed over her face.

"Okay," she whispered. "Okay, if you say so."

Reznick turned to go back to his trailer to close up his shed, throw away his bloody work gloves, and take a long hot shower.

Anna went to her trailer. The door was still open. She looked through the screen door and listened.

Kendra was still lying on the couch, snoring softly.

Dexter stood at the door, scratching on the screen.

Anna opened the screen and let Dexter out. He dashed down the steps and went out in the yard. Anna waited while he did his business. When the dog was finished, he came back up the steps and went inside, and Anna followed him.

215

She quietly went through the living room and hurried to the bedroom. She found a clean tank top and pair of shorts, then went to the bathroom. She pulled the shower curtain aside, reached in, and turned on the shower. Then she turned and looked at herself in the mirror over the sink.

She looked like something out of a horror film. She looked like Carrie after the prom. She looked almost as if she had bathed in blood. It was all over her. Her T-shirt hung on her, heavy with blood. Her hair was matted with it. It covered her face like some kind of exotic cosmetic mask. It was on her arms, and when she looked down, she saw it on her legs. It was caked now, thick on her, like a second sticky skin.

Anna wondered what she was going to do with the clothes. If she had a fireplace, she would burn them. Instead, she would put them in a bag, then put the bag in a garbage bag, and put them in the bottom of the big green garbage can outside.

She peeled the clothes off of her like dead skin. When she got into the shower, the hot water felt so good, she started crying again. But she cried silently. She pressed her lips together until they were white and held back the sobs, still unable to believe what she had done that night, that she had taken a life.

But he had deserved it, she felt no differently about that.

The blood looked black in the bottom of the shower as it swirled around the drain and was sucked out of sight.

Afterward, she dried off with a towel and put the tank top and shorts on. She looked at the flip-flops—they would have to go, too, because they were coated with blood. She went to the kitchen barefoot and got a brown paper bag from under the sink, took it to the bathroom, and stuffed the clothes and flip-flops into it. She went into her bedroom. There was a stapler in the top drawer of her night stand. She got it, folded the top of the brown bag over, and stapled it closed. She replaced the

216

stapler, slipped into her slippers by the bed, and took the bag outside and put it in the big garbage can. Back inside, she went to the kitchen and took the mostly full white garbage bag from the can under the sink. She tied the bag closed, then went to the bathroom and got the garbage in there. She carried the bags out to the green garbage can outside and dropped them in on top of the brown bag containing her bloody clothes.

Back in the trailer, she got herself a beer. She stood by the open refrigerator, enjoying the chill from it, as she drank it.

It felt good to be so clean again. But she was still stained. It was a stain that would never go away. It was the stain of having slid a blade into a man's gut again and again. The stain of spilling his blood. The stain of ending his life, no matter what he had done to deserve it. She suspected that stain would never go away. Part of it was now knowing how it felt to stick a blade into a man. She could feel it now—the blade pressing the flesh, then piercing it, then sliding in deep, then being twisted. It was a feeling like no other, and it would be with her forever.

She thanked God for Marc Reznick.

But don't forget, Anna—you owe me, he'd said. *You owe me big-time after this. And one day, I will (that is word used above, anyway) collect.*

Anna wondered what he'd meant by that. How did he expect to collect? Did he expect her to give him money? What did she have that he would want? *Her?* Did he mean he would want to *sleep* with her? It was the only thing she could think of that he could be implying. She decided she would not be averse to such an arrangement. Marc was a handsome man, and if he wanted to sleep with her, she would not argue or complain. The more she thought about it, the more she decided that was probably what he meant.

"Mommy?"

Anna closed the refrigerator and went into the living room.

"What, honey?" she said.

"Mommy, my finger hurts." Kendra was sitting up on the couch and her face was tightly screwed up in a look of pain. She held her left wrist with her right hand. "It's throbbin' real bad and making my whole hand hurt."

"Well, it's been awhile since you've had a couple pills. Let's get you a couple more, okay?"

"Okay."

The orange bottle was on the kitchen table. Anna went to it and shook out a couple pills. Then she put them in her pocket and went to the counter. She took a slice of bread from the loaf, put it in the toaster, and pressed the lever on the side.

"I'm gonna make you a piece of toast to eat with the pills so you don't get sick, okay, hon?"

"'Kay," Kendra said. There was pain in her voice.

Anna poured milk into a glass and took it and the pills to Anna. "Here you go, sweetheart."

As Kendra took the pills, Anna watched her and wondered. How did she bring it up with Kendra? How did she approach it? She had posed for those pictures—but how? Why? Surely she had not done it because she *wanted* to. Then again, maybe she really didn't know any better. Maybe she didn't think there was anything wrong with it.

Anna remembered all the times her sister Rose had lectured her about having The Talk with Kendra. Maybe if Anna *had* talked with her about the birds and the bees, she never would have posed for those pictures. Anna could not hold Kendra responsible for them, no matter what.

However Anna chose to broach the subject, she could not do it tonight. Her emotions were too close to the surface. She had just *killed* the man, for God's sake. It would have to wait. Maybe tomorrow night, or the next night, she could talk to

Kendra about it without flying apart in a million pieces like a plane slamming into the side of a mountain.

The toast popped up and Anna returned to the kitchen with the empty glass. "Would you like some jam on your toast, or just butter?" she said.

"Jam's good," Kendra said. "Do we have raspberry?"

"We sure do, honey. Comin' right up."

Anna got raspberry jam from the refrigerator and spread a generous helping on the toast, then put it on a small plate, and took it to Kendra in the living room. She was still watching the Game Show Network. *Match Game* was on. Anna sat down beside her and watched her eat the toast. She reached over and ran a hand through Kendra's long, shiny hair.

Kendra was almost done with her toast when she said, "How come you're starin' at me, Mommy?"

"I'm sorry, was I staring?"

Kendra smiled gently, as much as her pain would allow.

"I guess I'm just thinking about how much I love you," Anna said, her voice breaking. "You know, sweetheart … there's nothing I wouldn't do for you. Nothing."

"Me, too, Mommy. I mean, there's nothin' I wouldn't do for you, neither."

"Either."

"Either."

"How's your toast?"

"It's good."

Kendra finished the toast and handed the little plate to Anna.

Unexpectedly, even to Anna, she flung her arms around Kendra and held her tightly. Anna's eyes stung with tears and her throat felt thick. She kissed Kendra on the forehead, then stood and quickly turned and went back to the kitchen with the plate, before Kendra could see the tears in her eyes.

His hair still wet from the shower, Reznick stared at the pictures on his computer screen. He enlarged them one at a time and looked at them, studied them, absorbed them.

It was, indeed, Kendra. She did not appear to be under duress. Her smile seemed genuine, and her eyes sparkled. The sight of her naked body made his heartbeat quicken, made him harden. She was everything he'd expected and more. Her large breasts were firm and unblemished, with rosy, puffy nipples he could imagine touching with his tongue, tasting, sucking on.

Seeing her naked on the computer monitor only frustrated him more. He wanted her naked in front of him where he could touch her, hold her, kiss her.

And he would. He'd told Anna she owed him big-time, and that he would collect. Kendra would be his payment. Anna might never know about it, but if she found out, Reznick would not worry about it. He would not feel guilty as he would have before. Now, Anna was in debt to him in a big way, and if she didn't like it, a single anonymous phone call would send the cops in her direction.(hmm… not sure an experienced PI would think this way… he would know that if he called police, he could be arrested as well from the evidence they would discover)

He looked at the pictures over and over again. The last one was of Kendra's laughing face spattered with semen. She seemed to be enjoying herself. That was good to know—that she enjoyed that. That meant she would enjoy it even more because, after all, she had a crush on him.

Reznick did not plan to wait around, either. He planned to go to work late the next day, if at all. He planned to drop in on Kendra in the morning.

He would be gentle and loving. Much more than that cretin with the website, he was sure.

That night, Reznick did not sleep well. It was not the heat that kept him awake. It was thoughts of Kendra, of those pictures, and of what he would do the following day.

Twenty-Two

"How about some scrambled eggs, Andy?" Sherry said.

"Yeah, that sounds good," he said as he sat up in bed. He stretched his arms overhead as he opened his mouth in a big yawn.

Sherry slid her legs off the bed and sat up on the edge. She was naked and had slept without a single cover on. They'd gotten to bed late last night. People kept coming to the door. When Andy had pot to sell, they got a lot of visitors, customers coming to buy weed. Sometimes they stayed and chatted awhile if it was someone they knew, but the strangers only stayed long enough to buy the stuff. They'd come late into the night last night, once word had gotten out that Andy had some weed to sell.

"Hey," Andy said. He grabbed her upper right arm and pulled her back down on the bed. "I ever tell you how nice it is to wake up to your naked body?"

She smiled tiredly as Andy squeezed a breast, then put his mouth over the nipple and gently gnawed on it.

"Mmm," Sherry said, closing her eyes. "You want breakfast, or you wanna fool around? Tell you the truth, it's too hot to fool around. Too hot *already*. Jeez, I hate summers in Shasta County. Why don't we move to Oregon, or Washington, or somethin'?"

"You wanna move to Oregon or Washington? Maybe we will."

"Really?"

"Well, it's not impossible. I got a couple friends in Oregon and one in Seattle. We oughtta think about it, if you want. They like it real good there, my friends do."

"Really?" she said again.

"We oughtta think about it."

"Yeah, we oughtta."

"I'm hungry."

"I'll get breakfast goin'."

"I'm gonna fire up the lab later this evening," he said, "so get out the fans and open all the windows."

"Oh, shit. I hate that smell."

"It pays the bills."

"Yeah. Maybe I'll call Lissa. Maybe we'll go to a movie, or somethin'."

"That'd be good. Get outta the trailer."

Sherry got out of bed, put on a T-shirt and some shorts, and left the bedroom.

In the kitchen, she turned on the radio on the table, then opened the refrigerator. The icy chill felt good on her.

The radio was tuned to an album rock station, but the news was on. It didn't catch her attention until she heard the name.

"… Arnold Garvis, who was found dead early this morning in his Washington, D.C. apartment, the apparent victim of accidental carbon monoxide poisoning. His father, Senator Wilson Garvis, has retreated to his Louisiana home where he and his family are in mourning. Arnold Garvis was twenty-two years old. In the Supreme Court today, there will be …"

But Sherry had already tuned out. "Andy! Did you hear that?"

"Hear what?" he said as he came down the hall.

"On the news just now."

"No."

"It just said Arnold Garvis was found dead in his Washington, D.C. apartment early this morning, dead from accidental carbon monoxide poisoning. Can you believe that? *Carbon monoxide!*"

"Well, David said they'd come up with some other reason for his death. Sounds like they did."

"But what about us?" Sherry said with wide eyes.

"What *about* us?"

"*We* know he didn't die of carbon monoxide poisoning. How can they let us live?"

"Are you gonna start on that again?"

"I'm *sorry*, Andy, if you don't agree, but I happen to have a very bad feeling about this."

"You and your bad feelings. Am I gonna have to fix breakfast myself, or what?"

"No, I'll fix it, I'll fix it," she said with irritation, frustrated that he didn't care.

Sherry remembered the two men who had come to take Arnie away, the promise they had made to cause trouble for them if they didn't let them in to get Arnie. If they *really* wanted the world to believe that Arnold Garvis died of accidental carbon monoxide poisoning, why would they allow Sherry and Andy and Rob and Philpott and Lissa and David to live if they knew otherwise? It did not seem logical to Sherry. Why couldn't Andy see that? Why wasn't he *worried*?

Sherry was worried. Very worried. And she couldn't shake it.

She started breakfast and tried to push the bothersome thoughts from her mind.

———————

"I want you to go over to Aunt Rose's today," Anna said.

"No! I don't want to!"

"Please, Kendra?"

"No. I promise, I won't even go get the mail. I just want to stay here and watch TV. I don't feel good. My finger throbs."

Anna sighed. "You promise? You'll stay in the trailer?"

"I promise. It's already hot. It's gonna be too hot to go outside." Kendra wondered if that qualified as a white lie. What difference did it make if she went outside or not while Mommy was gone? It wouldn't hurt Mommy if she never knew about it, would it? It qualified as a white lie as far as Kendra was concerned.

"Well … okay. If you promise."

"I *promise*."

"Before I leave, I'm going to go get Marc's phone number so you can call him if you need anything, okay?"

"'Kay."

"How's your finger feel now?"

"It's throbbing."

"You can take a couple pills with your breakfast."

———————

Reznick was pouring a cup of coffee when someone knocked on his door. He took his coffee with him to the door and pulled it open. Anna stood outside. She smiled up at him.

"Hi, Marc."

"Hi." He pushed open the screen door and came down the steps. "What's up?"

"I'm leaving Kendra home alone again today. I was wondering if I could get your cell phone number, just in case she needs something. Would you mind if she called you?"

"Not at all. I don't think I'm going in to work today, so I'll be around."

"Oh, good. Thank you." She held a yellow Post It pad in one hand and a pen in the other. Reznick gave her his cell phone number and she wrote it down.

Reznick bowed his head and looked around. The blood stains were everywhere. Speckles of it lead to his trailer, then across the way to another trailer, then diagonally to another. It was all over the pavement and concrete.

"I'll see you later, then," Anna said.

"Yeah, see ya."

As Anna walked away, Reznick wondered how long it would take for someone to notice the bloodstains on the concrete and pavement, how long it would take for the police to get involved.

Anna walked slowly on her way back to the trailer, looking at the trails of spattered blood all over the cracked pavement of the road. It zigzagged here and there, and it had all come off of her as she'd walked away from the man she'd murdered.

The man she'd murdered.

When she'd awakened that morning, it had felt like a nightmare she'd had the night before. A horrible nightmare that clung to the backs of her eyelids in startlingly vivid images. Then, when she remembered it had not been a nightmare, when it all had come flooding back into her mind, the whole bloody, gory thing, she'd gotten out of bed and hurried to the bathroom, where she'd closed and locked the door, knelt at the toilet, and vomited, trembling, her head throbbing. It had gone on for a while, mostly dry heaves, as if her body were trying to expel her guilt. When she was finished, she'd washed her face and brushed her teeth, then stared at herself in the mirror.

She did not have time to worry about it. She had to go about her day. She had to go to work. She could not worry about how she was going to talk to Kendra about those pictures on the Internet, not now. She had to go to work. She couldn't call in sick or anything, not now, not with this new job. She had to be there, and on time.

Anna walked back to her trailer and went inside.

———————

While the coffee maker made coffee, Muriel Snodgrass opened her front door and stepped outside on the porch. It was going to be another scorcher. In her left hand, she held a letter to her sister in Bend, Oregon, sealed in a stamped envelope, and in her right, a cigarette, which she put in the corner of her mouth. It dangled there, sending up tendrils of smoke as she went down the front steps.

Her sister Alice had never gotten a computer. She was the only person Muriel knew who was not yet online. Muriel kept in touch with all her other relatives and friends by e-mail, but not with Alice. She had to stay in touch with Alice the old-fashioned way—with a letter in an addressed envelope with a stamp on it.

Muriel wore a sleeveless lime-green blouse, a pair of stretchy black shorts, and pale-blue mules on her feet. A sliver of her pale, hanging belly peeked out from beneath the bottom of the blouse. She started on her way to the mailboxes to post the letter to Alice. Her slippers shuffled over the cracked, broken pavement as she walked.

The cigarette dangled from the corner of her mouth and she puffed on it now and then, exhaling smoke through her nose. She had not yet put her teeth in, so her lips stuck out like a small bill.

Miss Dunfy's car backed out of unit eight, and pulled up beside her. Miss Dunfy rolled down her window.

"Hello, Mrs. Snodgrass," Anna Dunfy said.

"Hi, there."

"Look, Kendra's going to be home alone again today. She cut her finger really bad yesterday."

"Oh, I'm sorry to hear it," Muriel said, the cigarette bobbing in her mouth.

"Yeah, Mr. Reznick in space nine took her to the hospital and she had to have five stitches. She bled all over the place. Anyway, she's on painkillers, so she's not feeling so well. If you could keep an eye out for her today, I'd sure appreciate it."

"Be happy to, honey, you know me. I might even pop in on her today, see how she's doin'." A long ash fell from the cigarette.

"Thank you so much."

"You got a job?"

"Yeah, one of the temp jobs has turned into something a little more permanent. For a while, anyway."

"Well, good for you, honey. You have a good day."

"Bye-bye."

"Oh, wait," Muriel said. "You wanna do me a big favor?"

"Sure, what?"

Muriel held out the letter. "You wanna stick this in my mailbox and put the flag up for me on your way out? I'd sure appreciate it."

"Sure, no problem."

"Thanks a lot, hon. See ya later."

Anna drove away.

Muriel turned around to head back to the house when something caught her eye, something on the ground. She stopped walking and squinted down at the ground. Something dark was spattered over the broken pavement, a trail of it. It went this way and that, over there, over here. She couldn't get a good look at it—she'd left her glasses back at the house, and whatever it was, it was blurry. But it looked like …

"'Zat blood?" Muriel muttered.

She remembered Anna saying Kendra had cut her finger badly the day before.

She bled all over the place.

That must have been it. The poor girl had staggered and stumbled all over the place on her way to the trailer just next door. Probably the squeamish type, messed up by the sight of blood, especially her own.

Muriel's cigarette had developed another long ash, and there wasn't much left to it. She plucked it from her mouth and dropped it to the ground, stamped it out with her slipper. Then she went inside to get a cup of coffee and start breakfast.

———————

The day was scorching hot. By ten o'clock, the temperature was a hundred and five degrees. The trees above the Riverside Mobile Home Park, dry and rustling in the hot breeze, were filled with birds—their chirping and screeching clashed in a shrill cacophony that did not pause.

Shortly after ten, Reznick took Conan and left the trailer. The little dog followed him over to the Dunfy trailer next door. At the screen, Reznick knocked and looked inside and said, "Hello?"

"Hi," Kendra said. She came to the door and opened the screen for him. "C'mon in."

Reznick went up the steps and Conan followed him.

"I thought maybe Conan and Dexter would like to see each other this morning," he said. "I hope it's all right that I brought him over."

"Oh, sure, I like Conan. Hey, Conan, you cutie." She bent down and petted him.

"How's the finger?"

"Not bad right now," she said.

She wore a plain white cotton T-shirt and yet another pair of short denim cutoffs, this one with a yellow daisy sewn onto the back pocket. The T-shirt's material was thin and Reznick could see the faintest hint of her rosy nipples beneath it.

"You want somethin' to drink?" she said. "Mommy's got beer, or there's Pepsi."

"A Pepsi sounds good."

Kendra went to the refrigerator, got a Pepsi, and brought the can back to him. "C'mon in and sit down."

They both sat down on the couch.

"I was watchin' *The Joker's Wild*," she said. "You like game shows? I *love* game shows."

"Yeah, game shows are fun."

Kendra stretched out on the couch and put her bare feet in Reznick's lap. He looked down at them—the small, perfect toes with their red-painted nails, the paint chipping in places. He let his eyes move slowly up her long legs. He followed his eyes with one hand, running it up her leg, feeling the smooth skin, the lump of her knee, the firmness of her thigh. Then he looked at her.

She was smiling at him. She liked it.

He smiled back and said, "What have you been up to today, Kendra?"

She shrugged. "Just watchin' TV."

He nodded. "And … what have you been up to … *lately*?"

Another shrug. "Just layin' around since I cut my finger. The pills make me sleepy, but they also make me feel real good. I mean, they make me feel all floaty, like. I never felt nothing like that before."

"Yeah, codeine'll do that to you. No, I meant the last few days. I was wondering what you've been up to. If maybe you've been ... say ... posing for some pictures?"

The smile dropped off Kendra's face and her beautiful blue eyes popped open wide, lips parted, head tilted back just a little. She stayed that way for a long moment, frozen in place.

Reznick smiled. "I've seen your pictures online, Kendra."

"You ... have?"

"TrailerParkGirls.com. See, my work sorta brought me into contact with the man in unit five. What's his name again?"

"Steven. Steven Regent."

"Yeah, he's the one. Steven Regent. I needed to look up his websites for a case I was working on, and I saw your pictures on TrailerParkGirls.com."

For a moment, Kendra looked as if she were about to cry.

"They're beautiful pictures, Kendra," he said, almost whispering. "You're a beautiful young woman."

One corner of her mouth curled up into a half-smile. "Re ... really?"

"Looking at your pictures ... it excited me."

"It ... did?"

"Oh, yes. It made me *very* excited."

His hand was still on her thigh, moving back and forth slightly, and the sensation of their skin rubbing together made him hard. With his right hand, he pressed her ankle down against his erection.

The other corner of her mouth curled up, too. Her cheeks became rosy, but that didn't last.

"Do you like me, Mr. Reznick?" she said, tilting her head to one side.

"Kendra, you're one of the most beautiful women I've ever seen in my life," he said. "And I've wanted you since the first time I saw you on the roof of this trailer."

"You've ... *wanted* me?" she said, her eyebrows rising curiously.

"Yes. Wanted you. I've wanted to touch you, kiss you. I've wanted to make love to you."

Her breath caught in her chest and she held it for several seconds, then started breathing again, her eyes wide.

Reznick leaned over to his left and put a hand behind her neck. He pulled her to him and pressed his lips to hers. He gently pried her lips open with the tip of his tongue. When she exhaled against his face, it was with a high, tremulous sigh.

Reznick put his right hand on her breast and gently squeezed. Then he slipped his hand beneath her T-shirt and found the breast again, bare this time. His fingers passed over the hard nipple. He rolled it between thumb and forefinger and she made a small whimpering sound.

Reznick said, "Why don't we go over to my place and use the bed?"

"The ... bed?" she said.

"I'd be more comfortable. We can take the dogs with us."

She smiled. "Okay." Her smile faltered a little, and she asked, "What're we gonna do in your bed?"

He grinned. "Whatever we want to."

Reznick held the screen door open for her and she went up the steps. The little dogs followed her, their tiny claws clicking on the steps. Reznick followed them all into the trailer and pulled the screen door closed, then closed the door and locked it.

"Do you have any wine?" Kendra asked.

"No, I'm sorry. I don't have any alcohol."

"Oh. Okay."

"Would you like something else? I've got Diet Dr. Pepper."

"That sounds good," she said.

He went to the refrigerator and got her one, popped it open before handing it to her. She took several gulps, then released a long, satisfied sigh.

Reznick took her right hand and led her down the hall. The bedroom was dark. He sat on the edge of the bed with Kendra standing in front of him. He looked her up and down and realized his hands were trembling. He took the Dr. Pepper from her and put it on the night stand.

"Arms up," he said quietly.

She lifted her arms, and he pulled the T-shirt off over her head. He tossed the shirt onto the foot of the bed and stared at her, his lips parted, his eyes wider than he realized.

Her breasts were great round cushions in taut, smooth skin, topped with rosy nipples. He cupped them in his hands and lifted them up. He pressed his face between them and inhaled Kendra's scent.

"You like them?" she said, smiling. A little giggle escaped her.

"They're incredible," he said, pulling his head back and looking up at her face.

She dropped the shorts. She was wearing nothing underneath them. She kicked off the flip-flops and stepped out of the crumpled shorts. She stood before him naked and radiant. She moved around him and crawled onto the bed.

Reznick stood and quickly removed his clothes. He opened the top drawer of his night stand and removed a box of condoms, took one out, put the box back, and closed the drawer. The *last* thing he needed was a pregnant retarded girl on his hands. He tore the wrapper with his teeth, took out the condom. He set the wrapper on the night stand and put the condom on the wrapper where it would be ready and waiting for him. He turned to Kendra.

"You're hard," she said.

"Yes, I am. You do that to men, Kendra. You always will. You should get used to it."

"Can I touch it?"

"You don't even have to ask."

She wrapped her fingers around it and slowly moved her hand up and down. Reznick moaned quietly.

She put her mouth on him and he gasped. He only got harder and more excited. He clawed at the bottom sheet as her head and fist moved up and down on him.

"Oh," he said, "oh, oh, oh."

He did not want to come, so he reached down and closed his hand on her upper arm, made her stop, then tugged on her to come up with him. She moved up to join him and they kissed again, her right hand on his chest. She bent her right knee and moved her leg across his, pressed his erection down with her thigh. Her skin was soft as summer clouds as it moved over his.

Reznick reached down and found her center, ran his fingers through the downy curly hair, slipped his fingers between the moist lips and moved them, manipulated her.

Kendra pulled her face away from his and gasped.

He found her clitoris and she cried out, her mouth hanging open, eyes closed.

"You like that?" he whispered.

All she could do was nod jerkily.

He pulled away from her and moved down her body, then nestled his face between her legs. He reached up and massaged her breasts as he licked her.

Kendra's body wriggled as she moaned and cried out. She was feeling sensations she had never felt before, and it was getting the best of her. She cried out so loudly at one point, she frightened him. She kicked her legs, squeezed them together on his head for a moment, then spread them as wide as they would go. He worked his tongue on her as he pinched her nipples.

Kendra started crying. Not just crying out, but crying real tears.

Thinking he was hurting her, Reznick sat up and said, "Are you okay?"

"Don't! Stop!" she gasped.

He went back to it, smiling now.

After awhile, he crawled up her body, stopping to nibble and lick and kiss her here and there, finally stopping to kiss her on the mouth. Her eyes were puffy and wet. Reznick reached over to the night stand and got the condom.

"What's that?" Kendra asked, her voice breathy.

"It's called a condom. I put it on my penis and it keeps you from getting pregnant."

"Oh. Can I put it on?"

He smiled. "Sure." He rolled over onto his back and his penis jutted into the air.

Kendra crawled down to his penis and he handed her the condom.

"Do you know how to do it?" he said.

She frowned as she inspected the condom, then her face softened as she inspected his erect penis. She put the condom on the tip of his penis.

"It's upside-down," he said. "Turn it over."

She did.

"There you go. Now just unroll it down my penis."

And she did.

"And it's on and ready to go," he said.

"And now can we do it?" she said.

"Now we can do it." Reznick grinned as he took her in his arms and rolled over on top of her.

"Careful of my finger," she said.

"Okay."

She spread her legs and wrapped them around his waist and he slipped inside her with a gentle, tremulous sigh.

Twenty-Three

As morning turned into afternoon, the hot breeze that murmured through the trees overhead picked up and became a blistering wind. The dry, rustling trees crackled and shushed as the wind whipped them back and forth. Blossoms blew from the silk trees and fluttered through the air like a pink snow, skidded over the ground, bounced and spun. By noon, the temperature was one hundred and eight, and by two it had gone up another four degrees to one hundred and twelve.

The temperature reported on the radio and television and in the paper was always five or six degrees lower when it was that hot so as not to scare off tourists. The official temperature came from a thermometer at the airport, suspended over a cool, well-watered lawn in the shade, and it was deceptive.

All the swamp coolers in the Riverside Mobile Home Park hummed and rattled and dripped. Fans whirred and some swept slowly back and forth.

In unit nine, there was a lot of laughter.

Reznick and Kendra lay on the bed together, naked and with no covers on. They had been going at it all day.

He scooted down on the bed and rolled over on top of her. He put his face between her breasts, squeezed them together on his head, and said, "Now I can die happy."

Kendra giggled.

He pressed his mouth to her rib cage and blew hard, making a loud farting sound, and she burst into raucous laughter, saying, "That *tickles!*"

He propped himself up on his elbow and kissed her. They'd kissed so much that day, his lips were numb.

"*You* tickle *me*," he said.

"I want some more screwdriver," she said, handing over her glass.

"Sure."

Reznick took the glass, then sat up on the edge of the bed. The pitcher was on the night stand, next to a bowl of melting ice. He put some ice in the glass, then poured the mixture of orange juice and vodka into the glass. The ice cubes cracked and popped as he handed it back to her.

The mixture was mild, but it was working.

That morning, Kendra had said, "I want some wine. Steven gave me wine."

"Oh, he did, did he?" Reznick had said.

"Yeah. I liked it. It made me feel … goofy."

"Well, I'm sorry, but I don't have any wine."

"Can't we go get some? We could go to Handi-Spot, couldn't we? Just up North Street? Sometimes Mommy goes to Handi-Spot for cigarettes and beer."

Reznick had thought about it. He'd never had much taste for wine. Vodka had always been his drink.

"Ever had a screwdriver?" he'd said.

"No. What's that?"

"It's orange juice and vodka, and if you think the wine made you feel goofy, you should try *that*."

"Okay, let's go get some orange juice and vodka and make some screwdriver!" she said.

"You're feeling adventurous, huh?"

"Yes, adventure … ous."

A year of sobriety down the drain, Reznick had thought then. But when he looked at the naked girl lying in bed beside him, as he moved his eyes slowly up and down her pale, milky, voluptuous body, he was overcome with a desire to celebrate. He'd decided then that he would make the screwdrivers mild. He wouldn't overdo it, for his own sake and hers.

They had dressed and gone to the Handi-Spot Market in Reznick's car. In the store, he'd told her to go find herself an ice cream bar while he got the liquor. On the way home, she'd reached over and squeezed his crotch as he drove.

"Has anybody ever sucked on you while you drove your car?" she said. She took a bite out of the ice cream bar, licked ice cream from her lips.

"Yes, and it nearly got us killed, so thank you, but no thank you."

Kendra *was* adventurous. She'd been insatiable in bed, wanting to try everything. She had exhausted him, but at the same time invigorated him, so he was able to keep going back for more and more.

Now they sat up in bed with their backs to the headboard, and Kendra held up her glass in a toast.

"To, uh … to …" Her face brightened. "To *fucking*!"

"All right. To fucking."

They clinked their glasses together, then took a drink.

"This is the last, though," Reznick said. "You need to take a shower and sober up before your mommy comes home from work."

"Don't worry, I'll eat some peanut butter to hide the smell."

His eyebrows popped up. "How'd you know about peanut butter? That's an old alcoholic's trick."

"Steven told me about it."

"Oh. Good old Steven." Reznick remembered the sensation of stuffing the weights into Steven Regent's abdomen and tried to eject the memory immediately. It did not eject so easily, though. It was not what he wanted to think about right now. It made him frown, darkened his mood. He swung his legs off the bed and stood. "I'm gonna go check on the dogs. They might want to go outside."

He stepped into his shorts and pulled them up, then went down the hall to the living room. The dogs were napping side by side on the couch.

"How you guys doing, huh?"

They lifted their heads.

"Outside? You wanna go outside?" He opened the door, then the screen. "Huh? You wanna go outside?"

They stared at him sleepily, then put their heads down again, uninterested.

"Okay, suit yourselves." He closed the doors, then went to the kitchen, filled a glass with water, and drank it.

He thought of all the noises of opening up Steven Regent and stuffing his abdomen with weights.

The damp whisper of cutting him open.

Reznick turned on the faucet again.

The wet smacking sounds.

He filled his palms with water.

The farting sounds.

He bent down and splashed the water on his face and scrubbed his hands up and down a few times.

He closed his eyes and saw the body lying before him in the beam of the flashlight that Anna held. It had been opened up,

240

its dark guts glistening, milky eyes staring, mouth yawning open.

Reznick put both wet hands on the edge of the counter and leaned forward, let his head dip low between his shoulders. He felt nauseated. Part of it was the booze. It had been awhile since he'd had any. Yeah, that must be part of it.

But part of it was also those images on the backs of his eyelids, the memory of what he'd done the night before.

His temples began to throb. An ache developed behind his eyes. He frowned as he rubbed his eyes with his knuckles, then rubbed hard circles on his temples with his fingertips.

"Marc?" Kendra called. "Where'd you go?"

Suddenly, he did not want to go back to the bedroom. He'd had his fill for now. He felt far away from amorous. A shadow had fallen over him, a deep, dark shadow that had obliterated his desire.

He sighed and went down the hall to the bedroom.

"Time for you to go home, Kendra," he said.

"Aw, c'mon, not already," she said. Her whiny voice made her sound like a little girl, and it rubbed him the wrong way.

"No arguing. You need to get cleaned up and sober for when Mommy comes home. Eat some peanut butter, make sure your breath's clean."

"She might go dancing tonight. Can we get together then?"

"Maybe. But for now, you need to go home."

She sighed as she got out of bed slowly. She came around the bed and pressed her body against his. "You sure?"

He put his hands on her shoulders and gently pushed her away. "Positive," he said. "Get your clothes on."

"But I thought we were—"

"*Get your clothes on,*" he shouted.

Kendra flinched and her smile shattered and she stumbled backward.

Reznick immediately regretted snapping at her. He stepped over to her and put his hands on her shoulders again. "I'm sorry," he said. "I've got a bad headache. I didn't mean to bark at you like that. Get dressed and go home, and we can get together tonight while your mommy's working. Okay?" He tipped forward and kissed her forehead.

Her smile slowly returned. "Okay," she said. "I ... I had fun today."

"So did I. You're a beautiful, incredible girl, Kendra."

She smiled and bowed her head in embarrassment. "I'll get dressed now," she said in a whisper. "Hey," she said as she dressed, "you wanna coupla my pain pills for your headache?"

Reznick nodded. "Yeah, I'll take you up on that."

Kendra carried Dexter home and Reznick followed her. He got a couple codeine pills from her, then went back to his own trailer. He drank them down with a glass of water, then went to the recliner and stretched out, turned on the TV.

He frowned the whole time. His lips were pressed together tightly. He couldn't get those images and sounds out of his mind. All the blood. The smell of the blood. The reek of fecal matter. Those milky, staring eyes and that yawning mouth—as if it were trying to scream one last time but had no voice, no breath.

Reznick got up and paced for a while.

He went to the refrigerator, took out a cup of blueberry-flavored yogurt, and ate it. He tossed the cup into the garbage, washed the spoon, then paced for a while.

Outside, the wind continued to blow. Even as preoccupied as he was, he could hear the trees whooshing in the wind overhead outside.

Conan went to the screen and walked in lazy circles, then sat facing the door.

"Need to go outside, boy?" Reznick said. He opened the screen door and Conan shot out of the trailer.

He tried to leave the screen door open, but the wind slammed it around, so he closed it and listened for Conan's scratching as he continued to pace.

Open eyes ... open mouth ... open abdomen ... glistening black guts ... wet, farting sounds ...

Conan scratched at the screen door and yapped once.

Reznick let the dog in, then closed the screen door. He closed the door halfway, leaving it open to create a draft.

He went to the kitchen and found the bottle of vodka. He got a glass from the cupboard, some ice from the freezer, and poured some vodka over the crackling cubes. He put what was left of the vodka in the freezer. He took the glass to the living room and stretched out on the recliner again. He let the vodka stand on the lamp table for a while and chill.

He browsed the TV stations for something to watch and settled on an old movie with Clark Gable and Spencer Tracy. He watched the movie for awhile, tried to immerse himself in it.

Finally, he took the glass from the lamp table and took a sip. Then a gulp.

"Aaahh," he sighed, looking at the glass with its beads of sweat dribbling down the sides. "It's good to have you back."

Twenty-Four

The day had been hell for Anna.

It had been next to impossible for her to think straight all day. She could not get her mind off the previous night. The events of the night haunted her, at times scorched the inside of her skull with their screams.

You're a murderer, she thought again and again. Sometimes it was a nagging whisper, and sometimes it was a thunderous bellow that deafened her for a moment.

All day she had felt like someone with attention deficit disorder. But she did her best to hide it, and she was pretty sure, as she drove home, that she'd pulled it off.

At the wheel of her car, her hand relived the sensation of stabbing Steven Regent. Her ears heard the blade going in again and again.

She jerked her head back and forth, shook her thoughts up.

Anna stopped at the trailer park's entrance to see if Kendra had gotten the mail. She had not, just as she'd promised. Anna got the mail—junk and bills—got back in the car, and drove to her trailer.

Inside, she found Kendra asleep on the couch with a game show running on TV. Anna decided not to wake her. The codeine pills made her very sleepy. It seemed the cut—which had been quite severe—had taken a lot out of her, as well.

Anna changed into shorts and a T-shirt, then got a beer from the fridge, sat down at the kitchen table, and lit a cigarette. She closed her eyes and went through it again. Her right elbow rested on the table, her hand up, the cigarette between her first two fingers. The cigarette trembled there in her shaking hand as it all happened again in Anna's mind. The string of smoke that rose from the cigarette jittered in a zigzag pattern as her hand shook.

She realized how much she owed Marc Reznick. She would be in a huge mess without him—and he could be in a huge mess because of her. But throughout the day, it had begun to dawn on her that Reznick now had a terrific amount of power over her. She realized that, if he wanted to, he could destroy her with an anonymous tip to the police. So far as Anna knew, no one even *suspected* that Steven Regent was dead yet. But there was a bloody, gory mess in his trailer, and if he wanted to, Reznick could point the police straight to it. But why would he? He might be getting himself into some pretty deep shit, too. Unless he simply denied it. He'd covered his own ass pretty well all along. He was a detective, he knew how to do that. She only hoped he never decided to take advantage of his position over her.

She was hungry, but she didn't feel like cooking. It was too hot to cook. She grabbed her purse and went out to her car. She drove down to KFC and got dinner for her and Kendra.

The wind made traffic lights bob and sway. Trees and bushes bowed to its strength as Anna drove home. Her car was buffeted on the road by the hot, suffocating gusts.

Back in the trailer, she put her purchase on the counter.

Kendra stirred on the couch and slowly sat up, rubbing one eye with a knuckle.

"Hey, sweetheart," Anna said. "I just bought dinner. Kentucky Fried Chicken sound good?"

"Yeah. How was work, Mommy?"

"It was good. How was *your* day?"

"Okay. I slept a lot. My finger hurt real bad, so I took the pills, and they make me sleepy."

"I know they do. How's your finger?"

"It hurts again."

"Well, let's eat and maybe you'll feel a little better. Have you eaten today?"

"I had a peanut butter sammich."

Anna took the two dinners out of their bags and removed the plastic covers, then put them on the table. "Dinner is served."

Kendra got up and shuffled to the table. "You gonna dance tonight?"

"Oh, yeah, I have to after missing two nights."

"You're gonna let me stay here, aren't ya?" Kendra said. "I mean, I didn't even go get the mail today, and I've—"

"I noticed that, and I appreciate it. Yes, I'll let you stay here tonight."

"Thank you, Mommy."

They ate without speaking for a while, but not in silence. The wind battered the trailer and branches creaked overhead.

"Did Marc come over today?" Anna said.

"Uh, Marc? Yeah. Marc came over today. He brought Conan to see Dexter. They, uh, they went, uh, outside together."

"Something the matter?"

"No. Why?"

"I don't know, you just don't seem ... too sure of yourself all of a sudden."

246

"I-I'm sure of myself. Whatta you mean?" Kendra frowned a little.

"Well, don't get upset."

Kendra relaxed a little. Her frown receded. "I'm relaxed, I'm not upset."

Anna smiled. It was that crush again. Kendra got ruffled every time Marc came up in the conversation.

Suddenly she flashed on the photograph of Kendra smiling with Steven Regent's cock in her mouth. She took a deep breath.

"Kendra," she said hesitantly.

"What?"

"We ... we need to talk."

The blade sliding into his gut ... twisting in his insides ...

"About what?" Kendra said.

Anna put her elbows on the table and joined her hands under her chin.

... all that blood ... on her hands and arms ... on her face and in her hair ... splattering everywhere as she stabbed him ... and stabbed him ... and stabbed him ...

"Mommy? You don't look so good all of a sudden."

Anna didn't feel so good.

"Excuse me," she said as she left the table. She went into the bathroom, closed the door, got down on her knees at the toilet, and vomited.

Reznick sat up straight in the recliner with a sharp cry, his fingers digging into the vinyl upholstery of the armrests, his body drenched in sweat. His T-shirt clung to him and his shorts were so wet, they felt soiled.

He lifted his hands, palms up, and inspected them. They were not wearing blood-soaked work gloves.

It took him several seconds to realize that he'd been sleeping and having a nightmare.

He reached for the glass of vodka on the lamp table, but it was empty except for a little water left over in the bottom from melted ice cubes.

Reznick straightened up the recliner and stood, went to the kitchen for more vodka. But the bottle stood on the counter, empty. He narrowed his eyes as he looked at the bottle, trying to remember finishing it off. He could not.

He put the empty glass on the counter, grabbed his keys and wallet off the table, and left the trailer. He got in his car and drove down to the Handi-Spot market again, where he took a bottle off the shelf. Then he grabbed a second bottle. He thought about it a moment. He put both bottles back on the shelf and instead chose a liter of vodka.

He'd lost that feeling he'd had earlier, that wonderful buoyant feeling, that mind-numbing sensation that liquor bestowed. He wanted it back.

Reznick paid for his purchase and left the store.

A banner advertising Coca-Cola was stretched overhead in the parking lot and it snapped and fluttered in the scorching wind. The wind engulfed him like the fiery breath of a dragon. He got in the car and drove back to the trailer park, his mouth watering for another drink.

———————

Sherry and Lissa shared a joint at the bar. Sherry already felt good, having just had Lissa give her a fix from her kit. She was trying to stretch them out, though. She didn't *want* to be a junky. She was going to fight it, to wean herself off it. Her most recent dose had been a smaller one. The pot helped.

"You heard the news, didn't you?" Sherry said. "The news about Arnie Garvis?"

"No, what news?"

Sherry told her what she'd heard on the radio that morning.

Lissa's eyes widened a little. "No shit? Then David was right. They really *did* fake a death."

"Yep. And now I'm scared shitless. Andy says I'm just paranoid, but I don't think so."

"About what? I don't know what you mean."

"About them coming back for *us*. We're the only ones who know how Arnie really died."

"Oh, yeah. But … well … if they were gonna kill us, don't you think they would've done it that night? When they came to get Arnie? That makes more sense to me."

"Yeah," Andy said as he came into the kitchen. "Now *that* makes sense. If they was gonna kill ya, they woulda done it that night. You think they give a shit about you? Nobody's gonna believe anything you say. They don't care about you. You don't worry them a bit. So will ya quit worryin' about it, for cryin' out loud?"

Andy went to the refrigerator and got a beer, popped it open, and drank.

"Well, I can't help it," Sherry said. "It worries me."

"I'm gonna get started with this," Andy said.

"Okay, Lissa, you ready to go?" She stood and turned to him. "We're goin' to the movies. We'll be back in a couple hours."

"I won't be done by then."

"Yeah, I know, but that's when we'll be back."

"Okay."

The wind whistled around the corners of the trailer like some kind of howling beast. The trailer shuddered against it.

"You don't mind if we take your car, do you?" Sherry said. "You got air conditioning, I don't."

Lissa said, "No, I don't mind. I'd prefer it."

Sherry went to Andy and gave him a warm kiss. "See you later. You be careful with that shit, okay?"

"Hey, I'm always careful," he said. "I can't make any money off that shit if I'm dead."

The girls got their purses, left the trailer, and went out into the suffocatingly hot, windy evening.

Josh Garner punched in Steven Regent's cell phone number for the twentieth time that day. Once again, he received Regent's recorded voice, asking him to leave a message.

Garner severed the connection and looked at his watch. He could not understand where Steven might have gone all day long.

He punched in the number of Steven's trailer. He got the answering machine.

"Jeez, Steven, where the hell are you?" he said. "I've been calling your cell phone all day. I've got this woman coming over, this MILF—she's incredible, Steven, you've got to see her. I met her in the bakery at WinCo, of all places. She's a knock-out, and she's open to anything. I was hoping to get you over here, but she's gonna show up any minute now, and you're nowhere to be found. Look, just give me a call when you get in, okay? And it doesn't matter how late it is. By now, I'm worried. Even if it's late and you wake me up, go ahead and call. Just let me know you're okay. Talk to you later."

He turned the phone off and put it on its base on the kitchen counter, frowning. He'd never known Steven to simply disappear for a day. He was completely devoted to his work and would never just drop it and vanish for a while.

Garner was worried. He could not shake the feeling that something was wrong.

He decided that as soon as the MILF left that night, he would drive over to Steven's trailer. He had a key.

With her costume in a garment bag slung over her shoulder, Anna looked at Kendra seated on the couch.

"Now, you gonna be okay tonight, sweetheart?" she said.

"Sure, Mommy." She petted Dexter, who was stretched out beside her, wagging his tail.

Kendra stood and hugged her.

Anna could not shake a feeling in her gut. It was a bad feeling, like something was not right.

It's just because you're a murderer now, she thought. *Now nothing will ever feel right again because you've got* that *hanging over your head, and you never know when it'll catch up with you, when it'll fall and* land *right* on *your head. And it'll be with you forever, for the rest of your life. You'll always be a murderer.*

Always.

A murderer.

"Mommy?"

"Hm? Yes? What?"

"You were … starin'."

"Oh. Sorry. I got preoccupied with something."

"Mommy … are you sure *you're* all right?"

Anna smiled. "Yes, honey, I'm fine. Don't wait up for me. I won't be home till after two, and I sure don't want you staying up that late."

"Okay. I'll go to bed."

Anna left the trailer. She lay the garment bag out in the back seat of her car, got in, and started the engine.

That feeling stayed with her, the feeling that something wasn't right, that something bad was going to happen. Or was it just guilt? She really couldn't tell. There were so many feelings all mixed up inside her—all of them bad. As she drove out of the trailer park, she did not know how much longer she could live with them.

———————————

Kendra waited. She was afraid to go over to Marc's trailer. He hadn't been in a very good mood when she'd left that afternoon, and she didn't know if that had changed or not. If his mood had not changed, she did not care to be with him. So she decided to wait for him. If he was in a *good* mood, then sooner or later, he would come to her, she decided. But if he was still in a bad mood, he probably wouldn't want to be with her, either. So she would leave it up to him.

Or was she going about it all wrong?

She had no idea, and her mind reeled with confusion.

In the end, she decided to wait for him.

———————————

Reznick listened to the wind as he finished another glass of vodka. He'd turned off the TV over an hour ago and put on an old Elton John CD. Something from what he liked to refer to as his misplaced youth. He stared at the empty glass with his lower lip stuck out, Mussolini-like. He thought of Kendra next door. He looked at the clock.

8:09.

She was alone by now. By now, Mommy had gone to work, where she would take off her clothes for all the lonely, horny men. And if she was like half the girls at the Mt. Shasta Gentlemen's Club, maybe she'd take a few extra bucks for a handjob out behind the building, or maybe a blowjob.

Reznick stood. He went to the bedroom, got a couple condoms and stuffed them into his pocket. He went to the kitchen and opened the freezer, took out the big bottle of vodka. He tucked it under his arm and took his keys from the table, put them in his pocket.

Conan was curled up by the recliner. He'd eaten recently and was napping. But when he heard the screen door open, he lifted his head and looked at Reznick.

"C'mon, Conan, you wanna go see your buddy?"

Conan stood, stretched and yawned, then followed Reznick out. He locked up the trailer.

The shadows were darker. The sun would be going down soon and it would be dark. It was already pretty dark under the ceiling of trees in the trailer park. The hot wind slapped him hard and sucked his breath away. On it wafted a strong odor that Reznick recognized immediately—someone was running a meth lab.

He stopped walking and turned, tried to figure out from which direction it was coming. But he could not tell. He only caught the smell now and then, caught it on the buffeting wind. He didn't like the idea of a meth lab in his trailer park. In fact, it pissed him off. But what the hell was he gonna do about it? There was no way the managers—those two drunk, fat, albino manatees—didn't know about it. If they didn't care, nothing was going to be done.

Reznick's sigh finished as a low growl as he headed for Kendra's door.

Twenty-Five

He didn't bother to knock. He opened the screen door and went in.

Kendra was seated on the couch watching TV.

The swamp cooler rattled annoyingly.

Reznick went to the kitchen and put his vodka in the freezer. He returned to the living room, went to Kendra, clutched her upper arms, and pulled her to her feet. He put a hand over her crotch and squeezed brutally as he held her head and gave her a hard, punishing kiss. She moaned into his mouth.

When he finally pulled back and let go of her, she whispered, "You didn't eat any peanut butter."

"I'm not worried about Mommy finding out I've been drinking."

He went back to the kitchen and searched the cupboards for glasses, found one. He got some ice, took out the bottle and poured. Returned the bottle and closed the freezer, then took a couple healthy swallows.

He went to the couch, put his drink on an end table—there were no coasters and from the ring stains, he saw that nobody cared—then kicked off his flip-flops. He fished a condom from his pocket and dropped his shorts, stepped out of them, and sat down. He slapped his thigh and said, "Take off your shorts and come sit on my lap."

Without hesitation, she did as she was told.

———————————

When Sherry and Lissa returned to the trailer, Sherry was glad to find that Andy had set up the fans that blew the terrible smell out the open windows. But even that didn't help much. The smell was awful.

"How can you stand it?" Lissa said.

"I can't. That's why I try to get out of the trailer when he does it. You wanna beer?"

"Yeah, but I don't think I'll stay long."

As Sherry got a beer, Andy came into the kitchen.

"Like the movie?" he said.

"The movie sucked," Sherry said. "But it was a Tom Cruise movie, and I don't like Tom Cruise, so I should've known better."

"I thought it was okay," Lissa said.

"Blech," Sherry said before taking a couple gulps of beer.

"God, it's windy out," Lissa said.

"And it's such a *hot* wind," Sherry said. "Like it's comin' right outta hell."

"That's good," Andy said. "It'll blow the smell of this lab around, maybe. Make it harder to pinpoint. Oh, by the way, while you were gone, two guys dressed in black came lookin' for ya."

Sherry gasped and put down her beer.

"Yeah, said they were from the Secret Service."

She stared at him a moment, then her eyes narrowed. "Andy, you cruel shit. Don't *do* that. It *scares* me."

Andy laughed. "You're so easy to scare," he said before turning around and leaving the kitchen, laughing.

––––––––––––

The wind knocked over a few of the big green garbage cans, the ones that were empty. Dry, brittle branches, especially from oak trees, were broken off by the powerful wind and dropped on top of trailers or in the middle of the road that looped through the trailer park.

The speckling of light that came through the swaying trees was in constant movement as it was gradually extinguished by the setting of the sun.

Sunset did not bring a respite from the heat.

Trailers shuddered and shook in the wind.

Inside the trailers, people were on edge.

In unit thirteen, Roderick Cramer and his wife Chrissy argued loudly as their baby wailed in its crib.

In unit two, Donna Huber slapped her eight-year-old several times, her hand flying back and forth, because she caught her getting into her makeup.

In the Snodgrass house, Hank shouted at Muriel, "Shut *up* woman, my God, can't you just shut the fuck up for five Goddamned *minutes*? My ears are *ringin'* from all your fuckin' *yappin'*! And you can't stay on one topic for more than thirty seconds. Just give it a fuckin' *rest* for God's sake!"

The wind clawed at tempers and made emotions bubble to the surface like blood from a cut.

The darker it got outside, the darker it got inside.

––––––––––––

Anna danced to an old Rod Stewart song with a strong beat. She was topless, and she danced to emphasize her breasts. She worked the pole for a while, then moved slowly across the stage, peeling off pieces of her costume. She made her way down the runway, where there were already a lot of dollar bills, and some fives.

The whole time, there was a man seated at the runway bar, on the left, who seemed to be enjoying her performance more than the others. He was beefy and balding and he had a beard and mustache. He wore a blue shirt open over a white T-shirt. He kept whooping and hollering as she danced, raucously encouraging her to continue disrobing.

She'd been there for a couple hours. The hardest thing had been to keep smiling while she was dancing. That was important, smiling. But it was hard to smile when your mind was full of blood and gore and death.

Anna moved out on the runway, down to her G-string and heels.

The beard-and-mustache whooped and slammed his hand down on the stage, slapping a ten-dollar bill down.

Anna danced his way and shook the merchandise just for him.

"Yeah!" he shouted. "Fuckin' beautiful!"

He reached out and wrapped his big meaty hand around her calf and moved it up and down.

Her smile cracked. She tried to pull her leg away from him.

He closed his hand on it and pulled.

Anna started to fall backward and her arms flew out at her sides. She tried to compensate by throwing herself forward, but she overcompensated.

Anna fell face-first off the runway.

———

Reznick took Kendra on the floor and they both let go and got a little wild as the two little dogs watched them curiously a few feet away. Afterward, they lay side by side on the carpet, both naked, staring up at the ceiling. Reznick got up and got the ashtray from the table, returned to his spot on the floor and lit a cigarette.

"When does your mommy usually get home?" he asked.

"After two."

"Oh, yeah. Of course."

"Huh?" She turned to him. "Why'd you say 'of course?'"

"Oh, well, uh …" He shrugged. "I just figured, because … dancers work late."

"Oh. Yeah." She rolled over and put an arm and a leg across him, smiling.

Their bodies glimmered with sweat.

"I like doing this with you," Kendra whispered.

"Yeah, it's not bad, I'll tell ya that."

"Did you really want me the first time you saw me?"

"The very first time. I undressed you with my eyes. I held your breasts with my imagination."

Kendra giggled. "And Mommy was lying right there." She giggled again.

"Yep. Right there."

Reznick got up and found his glass empty. He made himself another drink and took a few swallows. He sat on the couch, still naked.

On hands and knees, Kendra crawled over to him, knelt before him, and rested her arms over his thighs, smiling up at him.

"You sure like that vodka, don'tcha?" she said.

"Oh, yeah. Oh, yeah. This vodka and me, we're old friends. We've been apart for a while, but we're together again. Together again." He took another drink, moved it around in his mouth a little, then swallowed, let it glide down his throat, burning as it splashed in his gut.

It kept away the bad thoughts. It kept the backs of his eyelids black, the way they should be.

Kendra lazily reached out and stroked him.

"Mmm," he said, "that's nice."

"I'm glad," she said.

The trailer trembled from the force of the wind.

———————————

Two of the other girls and Maxie, the bouncer, rushed to Anna's side. Maxie, a bald mountain of a man, bodily ejected the unruly customer from the club while the other two girls helped Anna up.

"How bad you hurt?" Wanda said.

"My back," Anna said, wincing. "My back hurts."

"Oh, shit," Desiree said. "I hope you don't got a back injury. Back injuries suck. C'mon, let's get you back to the dressing room."

Paul, the manager, followed them back there, eager to see if Anna was okay.

Her back radiated pain from one spot next her left shoulder blade, and she hurt her right knee. The knee would probably result in nothing more than a bruise, but she was a little more worried about her back.

"Look, Kitty," Paul said, "I want you to go straight home and get off your feet after that nasty fall. You hear me? You need to see a doctor? I'll pay for the first visit. Okay? Now, I don't want you to think about involving a lawyer in this, all right, honey?"

"Don't worry, Paul, I'm not gonna sue you," she said, wincing at the pain in her back. "It wasn't your fault, it was that damned drunk out there."

"Well, he's gone."

"I'll take you up on that offer to go home, though."

"You go on home and I'll let you keep all your tips tonight, sound good?"

Anna had to smile. He was nervous—he really was worried that she might sue.

"Sounds good to me," she said.

In less than ten minutes, Anna was in her car and on the road, headed home.

———————

Afterward, Kendra got a washcloth and soaked it with warm water, and returned to Reznick in the living room. She cleaned him up and then kissed him. He smiled as he buried his fingers in her long hair. She went to the bathroom and got rid of the washcloth, then came back and lay down on the couch with her head in his lap.

"Oh!" she said. "*Match Game* is on again! This is one of my favorite shows. It's so funny. Charles Nelson Reilly makes me laugh," she said with a laugh.

"Yeah, that Charles Nelson," Reznick said. He took another drink of icy vodka. "He's a riot."

———————

Josh Garner drove into the Riverside Mobile Home Park and stopped at unit five. He got out of his BMW and into the hot wind that blew loudly through the trees overhead. He went around his car to Steven's porch. He slowed down and frowned, his head down. It appeared something had been spilled all over the concrete, something dark, like motor oil, or chocolate syrup. He couldn't tell what it was because the porch light wasn't on, and it was dark.

Garner climbed the steps and knocked on the side of the trailer.

"Steven? It's Josh."

No response. He listened for the sound of movement in the trailer, but heard nothing.

Instead of knocking with his knuckles, he pounded with the side of his fist, shaking the whole trailer.

"*Steven!*"

Nothing.

He pulled open the screen door and tried the doorknob. It was locked. He took his keys from his pocket, found the right key, and slipped it into the doorknob, turned it.

Garner pushed the door open and found the lights on inside. He took one step inside and froze.

"Oh, Jesus Christ," he said, and it sounded like a genuine plea to the Savior. His voice wavered and he stumbled backward and swept an arm out to catch the edge of the doorframe so he wouldn't fall out of the door and down the porch steps.

There was blood everywhere. The trailer reeked of it, of soured blood and feces, and the blood was *everywhere*. On the floor, on the furniture, on the walls. But there was something *in* the pattern of blood on the floor. A shape on the carpet that was not covered with blood, a kind of smeared shape of a body. He could make out the head and the arms and legs and the torso. But it had been moved and blood had smeared onto the section of clean carpet.

"Oh, God," Garner whispered.

He found Steven's phone and called nine-one-one.

"This is nine-one-one, what is your emergency?"

"Uh, I'm at my friend's house, and I've found—uh, his trailer, I'm at his trailer, and I've found … well, blood, a *lot* of blood, and I haven't been able to reach him all day, and I think he's been murdered. I mean, if you could see how much blood there is here—I don't see how he could live."

"Where are you?"

He gave her the address.

"And you found your friend murdered, you say?"

"No, I think he's *been* murdered. All I found was blood."

"But there's no body?"

"No."

"Then there is no emergency."

"Well, *I* think it's an emergency, I mean, this looks like a fucking *slaughterhouse* in here, it looks like he was *butchered*! He's been missing all day, and I came to his trailer to see if anything was wrong, and the living room is *covered* in blood. And I think there's blood all over the concrete out front, too. Now if that's not an emergency—"

"We'll send a unit out, sir. What's your name?"

He gave his name.

"And you're at this address?" She repeated the address.

"Yes, that's right."

"Someone will be there soon."

"Thank you."

Garner sighed as he put the phone back on its base.

He turned to the living room again and put his hands on his hips.

"God, Steven. What the hell happened to you?"

———————

There was a grey Lexus ahead of Anna as she pulled off Interstate-5 into Anderson. The Lexus turned left onto North Street, just as she did.

Anna had always wondered what it would be like to own a luxury car. The kind of car that practically gave you a foot rub while you drove.

Up ahead, the Lexus stopped at the intersection of North Street and Stingy Lane, then turned right onto Stingy, just as Anna did. Anna was even more surprised when the Lexus turned left on Park Way. There were no Lexus owners on Park Way.

She was downright startled when the Lexus pulled into the Riverside Mobile Home Park.

It drove slowly ahead of her, so slowly that she assumed its driver was uncertain of where he was. He must be in the wrong place, she decided.

He passed up unit eight, where she pulled in. He kept going along the narrow road, on around the loop.

Anna killed the engine and opened the door. Pain pierced her back as she got out, and she groaned. She reached in the back seat and got her costume, closed the door. She noticed the Lexus stop outside unit seventeen across the road.

The hot wind slapped her garment bag around as she climbed the steps. She opened the screen door, then the front door, and went inside.

Twenty-Six

They were putting on their clothes when she came in. They'd heard her drive up. Kendra, of course, was quickly dressing as fast as she could, but Reznick was taking his time. He had nothing to hide. He was in no hurry. He didn't care.

She stood just inside the door, Anna did, her garment bag slung over her shoulder, her mouth open to its limit. She dropped her purse on the floor, then the garment bag. Her arms at her sides, her hands clenched into fists.

"Mommy, I'm sorry, really, I'm sorry," Kendra said, her voice high and quavering.

Anna's suddenly red cheeks trembled as her eyes bulged.

"Kendra," Reznick said as he pulled his T-shirt over his head, "why don't you take Conan and Dexter outside. They haven't been out in awhile, and they probably need to do some business."

"But Mommy, I don't want to—"

"Kendra," he said again. "Go ahead and take the dogs out. Your mommy and I need to talk."

Kendra's head turned back and forth between them, her mouth open. Finally, she called the dogs and slapped her thigh and made kissing noises with her lips, and they followed her out the door.

———————————

Monty Rudd drove the Lexus around the loop that encircled the barn-red house, then stopped his car in front of trailer number seventeen. He reached into the pocket of his short-sleeve burgundy shirt and unfolded the small piece of paper, switched on the overhead light, and sure enough, it was number seventeen. He put the slip of paper back in his pocket and killed the light, then the engine.

He got out of the car. The hot wind whipped at him and was noisy in the trees overhead making dry, harsh sounds. He wore black gloves and grey pants and black shoes. He was fifty-one, a pudgy man of medium height with a balding head of grey-shot brown hair. He leaned in and took his gun from the passenger seat. A Glock .45 equipped with a silencer. He racked the gun before closing the car door.

Rudd went around the car to the front steps of the trailer.

He could smell the meth lab. He'd been told it was a possibility. It was an unfortunate factor. The smell was foul.

Rudd silently climbed the steps. He opened the screen door, then simply opened the front door. It was unlocked, as they usually were. People were so stupid.

He stepped into the trailer.

Movement to the left.

He saw two young women sitting at a bar just to the left of the door. The one with dark hair had her back to him. The dishwater-blonde faced him. He shot her first. The gun made a thick, muted *phut* sound. A hole appeared just above her left eye and her brains splattered onto the refrigerator across the kitchen behind her. She was knocked over backward and hit the floor with a clatter.

He shot the brunette in the back of the head before she had a chance to turn around—*phut!*—and black-red matter sprayed over the bar. She fell forward on the bar and looked like she was sleeping.

Rudd took a clean white handkerchief from his back pocket and held it over his nose and mouth.

"What's going on out there?" called a male voice from down the hall.

Rudd headed down the hall toward the voice, his gun held ready before him.

———

Anna stood there staring at him, eyes wide beneath a frowning brow, head tipped forward. She tucked her lower lip in and ran the tip of her tongue back and forth over it.

"You look angry, Anna," Reznick said. "You need to calm down."

"You … you're telling me … to calm *down*?" Her voice was hoarse and unsteady.

"That's right." He walked slowly to the kitchen with his glass. The ice had melted in what was left of his vodka and it had become watery. He went to the sink and dumped it, then to the refrigerator, where he opened the freezer. He got more ice, then took out the bottle. He put the glass on the kitchen table. As he poured his drink, he said, "I told you that you owed me, and that I would collect. Well. I'm collecting."

She released an abrupt laugh as cold as a deadly-sharp icicle. "You're *collecting*. You think my daughter, you think my little *girl* is something you can *collect*."

"Your little girl came to *me*." He put the bottle of vodka back in the freezer. He turned around and froze.

"I thought we talked about that," Anna said. She stood just a couple feet away holding a steak knife with a narrow, serrated blade.

———————

Rudd was halfway down the hallway when a tall young man with curly, shaggy dark hair stepped out of an open doorway. He wore a white surgical mask. His eyebrows popped up.

Rudd raised the gun, but the instant he fired, the young man ducked back into the doorway.

Knowing he didn't have much time, Rudd hurried forward down the narrow hall. Arms outstretched, elbows locked, right hand resting in his left palm, he turned sharply to the right and entered the room.

The young man spun away from an open closet with a sawed-off shotgun and took two steps toward him.

All at once:

Rudd squeezed off a shot. The young man's left shoulder exploded in a spray of red, spinning him around and turning the shotgun toward Rudd.

Rudd fired again, and a red hole appeared in the young man's pale blue T-shirt, just below his chest.

At the moment that the young man fired the shotgun, Rudd got one more shot off. Rudd's shot took off half the young man's head. The shotgun nearly cut Rudd in half and he was thrown backward into the hall.

When Andy fell back, he landed on a structure of glass tubes and bottles.

There was a great ripping explosion.

A gout of flames and debris burst upward from the trailer.

267

The flames rose up and flared in the wind, and reached the dry, sweeping branches of the trees overhead.

"You want to think a minute, Anna," Reznick said as he picked up his drink. He took a couple swallows, them smacked his lips. "Your little girl isn't so little after all. She was hungry for it. And keep something in mind. I know something about you. Actually, I know a couple things."

"A couple things, huh," she whispered, glaring at him.

"First of all, I know you brutally murdered a man, and I could ruin you with a phone call. I'm pretty well covered, it would be your word against mine. Also, maybe it's about time somebody told your little girl what Mommy does at night. That she takes her clothes off for lonely, horny, drunken men. That maybe she does more than just take her—"

"How do you—how *dare* you—"

Reznick took another drink.

Anna attacked him with the knife.

He dropped the drink and raised an arm. The glass shattered on the floor and vodka splashed over his feet.

The knife sliced through the flesh of his forearm.

He grabbed her right wrist with his left hand, then with his right hand, he tried to pry the knife from her fingers.

She swung her knee up and slammed it into his crotch.

He doubled over with a grunt and she stabbed him in the neck.

That was when the explosion occurred, but Reznick was in too much pain to notice, and Anna's ears were ringing too loudly.

Kendra sat on the back edge of the trunk of Mommy's car, sniffling, with tears trickling down her cheeks.

Dexter and Conan were taking turns chasing each other back and forth along the edge of the road, yapping at each other, nipping at each other's tails.

Kendra felt horrible inside, like she was collapsing. She did not even notice the harsh smell that sometimes passed her by on the rushing, whipping wind. Branches creaked overhead as they swayed in the strong wind. Her long hair flew all around her head.

She was horrified that Mommy had seen her naked with Marc. Now she knew what was going on between them, which was supposed to be just their secret. Kendra wondered what she would do to her—what would her punishment be?

Why had she come home so *early*? She wasn't supposed to get off work until *two*!

Kendra was on the verge of a sob when she was momentarily deafened by a loud explosion that lit up the night a bright orange on the other side of the road, through the trees that grew between the two narrow lanes.

She lifted her head and her eyes widened, then narrowed, as she watched a trailer—the trailer in unit seventeen—explode in flames that rose up to the trees. The trailer became momentarily airborne, then crashed to the ground with a terrible clamber.

Kendra's breath was sucked from her lungs for a moment.

The flames rose up along with debris.

The flames licked at the whipping branches and caught almost immediately.

Kendra shot to her feet and called the dogs to her. They hurried to her, and she picked them up, holding one in each arm.

Flames crawled like great orange spiders through the branches overhead, spreading a fiery web.

"Oh, no," Kendra said, her voice high and shrill. "Oh, no, oh, Jesus, please, no."

———————

Somehow, Anna twisted her wrist around and stabbed the blade into Reznick's wrist. He blurted, "Ah!" and let go of her as blood began to flow.

With her lips peeled back over her teeth, she came forward, thrusting the knife at him. She got his left arm, his right arm again. Then his chest.

Reznick backed up against the refrigerator.

He slapped her face once, a backhanded swipe, hard.

Anna stumbled backward a couple steps.

He moved forward and reached for her wrist again.

Anna slashed the knife and caught the palm of his right hand. The blade sliced diagonally from the web of flesh between his thumb and forefinger, across his palm, and down to the heel of his hand. It was a deep cut, and blood came from it in a sheet that ran from his palm down his wrist and over his arm.

"You fucking men," she growled. "You all want the same fucking thing. *All* of you. You're useless. *Useless.*"

She darted forward and thrust with the knife. She got the inner elbow of his left arm.

She thrust again and again.

Reznick could not seem to stop her, so he tried to stop the *knife.* He grabbed for the blade with his bare hands. He got it once with his left hand, but she pulled it out—the blade sang on his skin as it moved along, slicing it open deep. Blood bubbled up and dribbled down to the floor in spatters.

He grabbed it with his right hand and tried to twist it out of her hand, grinding his teeth until they crunched in his head.

She threw herself forward, putting her full weight behind the knife while the blade was in his right hand, and he could not hold it.

The blade entered him just below his sternum and slammed him back against the refrigerator. It entered him all the way to the wooden handle.

Mouth open, he slowly bowed his head and looked at the knife sticking out of him.

"Mommy!" Kendra screamed outside, screamed at the top of her lungs. "Mommy! The sky's on fire! Mommy, come quick! The sky's on fire!"

Reznick's back slid down the refrigerator and he landed on his ass with his legs splayed out before him, the knife sticking out of his middle.

"Oh, my God!" Anna said when she got outside.

Hell had been unleashed overhead. The wind blowing through the trees had turned into flames. Burning branches were starting to fall as the flames roiled and whirled through the trees above. It spread rapidly in all directions, blown by the wind, until it covered the entire trailer park in a fiery sheet.

Anna hurried back to the trailer door. She went halfway up the steps, pulled the screen open, pushed the door open, and grabbed her purse off the floor. She reached into the purse for her keys as she went around the car.

"Kendra, get in the car!" she cried.

Holding the dogs, Kendra hurried to the passenger side of the car and got in.

Anna started the car and backed out of the carport.

It was like the end of the world. Fire rained down from the sky.

Other people were running for the trailer park's entrance on foot, and some were getting in their cars to drive out.

As Anna neared the exit, driving the wrong way on the right side of the road, she saw a police car with its lights flashing parked just outside the trailer park.

A BMW came out right behind her.

"What's happening, Mommy, what's *happening*?" Kendra said.

"I don't know, sweetheart, but we're gonna be okay."

"What about Marc? Where's Marc?"

"Marc's on his own."

Reznick crawled on hands and knees to the door, the steak knife still jutting from his middle.

He heard screaming outside, a lot of cars.

He grabbed the doorknob and pulled himself to his feet.

Blood dribbled from his cut arms and hands and neck. It ran down his belly under his T-shirt and gathered at the waistband of his shorts. He made a grunting sound again and again as he pushed the screen door open and went out on the porch. He stumbled down the steps.

The night was a shimmering orange outside. Reznick wondered if he was hallucinating. As he stumbled along the carport toward the road, he saw that it was raining fire, and he was certain he was dying and having some kind of near-death religious experience.

He staggered out into the road and looked up.

The sky was in flames. They danced and swirled and swelled overhead. They rained down on the ground.

People were running and screaming, and cars were rushing out of the trailer park.

Reznick waved at a passing car and cried out for it to stop, to help him. It drove by. Another came along and he tried to step out in front of it to get it to stop. The car simply swerved around him.

There was an explosion to Reznick's right, another to his left, and a rush of flame shot into the air from each one.

Reznick fell forward on the broken pavement and landed flat, driving the knife deeper into him.

He cried out, then retched. He coughed and sputtered and spat up blood. He pushed himself up on his arms.

Fire hit the pavement all around him and sparks spattered in all directions from it.

He coughed up more blood as he tried to crawl forward.

Something landed on his back. It quickly burned through his shirt. Reznick screamed in pain and rolled over to get it off his back. He rolled on the pavement, trying to stop the burning.

A pickup truck sped by and swerved at the last second to avoid him, but not quite enough. It rolled over his legs, and Reznick screamed again.

He saw the branch coming. It was a large branch, roiling with flames, big as he was. It grew larger and larger as it fell toward him.

It was followed by a whole tree.

Reznick did not feel them fall on him. One second he was screaming at the falling branch, and the next, he was unconscious, on fire, bleeding to death, broken in the road.

He did not live much longer.

Twenty-Seven

Nine people died in the fire. Propane tanks and water heaters exploded. Trailers went up in flames.

An entire flaming oak tree fell on the trailer in unit five, and the trailer burned to a crushed black skeleton.

The Snodgrass's barn-red house quickly burned to the ground with Hank and Muriel Snodgrass in it.

A shelter was set up in the meeting hall in Anderson River Park.

Anna and Kendra sat at a table drinking ice water. The building was crowded and noisy and hot. Dexter and Conan were on the bench beside Kendra lying side by side.

Kendra's face screwed up and she started to cry. "I'm so sorry, Mommy. I feel like this is all my fault 'cause I was so bad, Mommy, I'm so *sorry*."

Anna put an arm around her, stroked her back. "Don't worry about it, sweetheart. We got a lot to forget, that's all."

Kendra turned to her, tears coursing down her cheeks. "What happened to Marc?"

"Don't worry about Marc. Marc is one of the things we're gonna forget. We're gonna forget all about Marc, and Steven, and all that stuff, you hear me?"

Kendra flinched, stared at her mommy a moment, then nodded.

"We're gonna forget all about 'em," Mommy said. "We might have to stay with Aunt Rose for a little while, but we'll get back on our feet, and we'll start over. We'll start over clean. That's what we'll do."

"But what about Marc? I didn't see him when we—"

Anna turned to her with her lips pulled back, clenched teeth bared. "I said you're to *forget* about Marc. I don't want you to mention his name ever again, you understand me? *Ever.*"

"O-okay, Mommy."

Anna relaxed a little, took a collecting breath. Then: "You're to stay away from boys. And men. You understand me?"

"Yes, Mommy."

"They're all alike, and they're all bad. *All* of them. They all want one thing, and that's *all* they want. You're to forget all about them, you understand me, Kendra?"

"Yes, Mommy, I—"

"*You understand me?*"

Kendra's eyes widened a little. "*Yes*, Mommy. I understand."

"Good. Now. We're going to think new thoughts. And we're going to start over again."

Even at ten-forty-six at night, the wind was still hot as it whistled around the corners of the building, wailing like some pathetic creature, hungry, lost, and desperate.

About the Author

Ray Garton has been writing novels, novellas, short stories, and essays for more than 30 years. His work spans the genres of horror, crime, suspense, and even comedy. *Live Girls* was nominated for the Bram Stoker Award in 1988, and Garton received the Grand Master of Horror Award at the 2006 World Horror Convention. He lives in northern California with his wife Dawn, where he is at work on a new novel.

BIBLIOGRAPHY

NOVELS AND NOVELLAS
411
Bestial
Biofire
Crawlers
Crucifax
Dark Channel

Darklings
Live Girls
Lot Lizards
Loveless
Night Life
Meds
Murder Was My Alibi
Ravenous
Scissors
Seductions
Serpent Girl
Sex and Violence in Hollywood
Shackled
The Folks
The Folks 2
The Loveliest Dead
The Man in the Palace Theater
The New Neighbor
Trade Secrets
Trailer Park Noir
Vortex
Zombie Love

COLLECTIONS
Methods of Madness
'Nids And Other Stories
Pieces of Hate
Slivers of Bone
The Disappeared and Other Stories
The Girl in the Basement and Other Stories
Wailing and Gnashing of Teeth

Curious about other Crossroad Press books? Stop by our
website: http://crossroadpress.com
We offer quality writing
in digital, audio, and print formats.

Subscribe to our newsletter on the website homepage and
receive a free eBook.